C000049751

EVERNIGHT PUBLISHING ®

www.evernightpublishing.com

Copyright© 2020

Sam Crescent

Editor: Audrey Bobak

Cover Art: Jay Aheer

ISBN: 978-0-3695-0247-6

ALL RIGHTS RESERVED

WARNING: The unauthorized reproduction or distribution of this copyrighted work is illegal. No part of this book may be used or reproduced electronically or in print without written permission, except in the case of brief quotations embodied in reviews.

This is a work of fiction. All names, characters, and places are fictitious. Any resemblance to actual events, locales, organizations, or persons, living or dead, is entirely coincidental.

ALWAYS

DEDICATION

To all of my amazing readers

ALWAYS

ALWAYS

Next Generation: The Skulls

Part One

Sam Crescent

Copyright © 2020

❮◦ ◦ ◆ ◦ ◦❯

Prologue

Present day

"Holy shit, Tabby. Hold the fuck on!" Simon pushed her into the back. Daisy climbed into the front of the car. "I'll drive my fucking car!" He growled the words and pointed at Anthony. "Get in the back."

"Gladly, asshole," Anthony said, climbing in.

Simon struggled to allow another guy to touch his girl, but he didn't have much choice. He was the best driver; being a year older than everyone else, he'd had more experience.

"There's so much blood," Daisy said.

"Look away, Daisy. Now. You don't need to fucking see this," Anthony said. "Do you have any idea what the fuck you're doing? Tiny is going to go fucking mental, not to mention my dad."

"What about mine?" He knew Devil would fucking belt him if anything happened to Tabitha. His father had told him time and again to be careful, and if something happened to Tabitha, war would be declared between The Skulls and Chaos Bleeds. There was no way that could happen. He'd been told this years ago.

"You had no business starting shit. I told you from the start to keep away."

"She's mine, dickface. She will always be mine."

"Enough with the fucking shit. Stop your talking and get my sister to the hospital," Miles said. He'd jumped into the back.

Tabitha couldn't cope. The pain was too much.

"I've got you," Daisy said.

Her best friend in the whole wide world sported a black eye and split lip. She reached up, touching her face.

"It wasn't supposed to be this way, you know."

"Don't talk like that," Miles said.

Her brother. Her twin.

"This is bad, Miles." She groaned. Glancing down, she saw the blood. Daisy used one of the many shirts she wore to press on it, tears in her eyes.

"I've got you," Daisy said. "Don't you die on me. We've got so much to do. So much to live for. All the plans we made."

"I don't know if I'm going to make it."

"Don't fucking talk that way, Tabby. Don't you fucking dare!" Simon's scream from the front didn't offer her any comfort.

If she did die, Simon would follow her, but he'd leave nothing but chaos and destruction in his wake.

I don't want to die.

I'm too young to die.

I can't handle this.

I want my mom.

She closed her eyes.

"Fuck. Put your fucking foot down, Si. We don't have time for this shit."

Everything became a blur.

"Hurry up," Daisy said.

"Tabs, don't do this," Anthony.

I don't want to, but it feels really nice.

Chapter One

*A few letters and experiences between Simon and
Tabitha between ages ten and sixteen.*

> *Dear Tabby,*
> *How are you? It has been a long time and I miss
you. School is boring. There was a kid who tried to bully
me. He was some big-ass jock. Wanted to take out an MC
kid. That so didn't happen. I'm ten but I'm not stupid. I
kicked his ass ... kind of. The principal pulled us apart
and called our parents. Mom turned up and she went
mental. I got grounded and was forced to copy out the
dictionary. What do you think of my spelling? Dad's
decided lines and dictionary work will help me. I don't
know. It's boring but it means I get to think about you.
How are you? How is everything at Fort Wills? Is
Anthony still being an ass? Tell him I'll kick it for him.*
> *What are you doing right this second?*
> *This isn't going to be a long letter. Mom's busy,
and I've got to help.*
> *Take care, Tabby.*
> *Love you lots,*
> *Simon*

****

> *Dear Simon,*
> *Hey stranger. What am I doing right this second
is writing a letter to you, silly. Not a lot is happening
here, to be honest. Everything has been quiet. Babies are
always being born, and there's always a lot of parties.
Daddy says I'll not be going to a party like ever, which
sucks.*
> *Anthony is being an ass but I think that is because*

he loves Daisy. He doesn't just love her as a friend; nope, it's big, kind of scary. Daisy doesn't have a clue and I'm not about to spell it out for her. Good for you on whipping his ass. You did, didn't you? I hate that everyone gangs up on us. We're not an easy target, you know? Mom says not to listen to any of them. Some of the kids call us trash. I know we're not. It does upset me though. I don't show anyone because I know it will worry them.

Your spelling is much improved. I moved up a grade as well. So cool. I don't know what I want to be when I grow up. I'd love to sing, or maybe write, or maybe I could be a doctor like Sandy. I love going to work with her. She's so much fun.

I miss you. When are you coming back? Daddy says that it's going to be awhile 'cause you're all busy.

What do you want to be when you grow up?

I've got to go as well.

Bye.

****

Tabby,

When I'm there, I will kick anyone's ass that said you were trash. You're beautiful, Tabby. Don't listen to them, and don't give them that kind of power. You're too good for them.

Yeah. Dad was saying that money is tight at the moment. Something about a bad turn on the markets, and so we're recouping. They don't do the bad stuff, you know. We both know that some stuff cannot be talked about. I hate that I'm not seeing you as much. I'm hoping to get a laptop soon, and then we can stop sending letters and we can chat online. Would you like that?

I want to be prez when I grow up. I've always wanted to be part of the club, and I know I can handle it. I'm not being young and stupid either. You can be anything you want to be. Can you sing? I don't know if I've heard you sing before. I would totally love you to sing for me.

Would you be my old lady? I know you don't want to be part of the club, but I would totally support you, and there's no one else for me. You know that.

Now I feel stupid because I'm going to have to wait for your answer.

Yeah, still stupid, and I waited a couple of days but I'm not going to cross anything out.

Love,
Simon.

****

Text messages

Tabitha: **Mom says I can't be on here long.**

Simon: **Mine either. It's so annoying. Mom's looking all happy as she watches me.**

Tabitha: **It's because we're cute. It's what I hear Whizz or Lacey say. I like Daisy's parents. You know what I mean.**

Simon: **I do. I've got a question for you.**

Tabitha: **I'm waiting. I can't answer it if you don't ask me.**

Simon: **It's stupid and you're going to laugh.**

Tabitha: **So, it's never bothered you before.**

Simon: **Have you ever been kissed?**

Tabitha: **Yeah. Mom and Dad kiss me all the time. That wasn't a hard question, silly.**

Simon: **Not by our parents. By a boy!**

Tabitha: **Anthony kissed me once for a dare. It was so gross. He was eating tuna and he tasted really fishy. This was ages ago though.**

Simon: **I'm going to beat the shit out of him.**

Tabitha: **No, you won't. We were kids and young. Don't be a dick.**

Simon: **Do you want to be kissed?**
Tabitha: **Do you want to kiss me, Simon?**
Simon: **Yes, I'd really like that.**

****

Dear Simon,

Happy birthday. I'm so sorry I missed your birthday. What are you? Old now lol. You're thirteen, right? That must be totally awesome. You're a teenager. How is everything with you? Did you have a good birthday? I'm sorry we couldn't make it. I wanted to. Mom said we couldn't as we didn't have time to go. There's always Thanksgiving. I know Angel is inviting you guys home. Are you looking forward to coming to Fort Wills?

Sorry about all the questions. I'm just so curious and you know Dad always watches me when we talk. I don't know what his problem is. I'm your old lady, you would think he would be awesome about that. He never complains about anyone else. I don't know. He keeps saying you'll be with him over my dead body. He's old, doesn't he realize that you know, I'm younger? Lol.

Anthony has got it bad for Daisy. I heard Lash and Angel talking about him in the kitchen. When we were younger, like middle school, he would sit and listen to Daisy read to him. Whenever I'm at the clubhouse, I've seen him, Simon. He sits on a wall, and if Daisy's near reading a book, which she always is, he will get her to read to him. Honestly, it's crazy, and kind of weird, but I guess that is exactly what our families are like, weird. I think he's totally going to ask her out. I'm rooting for them.

When I talk to Daisy about Anthony, she just shakes her head as if I'm the crazy one. I'm not. I still haven't told her that Anthony is in love with her. I think a lot of people find Anthony weird because he doesn't talk all that much. He stares. They don't know him like I do. I see everything. Anything interesting happening on your end?

> *Take care, Simon.*
> *Love you.*
> *All yours,*
> *Tabby.*

****

> *Sweetest Tabby,*

I had a great birthday. My dad's teaching me how to fight. He says every man should know how to handle himself. I've told him what I want to be when I grow up, and he's really happy about that. I told him you were my old lady, and he laughed. Said I'd understand what a lady is soon enough.

I heard one of the guys at school talking about a blowjob. Have you ever heard what one of those are? I'm scared to ask my dad. What if it's one of those joke things that causes problems? I don't want to be seen as not knowing. Do you know what it is? I don't, and I can't check it out online. Ever since I stumbled onto two girls kissing, Mom put some parental things on the computer. I can't get on anything. Was Daisy able to get you a computer? I'm waiting for the text to let me know you're online.

I've got to go. This is so short but I'm hoping to see you soon.

> *Love you,*
> *Simon.*

****

> *Dear Simon,*

I don't know if I want to use the internet to talk. I think I like us writing letters. Daisy said she can set it up for us though if I want to. This seems kind of romantic to me, doesn't it for you? You're the only person I write to and I look forward to your letter every single day. I know it's going to arrive and each time the mailman comes, I'm so happy. I kind of attack him. Of course it means there's time between. I heard Angel the other day telling someone that distance can make the heart go stronger. My sister Tate says it doesn't work. I don't know. She got it to work with Murphy but there's a lot of stuff between them. There's so much about the past I don't know.

How is school? Are you still hanging out with the bully? You told me he was hanging around with you, right? You and him kind of got it tight? I don't know how you can do it. Be friends with an asshole. Oh, well. Not much is going on here right now. Grandpa Ned is coming to town again. It always makes everyone tense. I like him, but then he always feels guilty as I had that tiny almost-died thing going on. If you could see me, you would see me shrugging. It's all a little confusing right now, to be honest.

I don't give a fuck what my parents or the club are doing. It's their business. Daisy said it is my business but I'm thinking of getting out, you know? Being my own self. I talked to Mom about it, and she said it could be possible. I have dreams, you know, of being away from Fort Wills. Of course I'd want Daisy to come with me, but she seems content with the club life. I don't know.

I'm starting to feel sad as I write this. Got to go. Love ya.

****

Simon age thirteen, Tabitha age twelve

Simon looked out across the lake, feeling a deep sense of calm wash over him. Tabitha was on the blanket, her head resting on his leg as she read one of the books Daisy had given her. The breeze was warm, giving them some reprieve from the sun. It had been a hot summer in Piston County, too hot to enjoy. Simon stroked her hair, pushing it out of her face. Tabitha looked up. "Why are you smiling?"

"No reason. I'm with you, and that makes me happy."

She put the book down, taking hold of his hand and locking their fingers together. "I love being here with you too."

"One day soon, I'll always be here. We'll always be together."

She sighed. "I hate seeing you go and I don't want to leave you. It's the worst part of our time together."

With his free hand, he stroked her cheek. "I'm yours, Tabby. I told you that."

"And I'm yours, Simon. There's no one else but you. It will always be you."

"What about when you want to leave?"

She didn't speak and he looked down at her.

"I don't think I'll ever go."

"You wanted out of the club. To sing?" She had a beautiful singing voice.

"I know it's what I wanted, but everything changes. I've changed. I don't know what I want anymore. Everything has changed. Let's not talk about it."

****

Dear Simon,

Did you hear? We've had to join schools. Yeah, it's fucking horseshit is what it is. The high school closed and changed location to a larger building and now we're there with the fucking Monster Dogs MC. They're a pansy-ass club, and we now have to share it. What kind of shit is that?

Our school is now known as Peacebrook High! Piece of shit. I was supposed to go to Fort Wills High.

But not now. Nope. It's all changed. Sorry, everything is changing. The club, the school, even Daisy. She's different but I kind of understand the shit she's going through. Sorry, I'm angry. Really angry.

I miss you.

Also, I'm learning how to fight. Miles is shit and won't give me lessons. I'm sick of it, and now I'm taking lessons from Anthony. I told him not to treat me like a girl, and guess what, he doesn't. I mean, he doesn't hit me hard, and I try to dodge that stuff when I can. He's tough. I like it. The only way I'm going to survive is if I fight and if I'm better. Their club has girls as well, and let's just say lines have been drawn. I've got no choice. It's fight or die.

Daisy and I talked about changing schools. Our dads said an all-girls school would be our next option. Yeah, right. Not happening.

Besides, I'm there with the guys and if we make our mark, then it means the others don't have to. The Skulls always have each other's back, and I've come to realize that what I've been missing all of these years is that is exactly who I am. I'm a Skull. The club runs in my blood. Rather than hating it, I should be embracing it and that's what I'm going to do. Every single step of the way. My guys and my girls. I will have their backs, always.

I've got to go. I might not get a chance to write for a while but we can talk. You know I'm always here.

Love you,
Tabby

17

Chapter Two

Sixteen years old

"Please, Anthony. Please, please, please," Tabitha said, begging. She normally didn't beg, but right now, she didn't see any other choice. She would've asked her twin, Miles, but he could be a royal pain in the ass with his completely unnecessary demands, and he never kept his mouth shut either.

"I'm not helping you. You get caught, I'm the one who gets screwed."

"We won't get caught."

"Why can't you just see him tomorrow when everyone can watch you?"

Tabitha rolled her eyes. "Seriously, you're going to play that card?"

"No. I'm not doing it."

He continued to eat his Chinese food, and it just pissed her off. "I'll talk to Daisy," she said.

This made him pause, but he didn't say anything. He truly believed his feelings for Daisy were a secret. She knew exactly what to do to make him comply. Daisy had become her playing card with Anthony when she wanted something.

"No one has asked her out for the Halloween party, and I can probably make sure she goes, and you know, dances with you?"

Anthony glared at her. "I can see Daisy any time."

"Sure, sure, but you're on friend terms. What if I, you know, gave her a little encouragement to see you as something more?"

"You're going to use your friend to go see the

Chaos asshole?"

She glared at him. "I'll tell her that you're an asshole who is totally screwing three girls in high school, and probably has a sexual disease. You won't even get to hold her hand!"

Anthony continued to frown at her. "You know I hate you?"

"You don't, but come on, help me out."

"Fine! I'll cover for you, but I better get a dance and a fucking smile."

She leaned over, kissed his cheek, and smiled. "You will."

Tabitha didn't know what was going on between Anthony and Daisy, but either way, she was willing to help both of them out if it meant she got a few minutes alone with Simon. Sneaking out of the house was easy. She pulled her jacket around her, leaving The Skulls' compound and making her way toward the old park.

It wasn't safe anymore, and there was some kind of argument over the land being bought up, with houses built on it. She didn't know what else was going on with that, and she didn't really care.

Chaos Bleeds were in town, but they weren't staying at the clubhouse, at least not Simon. She figured it had something to do with her being sixteen and him pretty much seventeen and knowing all about sex. Simon had been the first one to find out about a blowjob, not that they'd done anything. Their parents didn't have to worry. Simon was the perfect gentleman with her. Either way, it didn't matter. Simon had texted her that he'd be waiting for her.

Ever since she'd grown boobs and started to ask sexual questions, Tiny, her dad, had become overprotective. She knew about sex and guys. Most of her life had been spent at the club, and even though they tried to stay on their best behavior, it didn't always work out. People talked and most of the time kids got forgotten about, which meant they opened their mouths frequently.

As she entered the park, it was too dark, and there wasn't much light. She couldn't make anything out.

Someone placed their hands over her eyes, and she smelled him before hearing him. "I didn't think you'd come."

"I had to blackmail Anthony."

Simon chuckled. He stood so close, she felt every inch of him pressed against her back. Even with his hands covering her eyes, she closed hers, basking in his closeness. They rarely wrote to each other now since she was given a phone. They didn't text, but they called all the time.

"What did you have to blackmail him with?"

"Daisy."

"Good." Simon released her, spinning her around, and she finally got to see him.

Cupping his face, she stared at him for a few moments, just taking him all in, before she went onto her toes to kiss him. He was way too tall for her. One of his hands gripped the back of her head, holding her close. He was getting bigger by the second. Tall, muscular, he owned the place. Gone was the puny little boy who'd tried to pick on her so many years ago. Not that it had lasted all that long.

"I'll have to be careful around you. You seem to have a way of getting what you want."

"I've learned from the master." She thought about her sister Tate who was much older than her. Tate had given her a few pointers on how to get what she wanted. Tabitha was happy to do most things so long as it didn't hurt anyone in the process. She couldn't stand the guilt. "I've missed this. I've missed you."

"Your dad would rather have me locked in cuffs than get close to you." He pushed some of her hair back, and she smiled. "Not that I blame him. You're so fucking beautiful. I never want to give you back. I bet all the guys are falling all over themselves to get with you."

"Stop. I've told you. No guy is going to take your place. I don't know if these moments are perfection or torture." She gripped his leather jacket, the Chaos Bleeds symbol on the back marking him as the property of the Chaos Bleeds leader. She remembered when Devil gave it to him.

He'd posed for her during one of their video chats.

Simon tilted her head back, and she smiled up at him. "They're perfection, Tabby. You can never reach that without a little bit of torture thrown in."

She giggled. "Are you trying to sound all philosophical?"

"Do you know what that word means?"

They were both laughing. "Do you?"

"I know that I will suffer everything to be with you, Tabby. The true torture would be never having these moments, knowing what could have been."

Just like that, he stole her heart once again.

He'd done so a long time ago.

There was no one else, just her Simon, like she was his Tabby.

She pressed her head against his chest. "I know you can't stay too long."

Simon sighed. "Dad has already told me we're heading out tomorrow. I've still got school come Monday, and all of their shit has been handled."

"I wish you could move here." She would love to have him here every single day.

"Do you think you could convince your dad to

move to Piston County instead?" he asked.

"Not a chance," Tabitha said, pouting. "It's bad enough when it's vacation time. I think the only reason he goes out is because of Mom. She needs the time and there's that whole age-gap thing." She shrugged. "I hate this."

"Sit with me awhile. Let's not think about tomorrow." He took her hand and they found a tree to lean up against. He sat down, drawing her between his legs.

Their moments were becoming less frequent. Lash, The Skulls' leader and current prez, tended to handle things a lot differently than her father had.

In the past twenty years, The Skulls had gone through so many changes. She'd only been around for sixteen years of them. Sometimes, she still had nightmares of some of the scarier moments. In recent years, they were legal. Doing everything by the book. The danger was still there, but it was limited. She couldn't remember the last time she'd been called in for lockdown.

It was nice.

She got to do pretty much whatever the hell she wanted to do, within reason. Her dad was still way overprotective and yet her twin, Miles, could do whatever the hell he wanted. The double standards were not lost on her. Even though Lash was moving the club forward, her father still had some old-fashioned views.

Staring up at the stars, Simon wrapped his arms around her, holding her close.

"One day, you and me, we'll be side by side. Like it was always supposed to be. We both know that's how it's meant to be."

A pain rushed through her chest. Was it?

For the longest time, she wanted nothing to do

with the club, either of them. The Skulls nor Chaos Bleeds were part of her future plans. That all changed. She didn't know how it happened. Just one day, she was pissed-off, angry, and the next, she knew without a doubt it was her calling.

She believed it was something Grandpa Ned had said to her.

"Honey, I know you don't want the club life, and you're right, it's not for everyone. It takes a lot of dedication and commitment. Running from this doesn't change who you are. You belong here. You need to understand there are people out there who have nothing. Who have no one. They would love to be in your position. To have family. You leave, your family will always welcome you back. You know how it goes. Don't for a single second believe you don't belong here. I know you're a strong person, and you're going to grow into a fine woman. The club, it's part of that. It has helped build you."

After their conversation, she'd been in tears. She finally realized that her place was as a part of the club and she didn't hate that.

"You've gone silent on me," he said.

"It's nothing. You know how it goes."

"We've never talked about what's going to happen when we're able to get married."

She tilted her head back. "You're still wanting to get married?"

"Hell, yeah, I'd marry you now."

She chuckled. "You're an impatient man, Simon."

He held her a little more tightly. "No, I just know what a beauty I've got, and how fucking lucky I am."

"Simon?"

"Yeah."

"Have you ever kissed another girl?" she asked. For some odd reason, she was thinking about his question from years ago.

"No, I've never kissed anyone but you."

She pulled out of his arms, turned, and sat between his spread thighs, crossing her legs. "You're sexy, hot. I go to school, so I know a lot of girls, hot girls, throw themselves at the guys. You've got ink already. You're like a rebel. Do you seriously expect me to believe that you're not, you know, with other girls?"

Anthony had a reputation at the school, but he never confirmed or denied the other girls' claims. Tabitha had never seen him with anyone and she knew he was smitten when it came to Daisy. She'd never given herself a chance to think of Simon with someone else. They had hours between each other. Towns, even cities that separated them. For so long, they'd been writing, texting, rarely emailing.

Simon reached out, tucking one of her blonde locks behind her ear. She'd asked Lacey to dye the tips a deep blue, but her mother had said no. She hoped Lacey wouldn't listen to her mother and just do it.

"You think any other girl would ever be able to take your place?"

"You're telling me you haven't?"

"Tabby, you've had me since we were kids. I'll always be yours."

"Love at first punch?"

"You got it. No, I don't kiss other girls. I don't screw other girls. I'm a virgin."

She smiled.

"Don't laugh."

"I'm not laughing. I just, really?"

"Yeah, really. Do I watch porn, yeah, but it's not you. I want my first time to be with you." He teased a strand of her hair.

"I'm not ready."

"Tabby, baby, I'm not rushing you. You ever thought I'm not ready?"

She leaned in close and kissed his lips. "You're telling me you're not ready? If I told you I was ready to get naked with you, you'd tell me no?"

"Don't put it like that. We both know you're not ready. Do I want to have sex with you? Yes, it's a stupid question. We've got the rest of our lives. I'm not going to rush you." He cupped her face. "This is enough."

Kissing him back, she released a moan, feeling a flutter throughout her body.

"I love you," she said.

"Not as much as I love you."

"It's not a competition."

"Oh, yes, it is." He pulled her close and within his arms, she felt warm, safe, protected, and loved. It was all she ever felt with Simon, and all she knew she'd ever feel with him.

****

"We good?" Simon asked Anthony.

"Why wouldn't we be?"

"I don't know. I asked you to keep an eye on my girl."

"Dude, I keep an eye on Tabs even when you don't want me to. Believe me, I know my place and it's taking care of everyone. You don't have to stress it."

"You know, a lot of people think you're weird," Simon said.

Rather than respond, Anthony continued to stare at him.

"Ah, the whole blank look. Does that still work for you?"

Silence.

"Right. Keep an eye on Tabby. Let me know about those guys. You know, the ones we caught out by the field that time."

"The Monster Dogs MC brats are pieces of shit. You don't need to worry about them," Anthony said. "I've got them handled."

"I don't like them."

"Who does? We shouldn't even be dealing with them, but I've got it covered and you need to stop worrying. Tabs would be pissed if she knew you wanted me to keep a close eye on her. She's a fighter. I should know."

"The Quad?"

"You got it. It's where we all go. The Skulls, we've got a reputation to uphold." Anthony glanced back at the clubhouse.

Simon followed his gaze to see Lash and Devil shake hands. Tabby stood with Daisy. She winked at him.

"I don't like her fighting."

"One day, you're going to watch her and realize she's a fucking queen here, Simon. Tabs isn't a person you need to be worried about."

"Does that make you king?" Simon asked.

He didn't like how Anthony was the shit in this town, or at least in their school. It wasn't lost on him that to some, Tabitha and Anthony should be together.

"You've got nothing to worry about, you know that."

"You keep your eyes on your own."

Anthony glanced down to where Daisy stood. "I've got shit covered. You keep telling me to deal, though, and I will hurt you in other ways." Anthony slapped him on the shoulder and left him alone.

That was the most conversation he got out of

Anthony. He didn't know if it was just because of who he was or what. There was no forcing shit with Anthony. The guy did what he wanted to do.

As he headed back to his dad, Devil told him five minutes.

He went straight to Tabby.

"Ugh, this is where you two do your romantic crap, isn't it?" Daisy asked.

"You can watch if you want?"

Daisy rolled her eyes. "I'll vomit. I'll be back inside."

"I'll be there in a minute," Tabby said, turning her smile back to him. "You love irritating her, don't you?"

"She gets you every single day. The least she can do is give me these few moments."

"You'll call as soon as you get home?"

"Yep."

"Promise?" Tabby asked.

"I promise."

She grabbed his shirt, pulling him close.

Sinking his fingers into her hair, he kissed her hard. These moments were the worst. He hated leaving her alone, but there was no way he could stay. Not yet. He'd asked his dad about moving to Fort Wills, but even though The Skulls and Chaos Bleeds worked together as a team on most cases, they were still separate clubs with their own lives.

Chaos Bleeds owned Piston County, and The Skulls had Fort Wills.

"Devil," Tiny, Tabitha's dad, said with a growl.

"Son," Devil said.

Tabby pulled away with a smile. "See you soon."

He wanted to kiss her again. Instead, he pulled away, nodded at Tiny and Lash, and gave the guys he was close friends with a wave.

Climbing into his dad's truck, he groaned. This wasn't the cool way to be leaving his girl. Most of the time, Devil rode with a couple of the boys when they were talking business. With him asking to come as well, the only way to appease his mom was to take the family truck. It was such a buzzkill as it reminded Simon of his parents constantly making babies. Sometimes he even lost count of the number they had.

They had just gotten out of Fort Wills when his father started to talk.

"I don't appreciate you sneaking out. Especially while we're in Fort Wills."

"You knew?"

"Son, I'm old but I'm not stupid. You and Tabitha are not going to turn me into a grandpa too early."

Simon burst out laughing.

"I'm being serious. Your mom wouldn't like it either."

"No, you're not going to be a grandpa too soon. Don't worry about it. Tabby and I don't get a whole lot of time together. You know how it goes."

"I have to say at your age, I don't. I was fucking everything with a pussy, Simon."

"I thought you were supposed to be the voice of reason with me?"

"I am. I'm not an idiot. I just want you to know what you've gotten yourself into. Your mom will be a little more delicate with you."

"You think?"

"I only want what is best for you."

"Tabby is what's best for me."

"And when your time comes to take a patch? I know that's what you want unless you intend to change that."

"No, I still want to earn my patch."

"You planning on killing me to get my club, son?"

Simon laughed. "Not a chance. I know you're going to be around forever. You'll give me the club when you're ready."

Devil snorted. "So you're still wanting to take a patch."

"Yeah. It's all I ever wanted." For as long as he could remember, watching his father run Chaos Bleeds, seeing his men be loyal to him, creating something that was just so much more than anything else, Simon knew he wanted to be part of that in some way.

"And you've talked to Tabitha about this?"

"Yeah, she knows."

There were a few seconds of silence.

"What are you not saying, Dad?" he asked.

"Nothing."

"Come on. There's got to be a reason you've gone all silent on me. Tell me what it is."

He waited.

"I've tried not to interfere when it has come to the whole Tabitha and you thing."

"You did try. You failed."

"Club shit always gets in the way, but you've got to understand, you're not a boy anymore. You're on the way to becoming a fine young man."

"Why do I feel a *but* coming on?"

"But she's still a Skull. Her place is in Fort Wills and the last time I checked, she's not planning on moving anywhere."

"Your point?"

"One of you is going to have to make a choice. Either she moves here, or you have to take your patch with them."

He saw his father's hands tighten on the wheel.

"We don't have to worry about that yet," he said. Simon wasn't stupid. He'd realized Tabby never confirmed they'd stay together. He didn't know how he was going to make it work, only that he had to. He had to do something. The thought of not having her in his life, of them not being together, it just didn't seem possible to him.

She was the only person he ever wanted, the only one he wanted to be with. He loved her more than anything.

Rubbing at his temple, he turned his attention out of the window.

"I know this is the kind of shit you don't want to know."

"I get it, Dad."

"I'm looking out for you."

"I know."

Silence once again.

Gritting his teeth, he tried to not think about anything. Driving away from Tabby was always difficult. The time they had together was a few stolen moments like last night. Everything else had to work. When he talked to his mom about it, she always offered him a sweet smile as if she knew what kind of trouble he was having.

He hated this. The feeling of insecurity.

Pulling out his cell phone, he sent her a quick text.

Simon: **Missing you already.**

Tabitha: **Always. Sucks seeing you drive away.**

"You've got to know I'm only worried about you," Devil said.

"I know, Dad. I know."

"I never thought I'd have a son, or have to worry, or even feel this way." Devil's hand opened up as he pointed ahead of him. "But it did."

"I get it. You met my mom, fell in love, and you've never been apart."

"I'm talking about you. I didn't expect to have kids. I only want what is best for you. Always."

He nodded. "I get it. We're not going to have one of those father-son conversations that creep me out, are we?"

"I hope not."

"Good. I don't think I can handle them. We can only deal with so much bonding."

"You're an ass," Devil said.

Simon snorted. "You want a soda?"

"Nah, you go ahead. Your mom's making lasagna for when we get home. Don't go snacking on everything, otherwise, she'll be pissed at me."

"Rather you than me." He tipped the can against his lips, got settled in as his dad turned on the radio, and stared outside at the passing scenery. All the time, his mind was on Tabby. His girl.

The woman he loved more than anything and yet, he got the feeling she wouldn't want to become his old lady when the time came.

Chapter Three

"I'm bored," Tabitha said.

"Then read a book." Daisy didn't even glance up from the book she was reading.

"I'm bored with reading."

"Then watch a movie." Finally, her friend lowered her book. "Let me guess, there's no movie you want to watch either."

"You got it." She dropped down onto the bed. "I suck, don't I?"

"Why? Because you're like most teenage girls and bored? Why don't you text Simon or something? That's what you do."

"I can't."

"Why not?"

"He's got this study thing he needs to do."

"Ah, right, the study thing where you went crazy not too long ago because you thought it meant he was seeing another girl?" Daisy offered her a smile.

"You don't have to be that way."

"I'm not being any way, just stating a fact." Daisy picked her book back up.

Tabitha recalled her deal with Anthony and groaned.

"What is it now?"

"Nothing," she said. It was hard to get anything past Daisy. Rubbing at her temples, she looked at her best friend. "You know Darcy and Ink decorated their place for Halloween?"

"I know. I seem to recall helping them. I picked up what they needed, remember?"

Great. Daisy went back to reading her book, and

Anthony would be pissed with her if she went back on a deal with him.

"So, er, don't you just love Halloween? I mean with all the partying and the fun. Dressing up. I love it. I can be whatever I want."

"No."

"What the hell is the no for?"

"I know you, Tabs. I know you better than anyone. Even Simon. Believe me. I get it. I know what's going on here and there's no way I'm going to any kind of party. I don't want to. Period."

"Ugh! It would just be for me."

"No."

"Come on, what's so wrong with going to a party?"

"I don't like to party."

"You're being a royal pain in the ass."

"And we both know the reason you're upset and angry and pissed off is because you want to go and head out to the Quad."

Tabitha was going to kill her friend. The Quad was where all the fights happened. She didn't know if her father or Lash, the current President of The Skulls MC, knew of the place, but she and the gang frequented the place often. Tabitha loved to be able to unload, especially if she'd experienced a shitty day, which seemed to happen more often than not.

"This has nothing to do with the Quad. I need you to go out on Halloween with me, to go to the party, at the high school. Is that such a bad thing?"

"You want to go to the high school where the Dogs will be? Seriously? You know it's bad enough going through a single day with them without you know, all the crap after school. I've seen them hanging out at the Quad as well. It's like this joint school thing has given them permission to come onto our land. It's not good."

She started to smile.

"What?" Daisy asked.

"Just, our land and permission. You sound very possessive all of a sudden."

"I am. Especially of the club. I've seen the way the guys are. Especially Luke and Ryan. They're pieces of shit."

"That I won't deny." She sighed. "This school thing. I kind of agreed with Anthony you'd be there."

"Why the hell would you do that?"

"You know, he likes you."

"Not that again. Please, not that. I can't stand that. I'll have to barf if you do that." She rolled her eyes. "Anthony has a gazillion girls he could date. You've seen the way they throw themselves at him."

"Yeah, but have you actually seen him kiss one? Hang out with one? Even touch one?"

"I don't even know why we're having this conversation. It's completely pointless."

"It's not. Come on. You'd be doing me a huge favor by hanging out with him. You know you want to."

"I don't know that I want to. In fact, I think I'd rather forgo the whole Halloween dance. Dad is going to rent a bunch of movies and we were all going to watch. Halloween candy, some kind of drink he's going to make up. It'll be fun."

"Sounds boring," Tabitha said. "Come on, you're only going to live once. Why not make it the best thing like ever? There's going to come a point when we're not going to be able to party and have fun." She held her hands together, begging. "Please, please, please."

There was a sudden knock on Daisy's bedroom window.

Tabitha turned toward the sound to find Simon, Miles, and Anthony all waiting in the tree.

"Oh, look, some of the gang are here." This Simon was her nephew, even though they weren't that far apart in age. Something he hated to acknowledge as he was actually older than her, even though she was his auntie.

Daisy climbed off her bed. She wore a pair of boy shorts, exposing her thighs. Tabitha watched as Anthony climbed through the room and seemed to try to get as close to Daisy as humanly possible. How was it no one else saw this? She'd noticed Anthony's obsession with her best friend years ago.

Her friend, as always, was oblivious to his devotion. It was kind of sad, but funny. For a long time, Anthony hadn't really spoken. He did his glaring thing, which seemed to scare off a whole lot of people. Not her and the group though.

"What's going on?" Tabitha asked, getting to her feet. She had yet to change her clothes for her pajamas.

"Big fight out at the Quad," Miles said. "Dogs are fighting. I thought it was time for us to see them in action. We've seen a couple of their boys, but not with any real competition."

"I can't," Daisy said. "My parents are downstairs."

"They're probably making out," Miles said. "We know what they're like, and with the Chaos crew just vacating, we've got time. We all know how this goes down with the parents. This is something we've got to do."

"You know he's right," Tabitha said. "We'll be back before midnight."

"I hope you know my dad already knows when we sneak on or off. He's got the whole place wrapped tight." Daisy's father, also known as Whizz, was amazing when it came to technology. He handled most of the security for the entire club and also helped to work the markets as he had a keen eye on investment. To The Skulls, he was the shit.

"Then what do we have to lose?" Tabitha asked. "They already know they're here. Let's go. Let's do this."

Daisy sighed. "Are we grabbing everyone?"

"No can do," Miles said. "I already checked in. They've got shit to do. It's got to be us."

"Of course, it does. I mean, why would we be strength in numbers?"

"You sound a little pissy there, Daisy. You okay?" Simon asked.

"She's fine," Tabitha said, interrupting. "She's just agreed to go to the Halloween party and we've now got to go shopping. Of course, this is all a treat on me."

"I did not," Daisy said.

"If you're going, that will be cool. The whole gang is going, right, Ant?" Miles asked.

Anthony, his silent self, just stared.

"See, confirmation." Miles pointed at his friend.

"He didn't even speak."

"But if you watch his facial expressions, you will see he is actually very easy to read. A certain brow lift. The sneer. You name it, he has it."

"We're all going," Anthony said. "Don't stare at my face for so long."

"Look, irritate him enough and he starts talking as if by magic."

She loved her twin. Miles didn't have a filter. A trait that seemed to run in the family. Their half-sister Tate was known for it.

Tabitha had learned young to bide her time, to

hold her tongue, at least, that was what she tried to do. It didn't always work out that way.

"I'm going. Fine. I'm going."

"We'll go shopping next week. Come on, get dressed. You know you want to."

Daisy rolled her eyes again, another little trait she'd decided to start doing. Rather than be pissed at her best friend, she rolled with it. It was what she did nowadays.

She knew, at times, Daisy was going through some crap inside her head. When she was ready, she'd unload, but until then, she got the pissy version from time to time. It wasn't like anything she couldn't deal with.

"Guys, leave," Daisy said. "We're not kids anymore. I'm not getting changed in front of you."

"Buzzkill," Miles said.

Anthony slapped him around the back of the head and made sure the guys left before he did.

Daisy changed into a pair of jeans, and like all of the kids of The Skulls, she quickly pulled on her leather jacket, labeling her as one. Whenever they visited the Quad, it was essential.

"This is stupid."

"You're going to love it."

"Watching a bunch of kids fight. Yeah, it's going to be so much fun."

"We are all still a bunch of kids."

"Yeah, well, I'm trying not to be."

"Oh, really, what are you trying to be?" Tabitha asked, climbing out of the tree.

"An adult. Do you expect us to keep on acting like this when we're older?" Daisy asked. "Should I put the window down?"

"You didn't make the bed to look like we're still

home and like you said, Whizz is going to know we headed out. He'd see it."

"True. I'll be grounded for this."

"We'll deal with that when the time comes." They were all often grounded as kids, but with how busy the club got, it was hard for their parents to keep a constant eye on all of them.

Down on the ground, Tabitha ran her fingers through her hair. Lacey had agreed to dye her tips, but now she was having doubts. Maybe she wanted a different color. Purple or green. She'd handle it then.

Daisy had such a kick-ass mom in Lacey, even though the woman wasn't her biological mother. Daisy's real parents had been pieces of work. Assholes who often forgot their daughter, and it was only because of her own mother and Angel that Daisy got any real kind of care. The Skulls had taken Daisy in, and well, she was family.

That was what The Skulls were, one big happy family. Tabitha or any of the kids could go to any of the club members' houses and there would be a bed for them, protection, and comfort. It was just the way the club was. Even for the prospects and the recently patched-in members. It was the way the club rolled.

She grabbed Daisy's arm, locking hers around her, as they walked down the street. It was only a twenty-minute walk to the Quad, but most of the time they took a car. Anthony had been learning how to drive and Simon actually owned a car. It was a gift from his parents, Tate and Murphy, but he still needed to pass his test.

"Do not try to make this right. You were a bitch up there," Daisy said.

"I know but I promise you, I'll make it right with you."

"You'll make it right? Your Simon will probably

sneak here and take you out. You'll abandon me, as that's what you do, and then it will be all over. I'll be at a party, on my own, wishing I'd stayed at home."

"It won't be that way."

Daisy looked toward her with a raised brow.

"What? It won't. I promise. I'll be good and I'll stay with you the whole time." With the entire gang going, she wouldn't get the luxury of sneaking off, and from her last conversation with Simon, he wasn't going to be able to sneak off either. His dad was pissed because he'd gotten suspended again for fighting.

He'd done this a few times. They both went to school with people who just seemed to enjoy running into their fists.

"I tell you, man, I can't wait to hit someone. I mean fucking mess them up," Miles said. He slammed his fist against his open palm and chuckled. "It will feel so fucking good."

"Miles, you're a dick," Tabitha said.

He burst out laughing. "Yeah, and you're a pussy."

Daisy sighed. "Really, I stopped reading for this?"

"Come on, Daisy. You know you love to watch a good fight. I bet if you asked nicely, Anthony would be all over that shit for you. Fighting, maybe even take his shirt off." This earned Miles another hit on the head.

Shaking her head, she held her friend's hand even tighter. "It's going to be okay."

"I don't doubt it."

"Come on, this is going to be fun. We'll enjoy this fight, your dad will be pissed, and then we've got Halloween to look forward to."

"And if this all goes wrong and it was a trick to get the cops here, our parents will be picking us all up from the cells. Oh, yay, what fun."

"What happened to my friend Daisy? You used to be cool."

"Thanks. Look, I'm sorry. I've got a lot on my mind right now."

"Is this because of your dad?" Tabitha asked, whispering so the guys wouldn't know. Daisy had confided in her that her real dad, the one who had given her up so easily, kept on sniffing around, wanting money. Threatening. She didn't want to take it to Whizz or get The Skulls involved because of everything they were going through, or put them at risk of killing someone.

Her real dad would be easily killed by the club, and he should have been a long time ago.

"Yeah, he called. It's fine. I'll deal with it. You know."

"Tell him to fuck off. He can't keep taking money from you. Piece of shit that he is." She hated him and didn't hide it.

"It's nothing. Don't worry about it. We should be focusing on what these guys are going to do."

"Ignore them. I do so often," she said.

Daisy chuckled.

Tabitha tended to know when her best friend was having a hard time—she turned bitchy. Between the two of them, Tabitha was more than happy to wear the crown of queen bitch, and Daisy was normally the sweet one. The one holding books, reading, and not getting into fights. They each had their roles to play and they did it well.

Arriving at the Quad, she saw it was busier than usual.

The moment they paid their entrance fee, Tabitha went on high alert. A crowd this big was dangerous, but it also meant the cops had been bought off.

"Dogs own this territory tonight," Mitch, the guard at the door, said. "You've entered at your own risk."

Keeping together as a group, they moved toward the main fighting ring. Ned had come to see this place with her a few years ago, and Tabitha had been addicted to it. Of course, neither her parents nor the club knew that Grandpa Ned had looked it over as a possible site he wanted to use.

Ned dealt in fighters back in Vegas. He was notorious for finding the meanest motherfuckers around. She also knew he wasn't a nice guy either, and so there were some fights that had a lot more odds on them, a fighter's life.

Those freaked her out. She couldn't ever imagine fighting for her life, nor did she want to. Still, this was fighting. It was fucked up, dangerous, but that was the way that it was.

"What are you thinking?" Daisy asked.

They pushed their way up to the edge of the ring. It was on a concrete pitch that was higher up as if on a pedestal. There had been wooden posts secured with rope to try to keep people inside. The trick was to not get slammed down. There were some rules to the fighting, seeing as it was mostly kids who took to the Quad. Some college boys as well. Those were the fights the club often went for. It meant bigger money as there was often some pansy-ass rich boy who thought he was the shit and got beat down a great deal because of it.

Anthony didn't go for fights he knew he could win.

Tabitha just loved to fight, and the thing about the Quad was they didn't care if you had a dick or a pussy. A fight was a fight. You win, you get paid. You lose, you go home empty-handed.

The club had yet to lose a fight. Out of the whole club, Daisy didn't fight, though. It wasn't that she couldn't fight, it was just better for everyone if she didn't.

Staring up at the two competitors, she spotted Luke facing off with a guy twice his size. Both had no shirt on. Luke was covered in ink. His arms, chest, and as he turned to dodge a ram, there was also ink on his back.

"You want him?" Daisy asked.

"Don't be absurd." She didn't want Luke but that didn't mean he didn't want her. Nope, she'd noticed Luke watching her. He was also the one who tried to keep things nice between the clubs. It was Dickface Ryan she had trouble with.

Luke was the President's son, and there was no denying he was a badass. He was also a bully. An asshole bully, but he didn't turn that shit on her, and when she caught him, she stepped right up into his face for it.

His technique was flawless. He hit hard and took no punishment.

It was good.

The guy finally went down and waved his hand in defeat.

The Dogs roared with victory.

Luke was embraced with open arms and then Ryan ran onto the pedestal. He was smaller than Luke. Still had plenty of ink, but he was a complete and total dick. There was no getting away with it. He believed his patch was what made him the shit, but it didn't.

If anything, it made him even more of an asshole. The guys couldn't stand him.

She certainly couldn't. It was bad enough having to deal with another MC, seeing as they'd been able to avoid it most of their school lives, but now, it made it even more so. Especially since some people considered

The Skulls as sellouts or weak. They weren't. They had just reached their end of horseshit and wanted a break.

Simple as that.

Ryan held his fisted hands in the air as if he was already going to be victorious.

"Can you believe this guy?" Daisy asked.

"Come on, are you all fucking pussies?" Ryan asked. He pointed out at the crowd. "I dare you. Come and fight me, fuckers!"

No one took to the pedestal.

"Are you all pussies? None of you can take me."

Tabitha watched as Anthony handed his jacket to Simon and then climbed up onto the pedestal. He wasn't scheduled to fight but there was no way Ryan could get away with that. Calling on others to fight when there was no real competition.

"Well, well, well, look what I've got here with me. None other than a Skull brat. Someone who needs his ass beaten."

Anthony didn't even bother removing his shirt or raising his fists. He looked bored.

The bell rang, which meant the fight had been accepted and now it was on.

Ryan raised his fists, and Anthony kept his by his side.

Tabitha tensed as Ryan went to charge him, but he went into the ropes that only just kept him in the ring.

Again, Anthony still hadn't lifted his hands.

When Ryan came at him a second time, he clocked him around the face, sending Ryan down with a single punch.

There were cheers, but the Dogs, they were pissed. She chanced a look over to see Luke watching her.

Averting her gaze, she saw Ryan get to his feet,

shake whatever it was off him, and charge again. This time, Anthony took him. Punch by punch. Ryan got a few in to the stomach, but Anthony blocked most of the face aims.

She winced a few times at the brutality of it but she was long gone past the days of covering her eyes. The shit she'd seen, the stuff she knew, it didn't make her weak, it made her strong. She was more prepared now than ever before, and she was ready.

Anthony threw the final punch, and this time, Ryan stayed down. Their boy had knocked The Dogs boy clean out.

Miles cheered, whooping in the air. "Suck it, Dogs. That's how it's done. That's our boy."

Anthony climbed out of the ring, went over to Mitch, grabbed their money, and that was it. They left the Quad. If Ryan hadn't been knocked out, there would have been a lot more crap to deal with. The Dogs wouldn't accept this. Ryan would demand a rematch.

"You know you fucked up there," Daisy said.

Tabitha's brows rose as Anthony came to a stop.

All of the guys did as Anthony turned to Daisy.

"I did?" he asked.

This was new. Daisy and Anthony were often in each other's presence but rarely on speaking terms. It wasn't odd for them. Anthony rarely spoke to anyone.

"Yeah. They're going to demand a rematch. You're going to have to go up against Ryan or Luke, or all of them."

"Oh, come on, our boy will take them all on," Miles said, clapping his hands in excitement.

"Are you all fucking insane?" Daisy asked. "There's only so much shit they're going to take before we have to face the consequences. You were only supposed to watch."

"We didn't say that," Tabitha said. She knew the moment they entered the Quad that the chances of them fighting would be pretty high. It was impossible for them to go somewhere with fighting and avoid it. It was like telling a fucking bee not to suck pollen. That shit wasn't going to happen.

"Were you worried about me?" Anthony asked.

Daisy stared at him.

Tonight was turning out to be full of surprises. Tabitha wished she could take her phone out to film this precious moment. At the very least, she could send it to Simon. That would give them something to talk about, and it would win her a bet, that said Daisy and Anthony would end up together. Simon didn't agree with her.

"You could have gotten yourself killed. It's not funny." She went to turn her back on him, but Anthony grabbed her arm.

Tabitha waited.

Silence.

Nothing.

Damn, the suspense was killing her.

"You better get home," Anthony said.

Tabitha kept on watching as Anthony let her go, and she was in shock.

"What the fuck?" she asked, mouthing the words to Anthony, who shrugged and kept on walking with the guys in tow.

She and Daisy headed back to her place. "What the fuck was that?"

"Nothing," Daisy said.

"Come on, it looked like you guys were eye-fucking each other. That has to mean something."

"It doesn't. You need to stop thinking you see stuff that is clearly not there. He could have gotten himself killed. I don't know about you, but could you imagine Lash over that? Angel would be dead, and Lash, he'd start a war. We all know how this goes. Then all of a sudden, our lives will change forever. I don't want that to happen." Daisy shrugged. "Anthony is part of us. We need to look out for each other, which includes him."

"You're blind, you know that?"

"Anthony and I are never going to happen."

"And why not?" Tabitha asked as they got to Daisy's home.

Daisy opened her mouth and closed it.

"See, you can't even give me a reason."

"Stop it, Tabs. You and I both know I'm not his type."

"You don't even know what his type is."

"It's not me."

"You don't know that."

"I know enough," Daisy said. "Come on."

"Why don't we walk in the front door? Your dad's going to know."

"If he hasn't time to check, I could get away with it."

They climbed up the side of the house, going into Daisy's room. As they came to a stop, Tabitha groaned. Not only was Whizz standing there, arms folded, waiting, so was Tiny, her dad.

Oops.

Chapter Four

"You're grounded?" Simon asked, laughing.

"It's not funny."

"You snuck out, went to a fight, and your dad was waiting for you when you got back. I think that's hilarious."

"Ha ha, very funny." Tabitha sighed. "It gets worse, he's picking me up from school. Whizz is doing the same for Daisy as well. We're being treated like kids."

"It's how you punish kids."

"You know I'd punch you if you were here."

He snorted. "I'm with your dad on this one. You shouldn't be going out."

"Kiss his ass, why don't you?"

"No, seriously, how are you?" Simon asked. Daisy had texted him late on the night in question in case he struggled to get in contact with her. He would've called Tabby's mother if she didn't answer. Her parents knew he loved her so it wasn't like he was saving any kind of face.

"How am I? I don't know. Bored. There's nothing to do when you're confined to the house. I'm not even allowed to go to the clubhouse so it's full-on grounding."

He leaned back, staring up at the ceiling. "Sing to me."

"Not happening. You know I only do that when I'm in the mood and right now I'm not. I wish you were here. Are you still not coming for Halloween?"

He groaned. "Not this year. I promised Mom I'd help out with the trick or treating. It feels like a hundred kids want to go and beg for candy. I'm sure if she asked, Dad would just buy them what they wanted and I'd be off the hook."

"Are you dressing up?"

"Probably, I think I'll go as a zombie biker."

She chuckled. "A hot zombie though, right?"

"Totally. You'd have to give me the kiss of death."

"I wouldn't kiss a zombie."

"If it was the end of the world and I was bitten, and for whatever reason the way to bring me back would be to kiss me, you wouldn't?" he asked.

"It depends. Will you have bad breath?"

"I'd be dead."

"Then you, my love, would have to stay dead."

"Charming, and here I thought our love would last a lifetime."

"Oh, it will. I'll keep you locked up and pet you."

"Like a dog?"

"No. A dog won't eat me. You would."

"You're willing to make me jealous of a dog."

"Totally," she said. "Thank you."

"For what?"

"Just this, being you. I don't feel like I'm going quite so crazy anymore."

"I'm always here for you. I don't know if I'd be able to cope with you being grounded. I'd piss your parents off, climbing into your window."

"Hiding under my bed?"

"Good times."

Her laughter came over the line and it warmed him from the inside out.

"I love this."

"Me too, but you haven't told me what you're wearing this Halloween."

"Daisy and I still need to go and get costumes."

"Will they even let you go to the party?"

"I figured if they don't let us go out shopping soon, I'll phone for reinforcements."

"Anthony?"

"You got it. He wanted her to go. I can't guarantee she'll see it as a date, and she hates me for it. She's not one to party, but it's what he wanted."

"I wouldn't wait around. Call him, get him to agree. They'll have some prospects go with you, or a couple of their guys. It's not like it'll be hard."

"I think we scare a couple of the prospects. Daisy hates being followed around. I think her father is sniffing around her again."

"Again?" Simon asked.

"Yep. She's in that bitchy mood which means she's keeping secrets. The only one I know, her dad. I don't know why she doesn't let Whizz handle it."

"You know why," he said.

"Yeah, I know but it's stupid. I'm sorry. I just, I hate it when it's like this, you know? Daisy shouldn't have to deal with it, but if he was killed, then she'd blame herself."

"Why don't you get Anthony to pay him a visit?" Simon suggested.

"Really, did you listen to what I said? Anthony would kill him, without a doubt. No question. He'd be dead."

"I'm just throwing it out there."

"It's a bad idea," she said. "I feel like I'm always talking to Anthony at the minute."

"He's going to take over as club prez," Simon said. "It makes sense."

"Yeah, he'd be a good prez. A strong one. Scary."

Simon thought about her twin. "What about

Miles?"

She groaned. "No, he doesn't have what it takes to be a leader. Besides, he's screwing everything he can get his hands on. It's sick."

"Sick?"

"Yep."

There was a knock at his door, and seconds later, Lexie poked her head around the door. "Dinner's in ten."

He nodded.

"You got to go eat?" Tabitha asked.

"Yep, and I'm starving, but I can eat it cold."

"Don't be stupid. Go and eat. Call me when you're done."

"Will do. Love you," he said.

"Love you too."

"Bye."

He hated hanging up and often didn't hear her say goodbye. As he climbed off his bed, Lexie had a large laundry basket on her hip, which he took.

"You don't need to do that."

"Don't worry about it," he said. "Dad would be pissed to know you're doing everything. You need to relax."

"How did I get so lucky with you?" She cupped his cheek with a smile. They headed downstairs. Elizabeth and Josh sat at the kitchen counter. The scents of tomato and garlic were heavy in the air. His mouth watered.

"Hello, loser," Elizabeth said.

"Takes one to know one, Squirt."

His sister stuck her tongue out.

"How's Tabitha?" Josh asked.

Simon glanced at his brother. He knew his brother had a bit of a crush on Tabitha, not that he'd admit to it.

"Fine, grounded."

"Of course she is." Josh went completely red in the face.

"Maybe next time you can go to Fort Wills and ask her out on a date," Elizabeth said.

"Enough," Lexie said, giving her daughter a pointed look.

"Oh, come on, this is so lame."

"Coming from the girl who has the biggest crush on Drew."

Elizabeth's face turned red. "Loser."

"Bitch."

"Simon, enough. Please, enough."

"What is going on?" Devil asked, entering their home. He had a large bag of groceries in his arms.

"Ice cream?" Lexie asked.

"Only the best for my woman."

"I love you." Lexie grabbed Devil's face and kissed him hard. "So freaking much."

"If it was only this easy to get in your good books, woman. I'd give you ice cream every single day."

"The kids."

"Ignore them, I do."

Simon snorted. He started to put away the groceries. They had a big family and it meant weekly shopping.

"How have you been feeling lately?" Devil asked, touching Lexie's cheek softly.

"Fine. Just a little tired. I'll be fine. You know me."

"I do." He gripped the back of her neck. "Take it easy."

"Always. One day at a time. It's what I do." Lexie pulled away. "Now, wash up. Dinner, kids."

Simon finished putting away the groceries and

stopped, looking at his mom as she stirred the sauce into the pasta, adding some cheese as she did.

"Are you okay, Mom?"

"Of course, honey."

"It's just Dad never worries unnecessarily."

"I know. He is just the kind of guy to worry about everything. Don't worry about me. I'll be more than fine. Trust me."

He did trust his mother, but … he couldn't help but feel they were hiding something from him. Lexie was always the kind of woman to do everything. She never wanted a nanny, even though there had been a short time one was in the house, but that was a long time ago.

"Will you pick up the costumes from Natalie tomorrow? She put some finishing touches to them and I totally forgot to ask her to bring them on by."

"I can do it tonight if you want?"

"Nah, it can wait until tomorrow. We've got plenty of time between now and then to get everything ready."

"Do you think we need to take them trick or treating? It's kind of lame."

"Lame or not, it's what I want to do. I love Halloween. I do appreciate you doing this for me. I know you like to sneak off to Tabitha's."

"It's fine. She's got something going on at the high school." He shrugged.

"How is she handling the grounding?"

"You already spoke to Eva?"

"Yep. Tiny was waiting for her when she snuck in."

Simon laughed. "She's doing fine. She hates being grounded but who doesn't?"

"Simon, I hope you know if I ever catch you sneaking out and back in, you won't be able to leave the house for thirty-plus years."

"Is this because you don't want to be a grandma?"

"I want to be a grandma," she said. "What makes you think otherwise?"

He raised a brow.

"Devil," she said. "Of course. The idea of becoming a grandpa seems to freak him out. Oh, well, just take care. I know we live in a good neighborhood, and the town is somewhat safe, but you know the risks."

"I know. I get it. I do, Mom." He hugged her. "I'll carry this in for you."

He took the food to the table. Elizabeth and Josh were already fighting and Devil merely watched while he put the cutlery down.

When Lexie came in, everyone was silent as she served up. Extra cheese was passed around to sprinkle on the top.

Simon took seconds, listened as his parents talked about school, and what some of the teachers had said. For all of Elizabeth's good-girl routine, she'd gotten into a few fights at school. Of course, he'd been there with a couple of other Chaos kids, but seeing as he was the oldest, he never meddled in their mess.

His dad had asked him to allow others to fight their own battles, and with him being older, he'd be in more shit if he did.

He had a couple of friends he'd kept with him who weren't club members. They were close, not as close as he was to some of The Skulls, but a close second. Dean and Eddie came from rich parents, but they were the kind that had a country club. Both of them were forced to wear polo necks and khaki shorts, and they both hated it. They didn't completely understand what it meant to be part of club life whereas the guys back in

Fort Wills did. He missed them. Tabby the most. He even missed Daisy. There was a time she offered an easy smile but now, she just seemed permanently attached to being a bitch, but again, he didn't know her. Tabby told him she was going through stuff and it wasn't his deal, so there was no reason to delve into that kind of drama. This was what made his life different to Tabby and The Skulls. Fellow Chaos Bleeds kids were younger. Even Vincent and Phoebe's kids were older than him. For the most part, he was alone.

After dinner, he did the dishes with Elizabeth, and his father called him out to the backyard as he picked up his keys. He'd gotten a text from Eddie about a meet-up at the back of the library.

Pocketing his keys, he walked out back to find his dad putting some chair together.

"You okay, son?" Devil asked.

"Yeah, I was just about to head out and spend some time with the guys. That okay?"

"What about school?"

"I'll be back. You know that."

Devil leaned on his knee. His father was near sixty but didn't look a day over forty, at least Simon didn't think so.

He suddenly realized that one day, he was going to wake up and his father wasn't going to be around anymore. The club would be his. He didn't like it. To him, Devil was going to live forever, but he couldn't deny his dad was constantly getting older. What would he do when Devil wasn't there?

After pulling out his cell phone, he texted his friends to let them know he wouldn't be there tonight, removed his jacket, and knelt down. "What do you need?"

Devil chuckled. "I can still put shit together, son.

No, I was wondering on our next run if you'd like to come with."

"Your run?"

"You know, when we have to go and pick out a woman or a family from a bad situation."

"Oh." That was what The Skulls and Chaos Bleeds did now. They worked as a protection detail with the Billionaire Bikers MC in helping families or women in fucked-up, abusive situations and provided them shelter, a home, anything they needed. Simon had also heard that they helped to rescue trafficked women. It was the Billionaire Bikers MC's MO. They helped lost women.

The Skulls and Chaos Bleeds were part of it. They helped where they could. There was a time a run meant delivering guns, drugs, whatever Ned Walker wanted, or whatever deal they had going. Simon had been young at the time. When both clubs had nearly been wiped out more than once by long-forgotten enemies, Lash and Devil had both agreed for the safety of their clubs and families that it was time to go legit. No more danger surrounding them. The days of lockdowns were so far in the past, he struggled to remember them. It was crazy.

It was during some of The Skulls and Chaos Bleeds lockdowns that he'd gotten close to Tabby. The love of his life.

"If you're not up for it, I understand. We never know what kind of shit we're walking into and it's not for the faint of heart."

"No, it's not about that. Believe me. I want to." He laughed, running a hand down his face. "You know, one day, I want to be like you."

"No, son, you're going to be better than me."

"I doubt that."

Devil stopped twisting a screw and looked at him. "Being a leader, the club President, you need to have doubt from time to time. What you need is to own up to it, and accept it. You've always got to be one step ahead of the game. You think I've been rooting for your education because of your mother, it's not. I need you to be able to think on your feet in case anything goes wrong."

Devil rubbed the back of his neck. "These runs, Simon, they're dangerous. I'm not going to pretend with you. I know how desperately you want to be part of the club, and if so, you need to know what you're getting yourself into."

"When do you know when a run is going to happen?"

"We get a call. We organize. We never go in half-cocked, unless we have to." Devil took a deep breath. "You still know how to shoot a gun?"

"Wow," he said.

"Yeah, wow. Some of the places we go, we still have to deal with people."

"By deal you mean kill."

Devil looked past his shoulder and nodded his head.

"I bet Mom already knows the kind of shit you have to do."

"Either way, I don't want her to know the full extent of all the bad shit that goes down. She doesn't need to be aware of it."

Devil ran a hand down his face. "You can go on out with your buddies."

"Nah, I'm good."

"Really? You're willing to spend time with your old man after all the shit I've heard about you being free to make your own choices and shit?"

Simon snorted. "Dad, I'm a teenager. Making your life hard is what I'm all about."

Devil shook his head. "One of the best days of my life with you was holding you."

"You never talk about it much. Why?" Simon asked.

He watched as Devil opened his mouth, closed it. "You know the drill. It was a hard time. Your mother and I, we didn't always see eye to eye."

"You know what I don't get," Simon said.

"What?"

"With Elizabeth, Josh, and all the others, there are so many photos of Mom pregnant. What happened to the ones with me? Mom doesn't have any with her being pregnant with me."

"They were lost, son, in a fire."

"Right." He stopped, wondering. "What kind of fire?" Simon asked.

"The kind that takes photographs. Go and grab me a soda, will you? I'm thirsty."

Simon shrugged, got to his feet, and headed into the house.

His mom was in the kitchen, stirring something on the stove. The scent of chocolate was heavy in the air. After all this time, Lexie was still trying to perfect the best hot chocolate that Angel had perfected years ago.

"Hey, Mom," he said.

"Hey, sweetie. I thought you were going out with some friends?" She turned to look at him.

"I was but I decided to help Dad."

"Ah, he's still pissed that his chair didn't come with instructions. He's determined to build it up from scratch."

"He's all manly. You know that. It's what he does."

57

She chuckled. "I love him so much."

He grabbed two cans of soda and closed the fridge. "Mom, can I ask you something?"

"Sure thing."

"What happened to pictures of you when you were pregnant with me?"

"Oh, I had them on my phone. It wasn't a great phone but it took pictures. It got lost and they were all gone."

"Right," he said.

"Is that all?"

"Yeah, that's all."

He headed outside and handed his dad a soda. "What's up, son?"

"Nothing. Nothing at all." He had to wonder why his mom and dad had a different answer for the pictures of her being pregnant.

****

"He asked tonight," Lexie said.

"What about?" Devil switched off the bathroom light, watching his woman as she put her book to one side.

She wore a sexy negligee that displayed her heavy tits.

After all these years together, he was never bored. Not once. His dick hardened at the sight.

"Me being pregnant with him."

He'd hoped this kind of conversation would never happen. "Yeah, he asked me too."

"Oh, no, what did you say?" she asked.

"I said they were gone in a fire."

She winced.

"What?" he asked.

"Er, I said it was on one of those phones and it got destroyed. Did he ask you about it?"

Devil shook his head.

"What do we do?"

"For now, we wait and see if he asks any more questions," Devil said.

"What if he does? What do we do? How do we tell him that I'm not his real mother? That she dumped him and then was killed?" Lexie covered her face and Devil went to her. He held his woman.

"You're his mother, baby. You will always be his mother and he knows this. You did everything you could to protect him."

"But he's going to hate us. We never told him the truth."

"He was too young to understand the truth."

"But what about now?" she asked. "We've left it too long and now he's going to think the worst."

Devil caught her face in his hands. "This was the decision I made. I will face whatever anger he has. I will not let it come near you."

"But—"

He slammed his lips down on hers. "No buts. No nothing. I wanted this. You don't have to worry. I'll take care of it."

"What if he finds out the truth?" she asked.

"He won't. Not until we're ready to tell him." Devil pulled her close, kissing her and using his hands on her body to distract her.

There was no way he would ever allow any harm to come to his woman. He would deal with his son when the time came.

****

"Man, you missed one hell of a party last night," Eddie said.

"Party? I thought you were hanging out at the library?" Simon asked.

Dean snorted. "Dude, we can go to the library any fucking day of the week. Nah, there was a party at Amber's, and guess what, she was asking about you."

Amber was the school queen. Most guys wanted to fuck her, and the girls wanted to be her. She was beautiful, rich, and popular. He didn't give her the time of day and he figured that was what pissed her off. She couldn't get under his skin and it wasn't personal. He was taken.

"Tell her I'm not interested."

"Is this all about that Tab chick?" Eddie asked.

"Don't, Eddie," Dean said.

"I've told you many times, Eddie, you don't understand, and if you talk shit about my girl again, I'll hurt you." He wasn't afraid of fighting. He'd gotten suspended a few times over the years for defending his club.

Piston County High, so original, was like any other school. The same groups of people. The jocks, the nerds, the hippies, and then of course there was him, the bikers. There were a few biker groupies as well. A couple of the guys liked to ride and play the part of an MC, but they weren't part of Chaos Bleeds.

"Sorry, man."

"I told you once and I'll tell you again, don't ever bring her into this." Tabby was for him and him alone. Eddie and Dean hadn't seen her yet. Whenever she visited Piston County, he rarely shared. His friends weren't a high priority during that time. Just his girl.

They entered the school. He carried his books but they headed to Dean's locker, which also happened to be next to Amber's.

Simon looked down the hall to see the little group of jocks. Wayne was one of them. Captain of the football team and all-around asshole. They'd come to blows a few times when they were younger. Now, they just had verbal sparring.

"What's happening tonight?" Dean asked.

"Got that thing with my parents."

"You're still doing the trick or treating thing? Come on, really?"

"Yes, really," he said. He looked at his friends. "What?"

"There's going to be a party and we figured seeing as you're here and all for the first time, you'd come with us," Eddie said.

"Not happening. I don't back out from my responsibilities."

"Hey, Simon," Amber said, coming to stand close to him. Behind her were five other girls. All of them wore short skirts and had this weird smile on their lips.

"Amber," he said.

"You weren't at my party last night."

"I was busy."

"Well, what about you make it up to me for Halloween? You be my date?"

"I've got nothing to make up for."

Amber pouted. She went to touch his arm and he caught her hand before she even got too close to him.

"Don't ever fucking touch me. Do you understand?"

This was the first time Amber had come on to him strongly. Sure, she'd smiled at him and tried to giggle and laugh. He'd ignored her. He had his woman back in Fort Wills. Anyone else wouldn't do.

Eddie and Dean said it wouldn't count if he wanted to fuck a chick. Tabby would never need to know, but he wasn't going to cheapen their time together by fucking another chick. What he felt for Tabby wasn't some quick flirtation. He loved her so damn much. He only saw his future with her. That was never going to change.

"Come on, Simon, don't be that way."

He got into her face. "I'm not someone you can control or manipulate. Go back to the pussies who want yours. I'm not interested." He let her go, turned on his heel, and walked toward his homeroom class.

Eddie and Dean weren't far behind him.

"Are you fucking crazy?" Eddie asked.

"I guess you can say that," he said.

"I can't believe you did that. No one has ever defied her at all. Holy shit, I think I've got a hard-on for you right now."

He laughed. "Don't be crazy." He took a seat in the back. Amber would try to piss him off again. He'd heard a few tales of what she liked to do to hurt the guys who wouldn't give her the time of day. He hoped if she tried, she was ready for a fight because he was more than happy to take her on.

The rest of the day went by without much event. Sure, people were pointing at him, but Amber kept a wide berth. At lunch, the tension mounted, but he sat at his usual table, staring at the jocks, waiting for one of them to come and try to defend her honor. He relished it, in fact.

Nothing happened. By the end of the day, he was a little disappointed. Unlike in Fort Wills, Piston County didn't have a fighting club. Any fights he got into were on school grounds, or sparring with a couple of the club guys.

After school, he arranged to meet up with Eddie and Dean later on that night, and stopped off at Natalie's to pick up the Halloween costumes. There were so many of them and she told him Lexie was expecting them at the club.

He didn't linger to chat, even though he adored Natalie. She was a lovely person. Instead, he made his way to the clubhouse, pulling his bike up at the end of the lot. Compared to all of the Chaos Bleeds crew, his bike looked so small and pathetic, but this was just practice for him. He intended to join the crew as a prospect as soon as he hit eighteen. He removed the large bag stuffed with all the costumes as he climbed off his bike.

Glancing past the bikes, he saw Dick on the ground, eyes closed, legs crossed, hands resting on his knees. He was one of the guys who had no choice but to put himself in rehab. Chaos Bleeds hadn't been strict on their rules and Dick had been a user, an addict.

"What are you doing?" he asked.

Dick opened one eye. "I'm meditating. What the fuck do you want?"

"Why are you meditating?"

"It helps me to find inner peace."

Simon couldn't help it. He burst out laughing. Now Dick was staring at him with both eyes.

"Inner peace."

"You ever tried it?" Dick asked.

"Hell, no, that shit doesn't work."

Again, Dick was staring at him.

"Does it?" Simon asked, trying to be polite.

"I won't tell you if it does or not. Piece of shit."

Again, he laughed. He just couldn't help it. He held up his hand in surrender. "I'm sorry."

"Leave him alone," Martha, Dick's wife, said, coming out of the clubhouse. "Lexie's waiting for you inside, and meditating helps." She sat in front of her husband and Simon watched as the two held hands, their knees touching.

Simon couldn't look away.

Both were staring into each other's eyes. Their connection clear. They breathed as one and were together. At that moment, he missed Tabby.

She would be his one.

Whatever was happening between Dick and Martha, they were a team and could handle anything that was thrown at them, together.

"Right, I better, go."

He didn't want to keep watching what he couldn't have, at least not yet. He hadn't heard from Tabitha that day, and he was already missing her.

Heading inside, he couldn't see his mom. Ripper was playing pool with Snake.

"Hey, guys, you seen my mom?"

"She's outside," Ripper said. "Judi's with her."

He nodded and headed out back to see Judi already helping with some of the costumes. A couple of the kids were in shorts and a vest.

After he dropped the bag, Lexie came at him with a hug. "You're a star."

"That's what I am. I'm hanging with some friends tonight."

Lexie reached into her jeans pocket, handing him some cash. "Don't forget to eat, and don't be too late. Your dad will be pissed."

He took the cash, kissed his mother, waved goodbye to the rest of the guys, and headed back to his bike. Martha and Dick were still doing some kind of breathing and totally digging each other.

Sending a quick text to his boys to meet him outside of the library, he took off and didn't stop until he was right there, going through the main street of the town, seeing it was still pretty busy, before riding around the back.

After turning off his ignition, he climbed off,

leaned against the wall, and saw on his cell phone that Eddie and Dean were having some kind of family crises and would be there as soon as they could. He was bored.

Pulling up Tabby's name, he dialed.

"Well, this is rather late of you," Tabby said.

"It's been a busy day." He told her about what happened in school with Amber, then the outfits for Halloween. "You talked to Anthony yet?"

"Yep, I did after we stopped talking yesterday. Daisy and I are going shopping tomorrow."

"That's cutting it a bit late, isn't it?"

"Yeah, but it's fine. I'm just pleased I'll get to get Daisy's ass into a costume. She's in her pissy mood. We'll see what happens." She sighed. "So, tell me more about this Amber chick."

"You're not jealous, are you?"

"No, but you don't think I don't know girls like her. I do and believe me, I don't like them. I don't like her being near you."

He couldn't help but smile at that. "I won't ever stray."

"Simon, I know you won't, and I can hear you smiling."

"I can't help but smile. You care."

"I'd be careful if I was you. It sounds like this Amber is a bad person and I'd hate for you to be on the firing line."

"All of the guys were there. Nothing will come of it."

"Don't be alone with her."

"I won't. Maybe you can come and meet me one day when you guys are visiting?"

Tabitha laughed. "You think she can take me?"

"I think you'll be the one being pulled off her," Simon said.

"What are you doing now?"

"Waiting for a couple of the guys."

"These the preppy boys?"

"One and the same."

"Why are you friends with them?" Tabby asked.

"They're good guys and besides, all of my friends are over there."

"We miss you," Tabby said.

"I know. I miss you as well." He sighed. "Wish you were here."

"I wish I was there as well. I'd show you how to have a good time."

"Really?"

"Yeah, and our clothes would stay on," she said.

"There you go spoiling it. Hey, Tabby, can I ask you a question?"

"Simon, this is what we do."

"I know, but, never mind."

"Talk to me," she said.

"Okay. It's stupid."

"It's only stupid that you're not telling me. Stop being a dick and just tell me."

He laughed. "Love you too."

"Simon."

"Fine, does your mom have pictures of her pregnant with you?" he asked.

"Yeah, why?"

"Are there any with my mom?"

"Not that I know of. I'd have to go and check, why?"

"I asked my parents about it and they each gave me a different answer," Simon said.

"What do you mean?"

He told her the two different stories.

"Simon, it was so long ago, I imagine they've

forgotten."

"Would they, though?" he asked.

"What do you mean?"

"I'm their first kid. Removing that memory, it's got to suck, right? You'd remember losing something so close to you."

"I guess. It could be that the memory of losing stuff is too hard. Shoot, Dad's home and he's been pissed. I've got to go. Don't overthink this, Simon. There's probably some kind of explanation that puts it all into perspective."

"Yeah, you're right."

"I'll talk to you later?"

"Yep."

"Love you."

"Love you too." He hung up just as Eddie and Dean arrived in a car. They didn't own bikes and as they climbed out, Simon couldn't help but laugh. They had some dress pants, a crisp pink shirt, and a vest over the top.

"Come on, man, don't laugh."

"I can't help it. You both look like nice boys."

"You're a dick," Eddie said.

"We hanging out or what?" Simon held up the cash. "My treat."

"I need pizza," Dean said.

"You start and I'll follow." He climbed back onto his bike and followed them just out of Piston County to one of the best pizza places in town. It wasn't as good as Mia's, but he couldn't expect her to cook for him whenever he wanted it.

There were a couple of cars he recognized.

"Really, you want to come here where the jocks and their groupies hang out?"

"They've got the best pizza. Come on, man, it

won't be too bad," Eddie said, slapping him on the chest.

Simon walked inside with his boys, and there was a spare booth. He clocked the jocks, including Amber. Giving them a wide berth, he took a seat, and the waitress was already there, ready to serve.

They ordered a couple of large pizzas, garlic bread, extra fries, and he was starving, so he had a couple of additional toppings on the side.

"Amber's watching you again," Eddie said.

"Yeah, she can watch all she wants, but she can't have." He ignored her.

"Simon, I want to ask you something," Dean said.

"Ask away."

"To get into your club, what do you have to do?"

Simon looked up, a little taken aback. "What?"

"You heard me."

"You want to join Chaos Bleeds?"

Dean nodded. "I can't take this shit much more, man. I'm…" He stopped, looking around the room. "They're organizing my wedding. I can't, fuck, I want my own life. I thought I could act with this shit, knowing I'll be able to make it out on my own, but that's never going to happen. I'm not going to get my chance." Dean ran a hand down his face. "I can't stand this shit. I just want a clean break from it all. Is it too much to ask?"

"It's not too much to ask, but being with the club, it's more than wearing a leather cut and riding a bike. It's family, man. It's about giving your life to them, trusting each other. Having each other's backs and shit like that. It's deep. It's not some quick decision you make."

"I get it, man."

"Do you? It's life or die."

Dean nodded. "I've watched you guys for years. I remember the first time I saw you all in the café, years ago. I was like five years old. My parents were so uptight and pissed. They have this superiority thing where they believe they count, but others don't. They're greedy and like to control. You can't be controlled. I need this."

He stared at his friend, who looked almost desperate. "Are you sure?"

"I don't want to get married at eighteen. If I do ever get hitched, I want to have some say in the woman I marry." Dean shook his head. "I can't, I've been thinking of getting emancipated."

"Well, shit," Eddie said.

"Is this happening with you?" Simon asked, seeing them both dressed the same way.

Eddie shook his head. "I had a family dinner."

"And you're still eating pizza?" Simon laughed.

"Did I say I ate it? My grandparents were down and when they are, we have to deal with proper protocol."

"Right," he said.

"It's just what happens."

"I don't know how much longer I can take," Dean said.

"Any lawyer you see through your family, they're going to know," Simon said.

"I know."

"I'll talk to my dad, if you want. He'll be able to find someone who'll handle this for you."

"You're serious?"

"If you're serious about leaving your family, and you know what you're doing, I can get someone to talk to you."

"Fuck, yes. Please, yes."

Chapter Five

"You're going to look hot," Tabitha said.

"I don't care if I look hot," Daisy said. "It's cold out."

The high school was already completely taken over by Halloween. Streamers, banners, spider webs, and all manner of decorations had exploded into each classroom and the halls.

Tabitha loved it. She loved everything to do with Halloween, even if her bestie wasn't the most well-receiving of it.

It was lunchtime and even though there was a chill in the air, they rarely sat indoors to each lunch. She wore a sweater to ward off the cold.

Anthony, Miles, Rachel, and Markus were already at their table. Simon had decided to cut class to go and get stuff ready for tricks he wanted to play. Blaise, Constance, Damien, and John were also present. They were outsiders. They didn't have MC parents, but they were close to them. They'd developed friendships with them along the way, and even though they didn't wear the leather cut, they had their backs.

"Look at the little rebels," Miles said.

"Bite me." Tabitha glared at her brother.

Miles just burst out laughing. "I can't believe Whizz called our dad. That was fucking cold!"

"Don't I know it," Tabitha said.

"It's not funny," Daisy said. "I've had my computer taken from me. I've only got my cell."

Tabitha looked toward Anthony. While her Simon was back in Piston County, she got her kicks out of watching these two. She didn't know if she was rooting for them, or wondering what would happen if they never got together. All of that was a problem for another day.

She had other things on her mind.

"Did I tell you some chick is trying to hit on Simon?"

"Piston Simon?" Miles asked.

"One and the same."

"Are you thinking we need to take a trip to Piston County?"

This was what she loved about her brother. No matter how much laughing or joking he did, he always had her back.

"I think it could be. What do you guys say, a trip to Piston County?"

"Is this just for you guys?" Blaise asked.

This always put her on edge with the outsiders. It was hard.

"I don't see why not," Miles said. "You got to get your parents to agree to a sleepover and visiting another town."

"Then I'm out," John said. "At times, I'm lucky they haven't thrown my ass in boarding school."

Miles laughed. "We'll send you postcards."

"I'd like to," Constance said. "My parents don't give a shit. I'm up for getting out of this shithole."

"Hey, this shithole is family," Markus said.

Constance looked at him, brows lifted. "Yeah, for you, who lives in a nice place with a dentist mother. Not for me with a mom in and out of rehab and a dad who won't let her move on. This is family to you, not to me. I've got you guys, that's it."

"You need some help with that shit?" Miles said.

"What shit?"

"Your family."

"Nah, I've got it covered. It's fine."

"You need help, you tell us."

"Will do."

Tabitha looked at Miles, who continued to look at Constance. She had already turned away. After a few seconds, Miles averted his gaze but caught her staring. She offered him a smile and he glared. "The fuck you looking at?" he asked.

"I don't know. You tell me."

"As interesting as all this is, Dogs are approaching and Ryan looks mad," Daisy said.

Glancing at her friend, she followed her gaze, and sure enough, the Dogs were on their way.

They all got to their feet. She and Daisy stood by Anthony's side. They all had each other's backs.

Some of the kids ran off in the opposite direction, clearly not wanting to be in the line of fire.

Tensed and ready, Tabitha watched.

Luke was at the head of the group. He always was. Ryan by his side.

"Do you think we were going to let that slide?" Luke asked.

"You don't bring Quad business here," Anthony said.

"Anything you got to say, you do so on Quad territory. You upset about getting your face rearranged, don't be taking on fights you can't win," Miles said.

"Ah, they have to hide behind all the nice little rules. They're a has-been club, baby. We should ignore them. They're not worth our time." This came from Daniella. She was a Dogs kid and considered the queen in her group.

Tabitha hated her. Daniella was a coward and had a reputation for taking her opponents from behind. It was the only way she could get ahead.

"We're weak, as opposed to the Dogs who are made up of easy pussy and whores?" Tabitha asked.

Daniella glared at her. "Takes one to know one."

"Don't talk to her like that," Daisy said.

"And what are you going to do about that?" Daniella asked. "You're the fat useless one of the group. You're not even a real Skull. You're a kid no one wants, and I bet your ass is going to be passed around."

Tabitha couldn't allow this to spiral out, so she did what any self-respecting friend would do. Daniella had stepped close to their group, thinking school grounds made her safe. She reached out, grabbed her hair, pulled her close, and slammed her face against the bench tabletop, smearing food from the trays that were left.

"You want to say that again?" She lifted her head up and slammed it back down.

Daniella cried.

She didn't have to worry about the Dogs rushing her. Her guys would keep everyone at bay, and that was why she landed a few more blows.

"Teacher coming."

Her guys moved, and she threw Daniella at her people, blood coming from her nose and a cut on her head.

Tabitha felt no remorse. Taking hold of Daisy's hand, she quickly looked all concerned.

"What is going on here?" Mr. Rivers asked.

"I don't know. She slipped," Daisy said, speaking up first. This did surprise Tabitha, but then her friend would always have her back.

"Yeah, man, she was coming onto Anthony, offering to suck his dick. I didn't realize the Dogs weren't packing good meat," Miles said.

"That is enough from you," Mr. Rivers said. "Daniella?"

Tabitha waited.

If she squealed, it would make their club look weak, and The Skulls would win.

Seconds passed.

"I slipped."

"Are you sure?"

"Yeah, I slipped. I fell. You need to learn to get decent cleaning crews on this shit," Daniella said.

Mr. Rivers looked insulted. "If that is all." He turned on his heel and backed away.

"This isn't over," Luke said.

Tabitha shrugged. "You can count on it."

The Skulls didn't move. The Dogs were the first to leave, and she breathed a sigh of relief.

"Badass, Tabs."

"You're going to pay for that at the Quad," Daisy said. "It's not going to be good."

"Don't care. She had it coming. Anyone who talks shit to you like that needs to be taught a lesson." Tabitha stopped talking as Anthony stood in front of Daisy. He reached out, cupped her cheek, and she waited.

No words were spoken.

Time stood still.

She nibbled on her lip, waiting.

Anthony stepped away, and the moment was gone.

"You've got to be kidding me," Tabitha said.

Daisy frowned. "What?"

The bell rang and lunch was over.

Tabitha sighed. "Time to get to class. Meet me before last period."

"PE, yay," Daisy said, hugging her friend. "Don't go hitting anyone else."

"I won't."

They all headed back into the school. She loved

how people stepped out of their way. The Skulls were feared even if the Dogs liked to think they owned the school.

Anthony and Miles left first, each of them dispersing down a separate corridor to their class. She now had English, and she entered the classroom, going toward the back, near the window.

She loved sitting near windows, staring outside at the passing world.

There was nothing more comforting to her.

Time passed.

Slowly.

She jumped as a book was slammed down on the table right beside her. Turning, she saw Luke sitting right beside her.

"This seat is taken," she said.

"Not today."

"Leave."

"Not happening."

"You think this is going to go well for you? My crew will eat you alive."

"And after that little show, I figured you were a hard-ass who didn't need anyone at her back."

"I don't."

The teacher watched them and she knew she couldn't allow this to happen.

"Go on, try it. You think any of the teachers are going to interfere with our stuff? They're too fucking afraid to be caught up in the line of fire."

"You want to declare war here?"

"We were at the Quad. You shouldn't have been there."

"There's no such rule to state only one of us can be there at any one time. Don't try to make possessive claims that don't belong."

"We were having fun."

"No one would take on your psycho. Our psycho did, and you don't like it."

Luke grabbed her arm and before she could stop him, he dragged her right out of the classroom. No one stopped him.

This was one of the few classes she didn't share with her crew. The only class with Luke.

Fuck!

"Let go of me."

This guy was strong. She wasn't used to being overpowered. The few guys she had fought hadn't been this strong, or they'd gone easy on her because she was a girl.

He threw her into a bathroom and she caught herself up against the wall, putting her hands out to stop her from impact.

She turned and glared at him. "Are you feeling like a big tough guy?" She slapped her hands together in applause. "Look at you, throwing me around."

He advanced on her, his hands slamming either side of her head. She didn't flinch, didn't even move.

"I'm trying to make it to graduation alive," he said.

"You've got two whole years to keep on fighting. We'll go easy on you."

"Dammit, Tabby, not this again."

She slammed her fist against his gut, but he didn't show any sign of that even hurting. "Do not call me Tabby." There was only one person who called her Tabby, and he was in Piston County right now.

Luke smiled. "Why, what are you going to do about it?"

He was pulled off her and she saw Anthony waiting. He threw Luke against the sinks.

No words.

Just actions.

Luke got to his feet with a laugh. "I should have known you'd be here."

"You think you can make a move on our girl and get away with it?" Miles came in.

Tabitha was even surprised to see Daisy standing there, arms folded. They all looked pissed. Rachel was there, Markus, even Constance, Blaise, Damien, and John.

Luke held his hands up. "Wow, can't even have a conversation without everyone. Is that what you all do? One big fucking orgy?"

Anthony struck him again.

Tabitha put a hand on his shoulder. He gave no sign of being distressed or pissed off. This was Anthony. Calm. Like it was merely an action. Nothing more.

Daisy stepped forward. "Walk away."

Luke glanced at Daisy before returning his gaze to hers. Tabitha folded her arms, waiting. She always thought Ryan was the stupid one.

"I suggest you leave school for the day," Miles said. "We wouldn't want anything bad to happen to you."

"And you're saying it would if I stay here?"

"We can't guarantee your safety," Daisy said.

"What you did was stupid," Tabitha said.

"No, but I also know someone in class has it in for the Dogs. Don't you see it? The school is divided. I was just curious to see which way it would fall."

"Don't fuck with my sister and get out," Miles said.

Luke smirked. "Until next time, Tabby."

She went to defend her name but Daisy was there, holding her back.

Luke left the bathroom and now Tabitha turned to

her friends.

"What the hell?" she asked.

"Don't talk to us like that," Miles said. "Do you have any idea what he could have done to you? How hurt you could have been? Next time, you don't go with him willingly."

She laughed. "You think I went with him willingly?"

"He's strong," Anthony said.

"I had it handled."

"Did you?" Daisy asked. "From where I was standing, it looked like he was the one in control. You, you were waiting for him to strike."

Tabitha shrugged. "You can believe me or not, I don't care. I'm telling you I had it handled. There was no way he was going to get past me."

"Why does he want to know about the school?" Rachel asked, coming further into the room.

"We better head back to class," Tabitha said.

"We need to meet up about this," Miles said, looking toward Anthony.

"Agreed," Daisy said.

"No!" Tabitha sliced her hand through the air. She'd heard enough. "Have you ever thought this is exactly what he wanted? Luke … he's not like Ryan. If this was fuckface, I'd say we've got to worry about his deal, but he's not. He's different. We all know this. No, I think this is him fucking with us. Trying to distract us. We don't bite. That's what we do."

"You're sure?" Daisy asked. "You seem to know Luke better than anyone."

"What the fuck is that supposed to mean?"

"Nothing. Wow, you're the one who has told us you keep an eye on shit like this. No need to be a bitch." Daisy shook her head and stormed out of the bathroom.

Tabitha winced. She had told the crew that, and now, fuck, she'd been mean.

"I'll let you deal with that problem."

One by one, her friends left until there was only her and Anthony.

"I didn't mean to bite her head off."

Silence.

She tapped her foot, impatient. "For fuck's sake, Anthony, tell me what you've got to say and then we can move on."

"You've got to learn to be careful," he said. "I don't trust the Dogs. We know their club is wrapped up in illegal shit. When we're old enough, the club will be ours, unless you've made your decision about moving to Chaos Bleeds."

"The club will be yours, Anthony. I'm not going to be your old lady."

He wrinkled his nose.

"Nice to know what you think of me."

"Be careful and make it right with Daisy." He stepped out of the bathroom.

Alone, she wrapped her arms around herself, wincing. Being thrown against a wall had hurt. She'd have a few bruises.

Leaning against the same wall, she tilted her head back and stared up at the ceiling. The Skulls, the club, this wasn't supposed to be so complicated.

"Fuck it, it's too soon to make any kind of decision right now."

Out of habit, she washed her hands, dried them, and headed back to English. Luke was still there and the teacher paused as Tabitha entered.

She kept her head held high and made her way to her window seat, right next to Luke.

Sitting down, she waited.

The teacher continued to teach the class.

A piece of paper was slid across to her.

She ignored it.

Luke pressed a finger on top.

Picking it up, she opened to find his note.

Are you okay? I didn't mean to hurt you.

There was no way she was going to justify an answer. Closing the note, she slid it right back to him.

Watching the teacher, she couldn't hear what he was saying. Holding her pencil, she copied everything off the board and she'd have to go over everything with Darcy, who was no longer in school because she was happily married to Ink and was still in recovery. She was another friend she wished was still in school.

She stifled a yawn but the note was slid right back to her.

Don't ignore me. It's rude.

Was this guy for real?

She didn't respond.

Again, he scribbled.

If you don't respond, I'll make another scene.

She responded.

Make a scene. I don't care.

Are you okay?

This is pathetic. I'm not talking to you.

I didn't mean to hurt you.

It takes a lot more than being thrown into a wall to hurt me.

I'm sorry.

You're sounding like a pussy now. I'm bored.

She slid the note over for him to read. Before he could respond, she snatched it back and tore it up. There, done.

The bell rang, and Tabitha was more than happy to get the hell out of there. She met up with Daisy and they hugged. Her best friend couldn't stay mad at her for too long, which she was thankful for. So long as she had Daisy, she'd be fine. Her best friend meant the world to her.

****

Eva, her mother, had gone all out in the Halloween decorations this year. Standing at the front gate, she laughed at the gravestones and the coffins with arms peeking out.

"You think this is too much?"

"Not at all. In fact, you better have a whole lot of candy ready. I just know we're going to get a lot of visitors."

"It was Angel's idea. Each of The Skulls with a yard have decorated the whole house."

She wasn't surprised about it being Angel. Being the club president's old lady, she'd brought it on herself to start working toward a better image to all of the people of Fort Wills. Angel worked so hard. She offered charity runs throughout town, helped with fairs, created food competitions, and anything with a fun edge, she was there.

For the most part, it worked.

"Look at you," Eva said, holding her arms out.

"Mom, don't." She stepped into her mom's arms, accepting her kiss to the cheek.

"You look stunning."

She'd gotten a costume of an eighteenth-century woman, complete with a corset. To help turn it into a Halloween costume, Daisy had helped her to tear the fabric, adding on some fake blood, and of course, there was more risqué with her boobs pressed tight and up.

She looked good.

She knew she did.

"It's a good thing Simon's busy. Dad wouldn't let

you out because he'd know all the kinds of naughty you'd get into."

"Oh, enough with you, Tate," Eva said.

Tate, her older sister, laughed.

"What do you think?"

"You know I think you look beautiful, and you do." Tate came toward her, hugging her tightly.

Once again, Tate was heavily pregnant. There were so many babies being born, it was hard to keep up with all the latest developments.

"Is Daisy ever going to come down?"

Just then, Daisy, complete in a nurse's uniform and long white socks, came downstairs.

Tabitha knew she was going to have to talk with Lash or Anthony about Daisy. When they'd been changing, she'd caught sight of Daisy's back and had seen a couple of bruises. One of which looked like it came from a foot, which said it had to be her biological dad. There was no way Whizz would do something like that, and no one at school would even dare touch her. They would have known if anything happened to her.

With the nurse's uniform, there were slashes across her arm, her face was heavily made up, and her long brown hair had been curled. Anthony was going to lose it.

"Wow, I mean, wow," Tate said.

Daisy stood, wrapping an arm around her middle, where more exposed flesh with claw marks lay.

"This is stupid. We're sixteen. Do we need to dress up?"

"We're going to be," Eva said. "I'm manning the door here until nine, and then at the clubhouse, there's going to be one hell of a party. It's going to be a lot of fun."

Daisy raised her brow, looking toward Tabitha.

"Do not think we won't be back to check on your guys. We will. If you're not home when we get back, your asses will be on the line."

Tate rolled her eyes and laughed. "Keep an eye on Simon for me, will you? Ugh, I'm sounding like a mom myself."

Tabitha laughed. "I will, and I hate to break it to you, you are a mom."

"I know but I remember when I was cool. When I didn't ask for my son to make me a grandma before my time." Tate shook her head. "Get out. Get out before I have a meltdown."

Tabitha grabbed two jackets as she laughed, but stopped, looking back at her mom.

"Mom, do you have any pictures of Lexie pregnant?"

"Of course."

"Do you have any where she was pregnant with Simon?"

Eva seemed to freeze. Even Tate coughed on her drink.

"Honey, why do you ask?"

"Simon and I were talking. It's nothing. I'm just curious."

"Lexie and I didn't know each other well enough when she had Simon."

She nodded.

"Have a good night."

She and Daisy left the house, heading down the yard, where ghoul and ghost sounds came from the trigger sensor.

"That was odd," Daisy said.

"What?"

"She referred to Simon as having him, not being pregnant with him."

"Why is that odd?"

"I don't know. Don't you think they acted weirdly?"

"I do. It was strange, wasn't it?"

"Why do you think they're behaving that way? Do you think Simon is adopted?" Daisy asked.

"Nah, he looks exactly like Devil. Remember?"

"True."

"Lexie can also have a lot of kids. We know, we've taken care of half of her population."

Daisy laughed. "What is with all the secrecy though?"

"Not a clue, but it makes me want to find out."

"Do you think I should try some hacking?" Daisy asked.

"Well, well, well, you're in a good mood. It's about time."

"Don't spoil it for me, then. Yes, I'm in a good mood. I am happy." She took a deep breath. "I don't like my costume but rather than be pissed about it, I'm going to embrace it."

"Will you be dancing tonight?" Tabitha asked.

"If you ask."

"And what if Anthony asks?"

"Don't. We're friends. That's all this will ever be."

"But if you and Anthony get together, that would put you in Angel's position."

"Tabitha, that is going to be your place. You're the queen here. If Tiny had still been the president of the club, Miles would probably be the first one in line."

"Don't forget they have to prove themselves, and my brother isn't like Anthony. He's too hot-headed."

"You and Miles are certainly hot and cold. Did you see the way he looked at Constance?"

"So you can see it in other guys looking at other girls, but not when they're looking at you?"

"Don't start. Anthony and I are friends. We're not going to be anything else. Stop pushing it."

Tabitha linked arms with her friend. "I will stop for tonight, but one day, you're going to see just how right I am."

"Until then, let's just have a lot of fun."

"You're talking about fun. What have you done with my best friend?" Tabitha giggled, resting her head on her shoulder.

"I've decided it's Halloween and I'm going to be taking a personal day off. I'm not going to think. I'm just going to be like every other sixteen-year-old who has finally gotten off grounding."

"You're going to drink way too much and make sure our parents wished they never let us out of the house."

"You've got it."

They both laughed and giggled together. "I love this."

"Me too," Daisy said with a sigh.

They got to the edge of the road and they didn't need to go far as Anthony arrived, complete with the crew. Miles, Simon, and even Michael were all in the back of the truck.

"You're driving tonight?" Tabitha asked.

Anthony was dressed as a doctor zombie. Her brother looked like a pirate, and Michael just looked the same. She couldn't see Rachel's outfit or Markus.

"Get in, sis, come on. Don't leave us standing around. We've got chicks to go find."

Rolling her eyes, she opened the door. "Doctor's first," she said, helping Daisy up into the truck. Her best friend looked like she wanted to say something else.

"Fun, remember?"

Daisy climbed up, taking the seat right next to Anthony. She followed inside, closing the door.

"Did you bring any booze?" Tabitha asked.

Miles stuck his head through the window. "Please, we know what our parents are like. Hypocrites to the end. We snuck it into the school."

Tabitha chuckled.

"Who's driving tonight?" Daisy asked.

"Don't worry about a thing. We've all got a plan." Miles patted her arm as if that was in any way offering comfort.

"He knows that freaks me out, right?"

"It's my brother. Don't expect anything he does to make any kind of sense."

They were all laughing, apart from Anthony, who was focused on driving or not irritating Daisy. She didn't exactly know what. Her cell phone was concealed in one of the secret pockets she was told about. She missed Simon. Most of the Halloweens, he was around to keep her company and she found today was hard for her. She wanted to be with him. Tapping her fingers on the doorframe, she tried to look forward to the party.

It was hard.

"Tonight is going to be kickass!" Miles screamed from the top of his lungs as if the whole world was supposed to hear him.

"Has he already been drinking?" Daisy asked.

Anthony nodded.

"It's going to be one hell of a night," Tabitha said.

Arriving at the high school twenty minutes later, Anthony parked the car on the edge of the lot, giving them plenty of room to make an escape if needed.

Climbing out of the car, Daisy needed a little help

as the skirt was so short and she didn't want to show off her panties to the rest of the world. "You had to pick the most risqué and daring skirt around," Tabitha said.

Daisy chuckled. "You helped me to pick."

Screams, laughter, and music all came from the school.

Staring up at the imposing building, Tabitha experienced the yearning deep in her heart for Simon. She always tried to ignore it because usually the fear of having to deal with questions, to have answers, to know what she wanted, was tough. To have Simon, she was going to have to make a choice.

"It's going to be crazy," Miles said, taking the lead as they headed into the school. There were already couples making out on the hoods of their cars.

Daisy put a hand through hers. "I hate this."

"Fun, remember?"

"Yeah, well, I don't like scary things."

"I thought you loved Halloween."

"I do. Movie marathons, silly candy, and names for food. I like the kiddy stuff."

"This is going to be fun."

They entered the school and a life-sized zombie doll dropped down from the doorway, causing Daisy to scream.

"I'm going to need a drink."

Kids were walking through the halls as there was supposed to be a haunted theme.

"There's a dance with food and drinks at the main hall," Tabitha said. "I'm going to head to the bathroom. I'll join you?"

"Sure." Daisy kissed her cheek and took off. Her friend knew what she wanted to do.

Anthony was already following after her. Her brother and the others were gone to enjoy their own stuff.

Taking a deep breath, she felt off about the whole thing, not connected.

She watched her friends, hoping Daisy finally realized Anthony's feelings for her and didn't dismiss them.

Still, it was a hard one.

She turned and headed toward one of the bathrooms. It was empty, and she went straight to the sinks, turning on the water and splashing her neck rather than her face.

Looking up, she stared at her reflection. She looked sad.

Stepping away, she made her way into one of the stalls and pulled out her cell phone. Picking the video option, she pulled up Simon's number. There was a chance he wouldn't answer. He did warn her how involved he planned to be with Halloween. She wished she'd offered to go and see him, but with the grounding, there was no way that was going to happen. She was lucky to be going out at all, and she knew if it hadn't been for Anthony, she'd still be grounded and enjoying a night like the one Daisy wanted.

"Hey, babe," Simon said, accepting her call.

He wasn't in his home and she saw past his shoulders, the streets of Piston County where he lived. His home was in a nice neighborhood. She'd visited him a couple of times. More often than not, Chaos Bleeds came to Fort Wills rather than the other way around.

"Hey," she said, hating how alone she felt.

"What's up?" Simon's smile was instantly replaced with concern.

"Nothing."

"Don't say that to me. I know you."

She took a breath. "You know me so well."

"Always. Talk to me."

"It's nothing. Honestly, I don't get it." She ran fingers through her hair. "I don't know. It's Halloween and I think it has been so long since you've been here."

"I'm missing you too. Where are you?"

"The school bathroom. The others have gone, fingers crossed, dancing and having fun."

"I command you to have fun."

She snorted. "You command me?"

"Yeah, I command you. I wish I was there but I've got to stick around here and make sure it all works. I want you to have fun. You've got a right to it. Take pictures. Send them to me. I want to see it all as if I was there."

"Simon, come on," a young girl said. His phone jerked as his arm was pulled.

"Go, I will go and do as you command."

"Good. You deserve to have some fun and I want to hear all about it."

"I will, sir!" She saluted him.

"Love you."

"Love you too." She hung up the phone and sighed, sitting on the toilet. She pocketed her cell phone and held in a groan as the doors opened.

"He's just so dreamy. I get that he has the whole bad boy vibe, but come on. I would so do anything for Anthony. I would love to see his head between my thighs, if you know what I mean."

Tabitha frowned. She didn't recognize the voice.

"I don't know how you can make a choice. Think about Luke," another girl said.

"One of the Dogs?"

"Yeah, I hear he's a monster in the sack."

She rolled her eyes. Seriously. They were talking about Anthony and Luke. Ugh.

"What about Miles? I hear Louise had sex with

him and she said it was the best she'd ever had."

She was going to be sick, really throw up.

"Come on, who do you think is better, The Skulls or the Monster Dogs?"

She'd heard enough.

Flushing the toilet, she let herself out of the bathroom to see four girls. Two of which she recognized from class but didn't actually know their names.

She washed her hands, loving the tension that mounted.

The urge to pummel both of them was strong. Instead, she dried her hands on a towel.

Turning back to the group, she smiled. "It's your lucky night. I catch you talking shit about my guys or my club again, you're all going to be mourning the loss of your pretty faces after I mangle them. Happy Halloween." She turned on her heel and walked out the door, heading toward the dance floor.

She found Miles and Daisy dancing while Anthony was on the sidelines.

Did she have to do everything herself? She was going to have to beat up her brother.

"You didn't ask her to dance?" Tabitha asked.

"How is Simon?"

"Don't change the question."

"I don't dance."

"Now you do." She grabbed Anthony's hand and pulled him onto the floor. She kept hold of his hands and moved them in a choo-choo train effect.

"You're mocking me."

"Dance." She threw her hands up in the air and danced.

"I don't think ladies danced like that back then." He pointed at her costume.

She laughed. "Come on, guys, let's take a pic for

Simon." She pulled her camera out. Daisy, Anthony, and Miles got in on the action. She stuck her tongue out, and it flashed.

"Dance with me." She stole Miles and urged Daisy into Anthony's arms.

"You've got to stop playing matchmaker, sis. It's not fair."

"You're not going to touch Daisy because you know he'll break your legs. Why do you keep insisting on coming between them? It's not fair."

"No, what's not fair is you clearly not seeing that Daisy is oblivious to all the shit you want her to see."

She and Miles turned in a circle.

"And what, I should just allow them to make their own mistakes?"

"Yeah."

"What if Daisy starts dating someone else?"

"Then Anthony will either kill the guy or make sure she doesn't date him for long. You've got to stop trying to protect them both. They're teenagers. Let them have some fun." Miles hugged her close and she looked toward her best friend.

She was laughing but was in Anthony's arms. They were so perfect together. She didn't know why her friend didn't see it.

"Look at them," she said.

"Daisy is having fun. She's already had a drink. Come morning, she's going to be a bitch again. Let them work their shit out at their own time. You don't need to keep helping them with this."

The dance ended and Tabitha moved away from the dance floor. She was thankful Anthony didn't allow Daisy to go.

She took her cell phone and started to snap pictures to share with Simon later.

Folding her arms, she watched the dancing and decided against being a lone partner. She wasn't going to be dancing with anyone but Simon. She had promised him all of her dances years ago.

Leaving the main hall, she started to wander down the corridor. Guys and girls were all laughing, drinking, making out, and having fun.

Sure, there was a lot of spookiness going on.

"I didn't think you'd be left alone," Luke said.

She turned to see him complete with vampire teeth but wearing leather. His hair was spiked, and blood spatter was on his clothing.

"Are you following me?"

"Nope."

"Good, then leave."

"I'm curious as to why you're all on your own."

"I'm not on my own and if any of my crew see you with me, they're just desperate for a fight."

Luke chuckled. "You think I'm scared of them?"

"What is this?" she asked. "Do you have some kind of secret crush on me, is that it?" She wasn't in the mood to deal with any shit. Her heart would always belong to Simon.

Nothing and no one was going to change that. Not even this guy.

"You think because I find you pretty I have some kind of crush?"

"Oh, so you find me pretty. Good to know." She rolled her eyes and kept on walking.

"You've got an attitude, you know that?"

"Yep." She wasn't about to deny something she certainly knew to be true. She had an attitude when it came to opposing clubs.

The Skulls and Monster Dogs MC should never have crossed paths. She wasn't an idiot. She knew this.

Everyone did, and the only reason they did cross paths was because of the school change. Her parents hadn't wanted her or Miles to go, but Lash and Angel had no problem sending Anthony.

Everything went fine, so long as the two clubs didn't mix. So far, their parental counterpart had yet to be caught in the same room. She truly believed for parents-teacher night, the school arranged for different days so nothing bad would happen.

Just because The Skulls currently had a deal going which meant they weren't involved in any kind of criminal activity didn't mean they weren't able to fight. In fact, there were a couple of times she'd snuck down when her dad, Tiny, had arrived back on a couple of the rides where they had to protect people, and he'd been pretty banged up. Bruises and bleeding, all sorts of problems. There had even been a couple of the guys who ended up in the hospital. Tabitha wasn't an idiot. To the outside world, people believed The Skulls had gone soft. They hadn't. They'd turned their skills towards actually helping people, rather than hurting them. The danger was still there and they put themselves in it on a regular basis, but again, she understood why. She'd seen some of the women and children, even men who they rescued, who needed their help. None of them were ever in a good way and on most occasions, serious therapy was required as well.

"You know, you don't have to be a bitch."

She stopped outside of a classroom and saw more people making out, even as spooky noises played in the background.

"Nice of you to be able to tell me that." She patted his arm.

"You know Ryan wants to get the jump on Anthony," Luke said.

This made her pause and turn toward him. "You do know by telling me this, in a way, you're picking sides."

"I'm not. I'm trying to get through high school. I didn't want this, and I doubt you did as well."

She ran her fingers through her hair. "When?"

"I'm not telling you that."

"By the jump, I'm guessing you mean he intends to play dirty?" she asked.

Luke nodded.

He didn't have to tell her.

"Thank you."

"No problem. You want me to escort you back to the dance floor? It's not good you being around all by yourself."

"I'm not. I've got you. My little white knight," she said.

"Be careful, Tabs," he said. "You never know who is watching."

"I know." She stepped past him but paused. "Thank you."

"I'm just trying to get through the school year." He escorted her back to the dance floor and she stepped inside. When she turned to talk to him again, he was gone.

Fine. Ryan was going to put the jump on Anthony. She had the warning clear.

Glancing across the dance floor, she smiled at her friends. She hadn't drunk anything but it was clear Daisy had. Her best friend was all relaxed.

She doubted for even a second Anthony had drunk anything. The guy was a master of control.

Folding her arms, she waited, watching everything play out. They all looked so happy.

Miles was the first one to come toward her.

"Come on, everyone is heading out by the lake for some fun." He kissed her head as Daisy stumbled toward her.

"Let's go to the lake."

"Are you sure this is a good idea?" she asked.

"Hell, yeah, it's a great idea." Daisy took her hands and spun her around.

Bursting out laughing, Tabitha felt a kick to her stomach. She missed her best friend being like this so much. One day soon, she was going to get to the bottom of what was going on inside that head of hers.

"We can't stay too long," she said, being the voice of reason for a change.

Daisy snorted. "Come on, it's going to be a lot of fun. I can't wait." She let out a whoop, spinning around, and Anthony caught her.

"No more alcohol for you," Miles said.

"Spoilsport. For the first time in like forever, I'm being fun and you guys want to take it away from me. No fun at all." She blew a raspberry.

After climbing into Anthony's car, Miles settled in the back to keep an eye on Daisy. They took off out of the school and the moment the building was behind them, she took a deep breath. They'd made it through Halloween without a single fight or problem. Progress.

They were headed just out of town toward the small lake that was often the site for families. There were always some kids who parked not too far to make out as it was secluded by the local woods and wildlife. Fort Wills had tried to build itself in the past few years as some kind of wildlife expert, especially since The Skulls hadn't brought any real trouble to town.

Anthony parked and out they all went. Blaise, Constance, Markus, Damien, and John also joined. Rachel and Simon weren't too far behind either.

John set up a small fire while Simon produced more alcohol. When he went to give the whiskey bottle to Daisy, Anthony took it from him, offering her some soda instead. Markus turned up the music from one of the cars, and that was it, they were all on their feet, dancing around the campfire. Along with Daisy, Tabitha kicked off her shoes.

Letting the music fill the night air, Tabitha threw her hands up in the air, closed her eyes, swayed her hips, and just let go.

There was no trouble, no danger, no acts, just her. She didn't have to worry about what the future was going to hold.

She was just a singular person.

Daisy started singing along to the words and Tabitha burst out laughing, joining her. Gravitating toward her, they held hands, screaming out the words, slowing down, staring into each other's eyes. The grass felt so good between their toes. When the song went loud and shouted, they joined in, stamping their food, emphasizing what they were doing and then both burst out laughing as the song ended and another started.

Taking a deep breath, they collapsed on the ground as the others continued to dance and drink.

"Thank you," Daisy said.

"What for?"

"For making me come out tonight. I loved it."

They were laid out on the ground and Tabitha was aware Anthony watched Daisy. He never stopped, not since they were a kid.

Turning her head, she stared at her friend, kissing her cheek. "Anytime. Tomorrow, you're going to tell me why you're always so sad."

Daisy sighed and tears sprang to her eyes. She licked her lips. "It's him again. He is..." She sniffed. "I don't want Whizz to hate having me. I know I'm not a great kid, nothing special."

Tabitha cupped her face. "Shut up. Don't start. Don't even for a second think like that. You're amazing. Whizz and Lacey know how good and lucky they are to have you."

Daisy nodded but the tears started to fall and then she curled up in a ball and started to sob.

Sitting up, Tabitha pulled her onto her lap and stroked her hair. "I've got you."

"I'm sorry."

"It's fine."

"No, it's not. I can't stand it, Tabs. Whenever my cell phone rings, I'm scared. I can't stand him. I don't want him to be around me anymore. Can't he just leave me alone? I've done nothing to him and all he keeps doing is invading my peace. I don't know how much I can take."

Tabitha stroked her hair, holding her close. Staring across at Anthony, there was no doubt in her mind what was going to happen. He watched Daisy.

There was nothing different about his face, but something in his eyes flashed. He'd heard Daisy's confession, the pain in her voice. The grief and the finality to her. Her father, the man who'd donated sperm, he was going to get one hell of a visit, but she wasn't going to tell him not to.

If he lived through it, he would get what was coming to him.

No one hurt one of their own and lived to tell the tale.

"It's going to be okay."

Chapter Six

"I thought you worked closely with The Skulls?" Simon asked.

The guys were staying at a hotel, a nice one that had been arranged by the Billionaire Bikers MC.

Simon stared out the window, wondering why Lash and the others weren't there.

"We do, on most cases. This is a little more delicate."

"How do you mean?" Simon closed the curtain and turned to see his father typing on his cell phone. He waited and after a few minutes, Devil put the phone down.

"Mom okay?"

"Yeah, she's fine."

"You want to tell me what is going on with her?" Simon moved toward his bed. They had decided to share a room with two beds, not that they needed to. He'd been more than happy with a single. He could have talked with Tabby. As it was, he now had to share all night with his pops. He hoped the dude didn't fart.

"What do you want to know the answer to more?" Devil asked. "If only given one question, what one would it be?"

He frowned. "Why would I only get one answer to one question?"

"Simple. In life, we have to learn to accept what we know and what we can't. You need to understand, down the road, you're only going to get one chance to know and understand. Do you think you can handle that?"

Simon sat on the edge of the bed. "Sure."

"So what would it be? Why we're here without The Skulls, or what is wrong with your mom?"

Simon ran his fingers through his hair. This was a test. His father had been doing these more often than not. He got it. To be a good leader, he needed to pick the right choices for the club.

Twiddling his thumbs, he stared at Devil. "Why are we here?"

"And why do you feel that is the most important question?"

"It's not the most important question in my life right now, but it's the most pivotal one. The men are relying on you keeping them safe. Of getting them in and out without too much trouble."

"That is where you're wrong, son. My men know there is always a risk when they come on these trips. I do what I can to make them safe but they know I'm not God. I don't have miracles up my sleeve."

"They all know?" Simon asked.

"They do. Even you need to know I can't guarantee something won't happen. Lexie knows this. She didn't want you to go."

"But I wanted to go." His mom had asked him if there was anything else he'd rather be doing. "She worries."

"But I know it's what you want to know."

"This is going to be dangerous then?"

Devil nodded. "It is. What you need to understand is we're entering a potentially dangerous home. The woman who called, she has three kids, all of which are under ten. But when we go inside, it could be the kids who cause an issue."

"What do you mean?"

"They've gotten used to the way life is and if they're loyal to their dad, they may have called him. It's a risk. It always is."

Simon nodded. "Are you afraid?"

Devil sighed. "I knew you were going to ask that."

"Sorry. I'm just trying to figure this all out."

"Are you?"

Simon looked at his dad. He didn't want to be considered a coward. The club was all he ever wanted and if his father thought he was a coward, he wouldn't be able to take over. "No."

"Wrong answer, son. You are. First rule here, don't lie."

"You're not afraid, are you?"

"No, I'm not. I've got no reason to be afraid, but here's the thing, son, I am as well."

"That makes no sense."

Devil chuckled. "Going into danger doesn't scare me. A guy with a gun. The shit I've faced, I know what I'm getting myself into and what's more, I'm more than happy to do it. I live for this shit." The smile went. "But the thought of never seeing Lexie again. Of her having to live without me, that's a cold, harsh reality I don't want to have to deal with. I love your mother, Simon. In fact, I can't stand the thought of going a day when I don't tell her that I love her. I'm sure you feel something just as strong."

"For Tabby. Being without her, it's like there is a giant, gaping hole in my chest but I'm not a fool, I know we're going to have a lot of problems."

"What makes you say that?"

"We don't talk about it, but I'm aware she's a Skull and I'm a Chaos. I know each time I talk about the future there's a chance, a slim one, we can't make it work. Even though our clubs work together, we're different."

Devil nodded his head. "You're right. We're different and knowing you're aware of this gives me hope."

Simon laughed. "Hope? Really?"

"Yes. It means you know that this thing with her is going to take some challenges. Tiny's been open and honest with me. For a long time, he knew she didn't want to be part of the club. It was only a few years ago that she embraced who she was, what she was. She could try to outrun the club, but there was no way she was going to leave this world behind. It sticks."

"Her loyalty is to The Skulls, not to me."

"You're wrong there. She's loyal to her club as is her right, but her loyalty is also to you. You've got something, and I tried to deny it. Figuring it was some kind of kid thing. You used her as a security blanket. Your childhoods, I tried to make yours as happy as could be but life, it was so fucked at times. When we managed to kill one evil, another came laughing in my face. There was no way I could keep it up. It's why I made the change. I thought the one constant for you was Tabitha. But then there was also Miles, Anthony, the other Simon, Daisy even. A few of the other kids but their names escape me. You didn't want to marry them or have their babies. You didn't vow to be their old man, or them your old ladies. She's special to you. I don't always understand it at such a young age. I was out, screwing whatever threw themselves at me, but the moment I met Lexie, she was like fire. She gave me a reason to breathe. The club was always part of my life, but she made me realize exactly what I'd been missing and I would never give her up, not for the world."

"Do you ever miss it?" Simon asked.

"Screwing random bitches?"

"No." Simon shook his head. "Riding. Being out

on the open road. I know you settled in Piston County as you felt the club needed a place to call its own, but do you ever miss just riding? Going from town to town?"

"Not anymore. The Nomad chapter is doing their stuff, you know. Remember Lucius?"

Simon nodded. "You haven't heard from him in a long time, have you?"

"No, but I do keep an ear out. I guess since Roxy's death, he's been trying to deal, you know, the only way he can."

Simon vaguely remembered the guy from the Chaos Bleeds Nomad chapter. Each of the clubs, even The Skulls, had a chapter that didn't live in any one area. They traveled. Lucius had been part of it, and so had Roxy. She'd been a club whore, a dearly loved woman, but she'd died. Afterward, Lucius hadn't been able to cope and had left. There was no sign of him, not even a dead body, unless Devil didn't want to tell him what had happened.

"Is that why you don't want to travel? What it would do to Mom?"

"No," Devil said. "The reason I don't want to travel is that I don't need to. I've done it all. I was reminding you of the Nomads, in case that's what you want to try. There's something freeing about being on the open road. You learn a lot about yourself."

Simon thought about it. "Right now, it's not something I want."

"Tabby?"

"I don't feel the need to be away from her any longer than I have to. Unless she wants to go with me."

Devil laughed. "I told your mom I'd give you the option. She was the one to tell me you wouldn't take it. She's right. Get some sleep, son. You're going to need it. There's no way you're going into that place without all of your senses focused." Devil got to his feet and escaped to the bathroom.

After kicking off his shoes and jeans, and removing his jacket and shirt, he lay down on the bed. He pulled out his cell phone and brought up the pictures. There were several Tabitha had sent him from Halloween. She looked so pretty dressed the way she was. Stunning even. He wished he'd been there. He would have danced the whole night away and had something to do with those bastards from the other club.

Scrolling past, he went to some of them together. Her lips were pursed, kissing his cheek as he smiled in the camera. Of course he had so many of Tabitha and Daisy. They were close and had been since they were kids. Anthony was there as well, looking mightily cute.

"That's not sleeping," Devil said.

"I'm just…"

"Looking at pictures of your girlfriend." He chuckled. "Don't go making me a grandpa before my time."

He rolled his eyes. "I won't."

"Do I need to have the sex talk with you again?"

"Please, don't. I like to not vomit in my mouth."

Devil chuckled, but it sounded evil and happy at the same time. This was what he loved about being with his dad. They were close, and he felt like he could talk to him about anything and there would never be judgment. Devil's cell phone buzzed. "It's your mother."

"You've got to rest as well, old man. You're not getting any younger."

"Cheeky little fucker." Silence passed. "Huh."

"What's huh?"

"It's nothing."

"Come on, Dad, what is it?"

"Lexie got a call from Eva. It seems Daisy's real

dad, not Whizz, the one who sold her to The Skulls, was found dead this morning. It looked like he was cleaning out his gun, and shot himself right in the neck."

****

Tabitha climbed up the wall outside of Anthony's bedroom window. The moment she'd heard her parents talking, she just knew. Climbing wasn't something she enjoyed doing and if her parents thought to check on her, she was going to be grounded again, but there was no way she was going to be able to hold off until the morning to ask him.

Getting to the window, she knocked on it. Anthony sat at his desk.

He glanced over at her and she pointed at the window. "Open it," she said, whispering.

Anthony looked like he was going to tell her no. If he did, she was going to beat his ass with a bat. She'd make Daisy kiss him and that would give her the leverage she needed to beat the shit out of him.

He opened the window and she climbed on through.

Again, no words.

"You did it."

Anthony sat at his desk and Tabitha started to pace the room.

"Parents are home," he said.

She stopped. "You killed him."

He didn't look up. His head was bowed over his books, a pencil in his hand. There was no real sign that he'd killed a man, but there was no way Daisy's father was miraculously cleaning a gun he didn't own.

"Damn it, Anthony, look at me."

He sighed, lowered his pencil, and turned toward her.

"You killed him."

Nothing.

"You're not going to say anything? You're just going to keep giving me the creeps with the stares."

"What do you want me to say? You want me to lie to you, Tabs? Is that it? No, I didn't kill him. He clearly was a drunk and I'm so sorry that he's dead."

"You're fucking lying," she said. "You heard what Daisy said at Halloween and it has been less than a week and he suddenly turns up dead. Don't lie to me. You owe me more than that."

He got to his feet. "Exactly what do I owe you, Tabitha?"

"I'm your friend. We're Skulls. We're a team."

"You're right. We're a family, and one of our team, one of our unit was dying inside. You want to know the truth, then yes, I killed him. He owned that gun, it was old, pretty much useless. I cleaned it up real nice. It fucking sparkled. I loaded that weapon and when he was drinking and trying to get more money out of her, I made him look me in the eyes, and then I pulled the trigger and I feel nothing. He is nothing. He was a piece of shit."

"If they find out—"

"They will never find out." Anthony slashed his hand across the air. "Period. They will never find out because I know what I'm doing."

"You're sixteen."

"And I still know what I'm doing. That will never change."

"You don't care? You killed a man."

"He was hurting Daisy."

"Is that all it's going to take from you? They hurt Daisy, and they're dead."

"Do you think the world is going to miss him? He was a piece of shit who needed to die. No one is going to miss him. Certainly not Daisy. He was killing her, little by little. I knew something was bothering her, I just didn't know who or what. When I did, I took care of it. Don't make me out to be the bad guy. I'm not. I did what I had to do for my loved one. I did what anyone would do."

Tabitha stared at him, shocked. "I think that is the most you've spoken."

"She never finds out. This is between you and me. Don't even tell Simon, and if you do, I will hurt you, Tabitha."

She gritted her teeth and stepped toward him. "I may not be fucking cold like you, but don't ever threaten me. I will end you, do you understand me?"

Anthony stared at her. "Understood."

Tabitha stood back and sat down on the edge of his bed. "I ... how was it?"

"You want to know?"

"Yes."

"I didn't care. He begged for his life but he had hurt her too many times to count. I was done with his bullshit." Anthony sat at his desk. "If you're found here, you're going to be grounded."

"What about you?"

"Dad would be happy that I've got a chick in my room."

"Have you ever been with those girls?" she asked. He raised a brow.

"Come on. Tell me."

"Tabs, no. Leave before I have to listen to you moaning about being grounded again."

"Would you ever ground your kid?"

"Yes," he said. "Especially if it's a girl."

"Double standards."

"Leave."

She rolled her eyes. "Have you heard from Daisy?"

"Nope, but I figure that's your deal. I won't be going to check on her."

"You want to?"

Tabitha climbed out of the window and fired the question at him, waiting. He kept on staring at her.

"You would?"

"Don't break your neck," he said.

He closed the window.

Asshole.

She climbed down and ran all the way back home, quickly climbing into her bedroom window. There was no sign of her parents. After stripping out of her clothes, she put on her pajamas and had climbed into bed, picking up a book when there was a knock at the door.

"Come in," she said. She hadn't run a brush through her hair. She hoped she didn't have any leaves or debris in her hair.

Her dad, Tiny, entered. She put the book down.

"I assume you heard?"

"I did. Does Daisy know?"

"Whizz and Lacey are going to tell her tomorrow. She hasn't been feeling well."

Tabitha nodded. "It was probably the pizza at school. That stuff isn't good for anyone."

"Do you have any reason to believe she could have anything to do with this?" Tiny asked.

"No!" She snapped the word out and frowned. "I mean, of course not. Why would you think Daisy would do something like this?"

Tiny shrugged, sitting on the edge of the bed. "It was … considered. He wasn't a nice person and we know he's been a bit of a problem in the past."

She nodded. "Of course, but Daisy wouldn't kill him."

"You'll go over there tomorrow. Be with her?"

"Yes. She may not be angry or upset. She might not even care."

"Probably not. He wasn't her real dad. We all know Whizz takes his role seriously."

"It's why he adopted her."

Tiny agreed and patted her leg. "Devil and a couple of the guys have invited us over for Thanksgiving."

"They have?" She hadn't been to Piston County in so long.

"Yes."

"Can I stay with Lexie and Devil? I promise I'll be good."

"Honey, you know they have a lot of kids."

"Dad, come on. I will be good. You don't have anything to worry about. I promise." She patted his hand.

"Do I need to talk to you about … what happens between a boy and a girl."

"No, Dad, please. You don't have to do the sex talk. I get it. Penis, vagina, sex, semen, babies. Protected sex. I get it." Her face was heating up by the second and she wrinkled her nose.

"I don't like how much you know. I wish you were still into ponies and dolls."

She giggled. "I was never into dolls."

"You were. If I could, I'd keep you as a little girl forever. I know I could keep you happy and nothing would ever hurt you."

"You're worried Simon will hurt me?"

"I know you're going to get hurt in life. I don't want that for you. For any of you."

"Dad, you can't protect me forever."

"And I know you've got to make some tough choices. Don't get me wrong, I hoped this thing with Simon would have run its course right now."

"You mean because we're in two different clubs?" she asked.

"Yes."

"Even with your friendship?"

"Honey, friendships aside, we're not the same. We don't always make the same choices. We work together where we can. Lash has taken the club in a direction I never even thought of. He's been a true leader."

She moved toward her dad, hugging him tightly. "I love you."

"I love you too, but when you have to make these choices, make them with your heart. Don't make them because you're being forced."

"I won't."

She was aware of what would be expected of her. Even if she put off the inevitable by going to college, there would always be that question. Would she remain a Skull, which would mean her relationship with Simon may have to come to an end? Or would she give up being everything she knew, and take on Simon's patch?

The thought of leaving everything behind scared her. She didn't know what choice to make. She loved her family and The Skulls were hers, but she also loved Simon, and there was no getting away from that.

"I'm going to leave you. Goodnight, honey."

"Goodnight."

She watched her father go.

Once she'd finished her chapter in the book, she put it down, turned out the light, and slid down, closing her eyes. Everything could be put off until tomorrow. There was no reason for her to make any decisions now.

None were expected of her.

Chapter Seven

"Put the gun down."

"Fuck you. You think I'm going to let you take my wife and kids from me? You're fucking crazy. I don't care who you are. Probably one of my wife's lovers. She's nothing more than a slut. Yeah, I know she spreads her legs for everyone."

Simon watched as the husband pointed the gun at all of them. This should have been so easy. In and out. His father had warned him last night and it appeared the seven-year-old son, who was now cowering in a corner, had called the father. The bags had already been packed but as Devil entered, they had found the dad waiting, gun pointed at them.

He didn't know if he could handle seeing his dad shot, not again. Memories kind of blurred all together.

Ripper was there, as were Pussy, Dick, and Snake. Several of the guys were outside as well.

Devil didn't take his gaze off the man. "You don't want to do this."

"What? I don't want to make her pay for what she's done? She deserves to die. I can't believe I even trusted her with my kids. Slut. Whore." Each word was shouted.

The kids whimpered.

His heart raced and he felt sick to his stomach. He watched the man as he suddenly grabbed his wife's hair. She screamed as he tugged her left and right.

"Enough!" Devil roared the word, and it caused silence to spill in the house.

The man laughed. "This is my house. How dare you come here! You think you can get away from me, slut? I promise you, you will never know peace. You're mine. Every single part of you is mine."

Past the man's shoulders, he saw Curse slowly making his way inside. Simon kept his gaze on the man, not wanting to alert him to another coming inside.

This could go wrong.

"I will make you all pay. I'll kill them all before you take them away from me."

As he pressed the gun against her temple, Curse reacted, jerking the man. The gun went off. Simon rushed forward, taking the woman as the others worked to get the kids. Out of the corner of his eye, he saw Curse fighting with the man. Finally, he landed a punch, which knocked the man out cold.

Taking the gun, Curse pocketed it and they were out there in a rush.

His dad was already behind the wheel and he joined him as they raced down the street.

"Are we housing them?" Simon asked.

He knew some of the people they saved and rescued were placed in either The Skulls' or Chaos Bleeds' care.

"No, we're dropping them off. The Billionaire Bikers are picking them up." Devil winced.

"Dad, what's up?"

"It's nothing."

His father put a hand to his side and it was then Simon recognized the blood. "You've been shot."

"It's nothing," he repeated, but he winced.

"Dad, getting shot is not nothing."

"I'll deal with it as soon as we get these to safety. Call Ripper, tell him to make sure the Billionaires are ready. Tell him I've been hit."

Simon did as he asked. Ripper cursed. "When we get there, escort them out, I'll take care of them, Simon.

Make sure your dad is taken to a hospital."

His hands were shaking. They left the town, and there was a small diner off the beaten track. It was completely empty and from the looks of it, it hadn't been open in quite some time.

Devil slowed down and Simon climbed out of the truck.

He didn't approach the men, but helped the woman and kids out, who were all crying and shaking. There was a protocol, but right now, he had to get his dad to a hospital.

"Son," one of the men said.

He couldn't think of the Billionaire's name right now.

"The guys are seconds away. My dad has been shot. We need to get him to the hospital."

"There's one twenty minutes out. We'll make calls," the man said.

He didn't even say thank you. Rushing to the driver's side, he saw his dad had moved along. After climbing behind the wheel, he pulled onto the road and pressed his foot to the gas.

"Don't panic," Devil said.

"I'm not going home and telling Mom you didn't make it." He focused on the road. The cell phone rang and Devil reached out a blood-soaked hand.

"Ripper, what's up?"

"I've dealt with the handoff. James is organizing what we need."

"Good." Devil coughed.

"You with me, old man?" Ripper asked.

"Fuck you. What is with people calling me an old man? I'm as healthy as can be. I can take all of you, and you all fucking know it."

There was a chuckle but Simon heard the

concern.

"Put your foot down, Simon. The Billionaires are handling everything."

Simon broke speeding laws, seeing the sign for the hospital. He'd never felt so much relief as he came to a stop. After slamming the door closed, he moved to his father's side, helping him out.

"When did you get so tall?" Devil asked.

"I'm your son. It's in my genes."

Devil laughed.

They stumbled into the hospital. "Please, my father has been shot. Help."

There were already doctors waiting. "Devil? Chaos Bleeds?" one of them asked.

"Yes."

"We got the call. We've been waiting for your arrival. We can take it from here."

"No, I can't leave him."

One of the doctors put a hand on his arm. "We've got it from here. There's nothing you can do right now. We will be out to tell you more."

Simon watched as his father was escorted on a bed away from him.

His hands shook and he felt sick. He wanted to call his mom but she would be too worried. Devil wouldn't want him to do that.

Taking a seat, he stared at the doors.

He held his cell phone in his hands. Tabitha's name was there. Clicking on her name, he put the cell to his ear.

"Hello, stranger," she said.

Just hearing her voice lightened his heart and made everything come into focus for him.

"Hey," he said.

"Simon, what's wrong?"

"Nothing."

"Don't lie to me. I hear it. Talk to me."

He looked down at his hand and saw the blood. Heart racing, he felt sick to his stomach.

"Simon?"

"I shouldn't have called you."

"Don't do this. Don't shut me out. We promised each other that no matter what, we'd be there for each other. You need to lean on me, do so."

He got to his feet and headed toward the bathroom. "My dad's been shot."

"Holy shit," she said. "What's going on?"

Simon told her about what had happened, how the gun had gone off, and he didn't think to check to see who got hit. "He still drove, Tabby. I mean, he must be completely crazy."

"Do you want me to tell my mom?"

"No, she'll call mine and I don't want her worrying." He put the phone on speaker as he put it near the sink. He slammed his hand against the soap dispenser, turning on the tap and washing his hands. The soap went pink, and the water turned the same color. He felt sick. This was his dad's blood.

"Simon, you there?"

"I'm there. Just washing my hands."

"God, I'm so sorry. He's going to be okay though, right?"

"I don't know. The doctors took him away. What do I do if he dies?"

"Don't talk like that."

He removed the speaker and put the phone to his ear as he made his way back outside to the waiting room. No one was looking for him. He took a seat.

"I'm still here, Simon. I wish I was with you right now. I'd hug you so damn tight and never let go."

"I want you here."

"We'll be coming for Thanksgiving. Dad tried to give me the talk."

"You're trying to distract me."

"You're there on your own, aren't you?"

"Yeah."

"Where are the others?"

"Doing what needs to be done."

"I hate this," she said.

"I don't want my dad to die."

"He won't." She sounded firm. He could imagine her frowning right at him, so he knew she meant business.

"I love you," he said.

"I love you too. He will get past this. With all due respect, he's Devil. Prez of the Chaos Bleeds, he won't die for anyone until he was fucking ready," she said.

He laughed even as tears filled his eyes.

Looking up, he saw the rest of the crew coming in. "The guys are here. I better go."

"Love you."

"Love you too."

He hung up, got to his feet, and filled them in on what had happened. All of them looked grim as they took a seat. Ripper was the one who went to the main desk.

"Your dad will make it," Dick said. "No bullet wound will ever stop him from walking."

"You're sure?"

"I know this man. There's no way this man will let anyone else tell him when his time is up." Dick slapped him on the shoulder.

It was of little comfort to him.

Time passed.

He watched the clock click, seeing the hands slowly tick along around, mocking him. He'd long wiped the tears from his eyes. Right now, his father needed a man, not a boy.

Squaring his shoulders, he waited, prepared for the worst.

When the doctor finally came out, Simon was expecting awful news as his face looked grim.

He was going to lose his father, he just knew it.

****

Two days later

"Ouch, woman," Devil said.

"Keeping me out of the loop. Not telling me my own husband was going to die," Lexie said.

"I didn't die."

"You will when I get my hands on you."

"You're going to make me pay for being a naughty boy," Devil said.

"I think I just threw up in my mouth," Simon said. "Ouch." He rubbed the back of his head from where his father had slapped him. "Not exactly fair."

"Don't think I'm not mad at you as well, young man. Not telling me about your father being shot. You told me this was going to be a simple mission. In and out, no problem."

"Baby, I have always warned you of the risks. They don't go away. Not for anyone."

She made some weird snorting noise. "I have a good mind to tell those Billionaires where to stick their little mission requests."

"Not happening, baby. You and I both love it when we get our rewards."

"I need to leave," Simon said. "This has got to be some form of child abuse, seeing my parents hump each other."

Devil had an arm wrapped around Lexie and he'd pulled her into his lap. There was no mistaking where his thoughts were going, and it was gross. Really gross. Disgusting.

"Son, close the door on the way out."

Lexie giggled. "This is not happening."

"Rather than shout at me, tell me how much you have missed me."

He closed the door as he heard the first moan.

Elizabeth stood there, waiting. She looked a little pale. "He's going to be all right, right?"

"Yeah, he's going to be fine."

"Was it scary?"

"Not too bad."

Elizabeth nodded. "I sometimes allow myself to believe the bad times are over."

"They are over. There are no more lockdowns. We're safe." He patted her arm.

"But what if someone decides to hunt them down? You know, like, the bad guys who Dad goes and takes from?" She frowned. "I know I'm not explaining this well."

"You're worried that the bad people will want revenge?"

"Won't they? They can't be good if they are always dealing in people."

Simon agreed. "You're right. We don't know for certain. I know our dad, I know the club. They would never do anything to jeopardize our safety."

"It's not about our safety." Elizabeth wiped beneath her eye. "I ... I know he's our dad and everything but I don't want to lose him. Not to anyone."

He opened up his arms and she stepped between them. "It's not going to happen. Believe me, no one is going to take Dad until he's damn good and ready."

"You know that for a fact?"

"I do. Come on. No one is going to tell him when

he will die. Only he will."

She let out a breath. "That's good to know."

"You don't want to go in there, trust me."

"Are they being all lovey to each other?"

"You got it."

Elizabeth wrinkled her nose. "I'm going to go and study."

And he had babysitting duty for the time being.

He grabbed the laundry basket from the bathroom and carried it downstairs to the laundry room. He folded everything up that was in the dryer and organized a load of washing to do. His mom had taught him how to do this years ago. With her constantly pregnant, she always needed the help and besides, he knew it gave him benefits in the long turn.

Just as he finished one load, the doorbell rang.

Leaving the room, he headed to the front door as his mom came downstairs, fixing her clothes. It didn't take a genius to work out what was going on there. Her cheeks were red.

"I'll get it," he said.

Opening the door, he saw Eddie and Dean were waiting for him.

"You want to head out? A bunch of us are going to the..." Dean started to speak but saw Lexie close. "The bowling alley. You know, have some fun."

Simon wanted to put him on the spot and ask a whole load of questions but thought better of it.

"Go out, have some fun. You've been a big help and you deserve it." Lexie said.

See, he got paid for being awesome, tenfold. "You sure? I don't mind sticking around."

"Please, I can handle this. Go and have some fun. You won't be young forever." She kissed his cheek.

Grabbing his jacket, he headed out. They had

turned out of the driveway when he snorted. "Bowling alley, seriously?"

"I panicked. I didn't know what to say."

Eddie laughed. "Do you think she believed him?"

"Not a chance. My mom was young once too."

"So were my parents, but I truly believe they spent their fun time looking at the cutlery to see how expensive it was," Dean said.

"How are you guys getting out so late? Don't you have your little engagement to plan?"

Devil was currently working with a lawyer to help with Dean's emancipation. Until they had a clear plan in sight, everything was being dealt with privately. Dean's parents didn't even know what he was doing.

"Don't start. Any news from your dad about … you know?"

Dean was so paranoid, he tried not to discuss it for fear of people listening. It was sad how far his fear went, that he believed he was followed.

"He's just getting over being shot at the moment. I'll ask him when I get back."

"Shit, yeah, I'm sorry about that, man," Dean said.

"How is he holding up?" Eddie asked.

"He's got my mom all to himself. Believe me, he's lapping up the attention."

"Dude, I don't get how your parents can still be digging each other," Eddie said.

"Tell me about it. My parents each have flings. Dad's currently screwing the new maid and mom's doing the pool boy. They have lovers in the city as well. They can't stand to touch each other," Dean said.

"I don't know if that makes me lucky or not," Simon said. "Believe me, it can get pretty gross."

"I think you've got the best life," Dean said.

"Dude, his dad just got shot. At least our dads only have to deal with gold-diggers," Eddie said, slapping his friend's shoulder.

"Don't worry about it. We don't have to start comparing the best parents," he said. "So where we going, anyway?"

"Out by the creek. There's going to be a bonfire. Partying. The whole deal. A couple of chicks there," Dean said. "I know you've got the whole chick thing covered but we don't. I need to get laid, like, right now."

"Eddie will do the honors," Simon said, shoving his friend closer to Dean.

"Ha, ha, very funny."

Simon laughed. "Come on, you two would make one hell of a couple. I can see you guys adopting and all sorts."

"Fuck you, Simon," Dean said. "I'm starting to believe this girl of yours is make-believe, and you're really in love with both of us."

"You can eat your words. My girl is visiting Thanksgiving and you suckers are going to so be mourning the fact I got to her first. She's my girl and will always be mine."

The guys ribbed him all the way to the creek where the bonfire was already in full swing. Beer cans lay on the ground. Music spilled from cars. People were making out, smoking pot, and Simon looked at it all with a sense of boredom.

None of this meant anything to him.

They all thought it made them tough, rebelling against what was required of them. After being hunted, shot at most of his life, this was all childish to him. He rubbed the spot on his chest from when he and Tabby were shot. They'd been standing together and it had been a through and through. Tabby had the same scar. Even though they'd both been shot together so long ago, he could still remember the day so clearly. Not just the pain or the fear, but also the aftermath of when Tabby was in the hospital.

He looked across the hospital room and saw Tabby struggling to sleep. She was whimpering, crying out, and it hurt him to see it. Climbing out of his bed, he gathered up his equipment when the large guy Gavin came into the room. He was a friend of Ned's, and had been ordered to take care of them. His mom had to go home, as had his father. He wasn't stupid. Simon knew the threat that had put them in the hospital was still out there.

"Get back to sleep, little man."

"My girl is hurting, and you're not going to stop me." He climbed off the bed, ignoring the pain. Simon had made a promise to Tabby. As long as he was alive, he would do everything to make her safe. Bad dreams included, and he wasn't about to break his promise. Even if his father threatened to stop him from calling her, he wasn't going to stop. Gavin took a step closer, and Simon held his hand up.

"I will scream if you come any closer. I'll make sure the nurses don't let you near me."

"Look, you little shit—"

Stepping up to the large man, Simon glared. "Finish that, I dare you. My father is Devil, President of the Chaos Bleeds MC. I am going to follow in his footsteps. That club will be mine one day, and I will not forget about this. I will hunt you down and hurt you in ways you can't even imagine. My girl is hurting, and I promised to help her. I'm not going to break that promise." He'd listened to his father command in the same voice. Simon had spent hours practicing so that he could be exactly like him. Devil was respected and feared. Simon intended to make sure he was the same. Gavin kept on staring. "I'm going to lie down with her. That's all." Stepping away from the man, Simon made sure not to turn his back. It was one of the first warnings his father had given him.

"Fuck this. Little shit…" Gavin kept on muttering as he left the hospital room.

Wheeling his medication, Simon placed it opposite Tabitha's and climbed into bed with her. The movement woke her up, and she gasped, staring at him.

"Simon?"

"Yeah, it's me. You were having a bad dream."

"I just want them to go away. All the dreams to go away." She lay down, and before her head rested on the pillow, he gathered her up in his arms. She rested her head on his arm, and he stared down at her. He didn't know what it was about this girl, but Simon couldn't stop thinking about her. Love. That's what it was, love. He loved her more than anything. She called to him in ways he didn't even know was possible. "I'm here now. Dreams won't hurt you."

"Do you have bad dreams?"

"I dream about you."

"You know Miles has a girlfriend. Her name's Bertie, and she goes to our school. I don't like her."

"You're my girlfriend."

She giggled. "Yeah, I am. Mom says I'm too young to have a boyfriend."

"What do you say?"

"I don't care. You've always been mine." Her eyes started to droop. "Don't go."

"Never." Simon held her as she fell back to sleep, falling himself. This was how he wanted the rest of his life. To fall asleep with Tabby in his arms.

Damn, he remembered that moment. Being with

Tabby, she was his life. Then and now. He didn't bother to grab a beer. Shoving his hands in his pockets, he watched as his buddies left to go find some girls to dance with. He wasn't going to be screwing random girls, but he wouldn't get in the way of his friends wanting to party. He wasn't totally cruel.

Finding a spot near the flames, he watched them. His cell phone was on loud, so he could hear it ringing if his mom needed him.

"Well, well, well, look who I found here all by himself," Amber said, slurring her words a little.

He rolled his eyes and glanced at Amber. She wore a small skirt and a shirt that exposed most of her tits.

"Is this necessary?" he asked. "You must be fucking cold."

"I'm not. In fact, I'm hot, Simon." She took a step closer.

He moved back and she pouted.

"I hate it when you make me work hard for it."

Simon had no choice but to turn on his cell phone and start recording. He knew his cell phone's layout off by heart so he started to record.

"Amber, I don't want anything to do with you. Leave me alone," he said.

"But I don't want to. I mean, why do you keep turning me down, Simon? I want you. I'm willing to give you whatever you want." She tried to lean in close and she stumbled. "You know a lot of guys would beg for what I'm willing to do."

"Not interested."

She growled. "You think playing hard to get makes you cute. You will be mine, Simon and if you won't play along, I'm going to tell everyone you forced me. Raped me."

He threw his head back and laughed. "You know what, Amber? Go ahead. You think I don't know what kind of game you're playing? I do. I'm prepared for whatever you want to throw at me."

"Hey, man, we saw the viperous bitch and figured you needed some backup," Dean said.

Eddie was there as well. Both of his boys had his back.

"Thanks, guys. I can handle this bitch. Get gone."

"One day, Simon. One day you're going to want me and then I'm not going to let you have me."

"Yeah, like that's ever going to happen. You should be careful, Amber. I hear his girl is coming to town and she's a mean bitch who likes to punch," Eddie said, shouting to be heard.

Amber stumbled away.

Any idea of partying was lost to him. "I'm going to head on back. You two want me to walk you home?" Simon asked.

"Nah, we're good, man. We've got a couple of dates. See you in a bit."

He waved them off and left the creek, heading home.

It was late as he arrived home. As he let himself in, his stomach growled. After removing his jacket, he put his keys in the dish and walked into the kitchen to find his mom crying at the counter.

"Mom, are you okay?" he asked.

She nodded, lifting her head. "I'm just so relieved, you know." She wiped the tears from her eyes. "God, I can't bear to lose him. I love him so damn much."

He went to her, holding her tightly. "I've got you."

She rubbed his hands. "Thank you, for driving

him to the hospital. I can only imagine the fear you must have felt."

"I knew if I didn't bring him home, you'd be pissed."

She laughed. "That's another dollar for the jar."

"I don't care. I know you love him, Mom. Just like he loves you."

"You know, I always hoped you guys would find the same love I've been lucky to get. I know it's going to happen with Tabitha. Your dad wants me to talk to you about her," she said.

Simon groaned. "Do I want to know why?"

"She's coming for Thanksgiving. Tiny wanted to rent a motel room, but we won't have that. This house is plenty big enough for them. I know Angel and Lash are coming as well. We will make it work. You know how I love to have everyone around."

"I know. Is this about sex?" Simon asked.

Lexie's cheeks heated. "I'm trying not to be too embarrassed. I know you're going to have it one day, if you haven't had it already."

Simon covered his face. "Mom, please, I'm a virgin. Let's keep it at that."

"What? You are?"

"Yeah, I haven't been with a girl. Ever. The only person I want is Tabby and we're not ready yet."

"So your father's been worrying for nothing."

He nodded. "Yes, he's been going through a whole lot of worry for no reason. Tabby and I, we're not going to rush this. Believe me, we're going to take our time."

Lexie ran a hand over her forehead. "Phew."

"Okay, I think I can eat a sandwich and go to bed."

"I can make you something."

"Mom, I can do it."

"Sit, I will make you a sandwich. How was the party?" she asked.

"Dean didn't fool you once, did he?"

"With the bowling alley?" She snorted. "Hell, no. Besides the fact I was young once, and you're Devil's son, the bowling alley is closed for the next couple of weeks for refurbishment."

"Oh."

"Yeah, tell Dean to come up with a better lie next time."

"I will."

"Cheese and pickle?"

"You got it."

He watched as she made him a cheese and pickle sandwich. "Your pregnant again, aren't you?"

Lexie shook her head. "I'm not pregnant, son. Your dad took care of that. We can't have any more kids."

"Then what is it?" he asked, concerned.

She sighed. "There was ... I've had a few tests, and I'm due to have some more. It could be nothing. I don't want to worry you with the details."

He stared at his mom, wanting to know more, but he didn't press. She was pale and he saw she was already stressed out. He refused to add to it.

After picking up his sandwich, he took a bite and moaned. "This is so good."

She smiled. "Good."

Whatever was going on with his parents, it had to be bad. They were keeping it a secret and his father had been home a lot more over the past few weeks. He hoped nothing was wrong with his mom because he couldn't bear for her to be suffering from any illness of any kind.

Chapter Eight

Running out of the house, Simon caught Tabby running toward him. She threw herself into his arms, and he spun her around. It had been too damn long since he held her in his arms.

Sinking his fingers into her hair, he kissed her lips, hard.

She moaned, and he slid his tongue inside, meeting her halfway. Slowly, he lowered her to her feet, still kissing her.

Someone cleared their throat.

So did someone else.

Still, he couldn't stop.

She tasted good. Like breathing and fresh air. She was his life and he loved her. He didn't want to let her go.

Again, another throat clear, and this time, he pulled away. His dad and Tiny were close, glaring at them.

"Hi, Devil," Tabby said.

"Hello, Tiny," he said, looking at her father.

"I think it would be best if we went to a motel," Tiny said.

"Don't be ridiculous. They're only kids and they know the rules. They won't break them. Will you?" Lexie said, laughing.

"Nope," Tabby said.

He had every intention of breaking them. He crossed his fingers behind his back as he agreed to be good, while already planning to fall asleep with her in his arms.

"Hi, Tabitha," Josh asked.

Simon watched his younger brother as he came closer. The redness of his face gave away his embarrassment.

"Hey, Josh, you're sure growing up fast." She ruffled his head.

His brother ran away and Simon winced.

"What did I do?" Tabby asked.

"He's got a crush," Elizabeth said.

"Elizabeth!" Lexie snapped her name.

"What? He does. Tabitha should know. Ugh, what is the big deal with everyone?"

"This coming from the girl who has a thing for Drew?"

This time, Elizabeth stomped away.

"She does?" Tabby asked.

"She does. Come on, I'll show you to your room."

Tiny cleared his throat. "I don't think that's necessary. I'm sure she knows the way to the bedroom."

"Dad, please, trust me. We're not going to be having crazy sex or anything," Tabby said.

"Honey, we have kids who don't need to be repeating words," Lexie said.

Tabby winced. "Sorry. Trust me, Dad. I won't disappoint you."

"It's not you that I'm worried about," Tiny said, looking at him.

"It will stay in my pants, sir."

Devil clipped him around the back of the head. "No grandbabies are being made in this house, Tiny. Believe me."

Simon laughed as he finally got to take Tabitha away from the driveway and showed her where she would be staying. What he didn't expect was Miles to be hot on the heels.

"Go away," Simon said.

"No can do. I'm sharing a room with Tabs," he said.

"No," Simon said.

"Can't change it, I'm afraid. Dad is much happier with this arrangement. There are two beds, and don't worry, I won't spill the beans that she's going to be sneaking into your bedroom like you do every sleepover," Miles said. "Now, are there any decent chicks in this town?"

They entered Tabitha's room, and of course there was now a second bed. Simon hadn't even realized a second one had been put into this room. He was going to kill his dad. There was going to be murder.

She dropped her bag onto the bed.

"I figure me being all nice and everything, Tabs, you'll unpack for me. I've got some hunting to do and besides, laundry is woman's work."

"I'm going to kick your ass," Tabby said.

Miles was already long gone.

"Woman's work. Remind me the next time I see him to knee him in the nuts. I'm going to stop him from ever fathering children."

"Consider it done." He moved over to Miles's bag and tipped out all of his clothes. "Your brother's a slob."

"And you're much better?" Tabby asked.

"Hell, yeah, I mean, look at this. At least when I pack, I fold shit neatly."

Tabby chuckled. "You sound so posh when you say stuff like that. Especially because I know your mom packs everything for you. You're just trying to get in my good books because of the whole woman's work." She moved to him, putting her hands on his chest. "Do you think this is all woman's work?"

"No, and you're wrong." He put his hands at her waist. "I do the laundry. I've been packing my brothers' and sisters' stuff, as well as mine for a long time now."

Her eyes went wide. "You have?"

"Yeah, I have. I'm damn good at doing women's work." He kissed her lips. "I've missed you."

"I've missed you too." She kissed him, patting his chest. "Come on, I've got to do this. Dad will come and check and when he sees nothing done, he will want to castrate you."

"I don't even think he would trust me if I castrate myself. When he's going to realize we're not going to start screwing each other?" Simon asked.

"He's never going to believe it. Devil's still hung up on being granddad, isn't he?"

"Yep. I think it's his complex of getting older." He shrugged. "Who knows."

"Can you imagine him being a granddad?"

"He keeps saying *grandpa* as if it's some kind of disease." He hung up all of Miles's clothes, dumping his boxers and socks into the drawer.

Next, he helped Tabby, liking some of the dresses.

They had just finished as Tiny entered the room.

"Don't worry, Dad, we kept our hands and body parts to ourselves as we unpacked. Miles is a slob, though."

"Miles should stay here."

"You trust him," she said.

Simon decided to not say anything. The last thing he wanted to do was upset Tiny. The man was huge. Even though he was old, he knew for a fact the man could still wipe him clean out if he wanted to, and he certainly wasn't going to test the man's skills when it came to fighting.

Tiny glared at them.

"Daisy and Anthony are waiting downstairs," he said.

"Yay," she said. "I figured you could show me around."

"You've been to Piston County all the time."

"I know, but you can like, introduce me to your friends," she said. "You always keep me to yourself, now you get to show me off. I'm no longer the phantom, imaginary girlfriend. I'm real." She took his hand and he followed her.

Anthony and Daisy were waiting. They stood close together. Daisy offered him a smile, which he returned.

"I hear condolences are in order," Simon said.

"No, they're not. Believe me. My parents want to put me into counseling, I'm sure of it."

Considering Whizz and Lacey were her parents and the rumors he'd heard about the two of them, that was a shock.

"Why?"

"They told me and I danced. I was so happy." She giggled. "I know, it's awful. I'm a horrible person, but I can't help it. I'm free."

"Yeah, imagine that. You're free," Tabitha said.

Simon looked at his girl, who was staring at Anthony. The two were having a stare-off, and he chuckled. "Okay, now that everything is awkward, let's go and show you guys off to my boys."

"You actually have friends that are not us?" Daisy asked.

"Yeah, of course. You think I live my life here wondering about you guys? I can socialize without you."

Daisy pressed a hand to her heart. "Now you're killing me."

Her father's death hadn't hurt her at all. She looked happier than he could ever recall seeing her.

Wrapping his arm around Tabby's waist, he kissed her cheek, her neck, as they headed out. It was cold as fuck, but he didn't mind. Daisy fell into step with Anthony.

"Are you okay?" he asked, whispering the words against her ear so only she would hear them.

"Yeah, I'm fine. It was a tough trip down is all. Do you have any idea what it was like listening to Mom and Miles argue about who cooks the best turkey? I think I'd had enough."

"I'm thinking of giving up all kinds of meats this coming year," Daisy said, suddenly joining the conversation and taking hold of Tabby's arm.

"Really?"

"Yeah, why not? It'll be nice to do something different for a change. You want to do it with me?" Daisy asked.

Simon responded with a hell no.

Anthony chuckled.

Tabby didn't say anything. "Really?"

"Why not?"

"You know it's going to piss your mom off?"

"Actually, it won't. Mom's giving it a try. She's also getting my dad to eat healthy as well. She's told him he can be buff all he wants to but she's now in charge of everything he eats. I think he's taking puddings from the club, but whatever. It looks like a lot of fun and it will help me lose weight." Daisy patted her stomach.

"You don't need to lose weight," Anthony said.

Simon's brows rose. The guy could actually speak. He knew he was more than capable but even still, it was a fucking shock to hear him.

Daisy stopped, which made them all stop.

"Thank you," she said.

"You're fine the way you are and beautiful. Don't change that."

Silence rang out.

Tabby tilted her head back and gave him the biggest smile which he couldn't help but reward.

"Okay."

They started walking again.

"I'm still going to give it a go. It looks like fun."

"Doesn't your mom suck at cooking?"

"Pretty much. I think she's trying, you know. What does she have to lose ruining a bunch of vegetables?"

Simon laughed. "You'd be surprised."

"She's determined and I support her."

"Then you know what, I will support her as well. It could be a lot of fun."

"You're going to starve," Simon said.

"You'll get to come to my rescue."

"I always knew there was a good deal in it for me." He pulled her close again, kissing her head, breathing her in.

She always smelled amazing. Like fresh air and hope.

"What do you do for fun around here?" Daisy asked.

"Not a whole lot. At the moment, I tend to stick close to home. Something's going on with my mom and it's not pregnancy."

"There is?" Tabby asked. "You didn't tell me."

"I don't know what to tell. She's pale, tired, and Dad's sticking close to home. I don't think he's stayed at the clubhouse once. I tend to babysit so they can have a day or two together."

"I hope it's nothing serious," Daisy said.

"Me too." He loved his parents. Unlike Dean, his friend, his family supported him and Simon knew without a doubt they would never lie to him or force him to be someone he didn't want to be. They were constant rocks in his world. They took a few shortcuts he'd learned through his time and arrived in town.

It was busy. Shoppers trying to get all the last-minute preparations for Thanksgiving. The library was closed. They made their way around the building, and sure enough, Dean and Eddie were sat there smoking.

"Really, this is your hideout spot?"

"Not all of us have the luxury of the Quad back at home." He held his hand out, shaking Dean's and then Eddie's hands. "My boys, I'd like you to meet my girl in the flesh."

Tabby rolled her eyes. She held her hands out and gave a little twirl. "Not a ghost, guys. Very much living and breathing." She even gave a curtsy.

"Wow," Dean said, getting to his feet. "I thought you were some made-up chick."

Daisy laughed. "You think Simon's capable of making stuff up?"

"Harsh, girl, harsh," he said.

"So you're The Skulls?" Eddie asked. He was on his feet, approaching them. He went to touch Daisy's shoulder but Anthony grabbed his hand.

"Don't touch."

Simon watched as Anthony applied enough pressure for Eddie to back off.

"This isn't all of us," Daisy said, stepping back against Anthony.

"Yeah, my evil twin brother probably has his tongue down someone's throat right about now," Tabby said. "You're my guy's friends."

"Yeah."

"You have his back?"

Simon touched hers. He had to put his hands on her, to feel her against him. It had been too long since they'd last been together.

"Always," Eddie said.

"You two know how to fight? I hate to say it, but you look like two rich boys who have everything done for you."

Dean tensed up.

"They are two rich boys but believe me, they've got my back." He kissed her neck. "I love that you worry about me."

"I don't like leaving my boy behind. You have his back, I've got no problem with you. You let anything happen to him, and you're going to have to deal with me."

Dean whistled. "Are you going to have a talk with Amber about that?"

"Amber?" Tabby asked.

"Viperous bitch who wants in my pants. Trust me, I've got her covered."

"Do I need to have a word with her?"

Simon cupped her face. "Not to spoil our Thanksgiving weekend. I don't want your parents having to take you away from me."

"Are they always like this?" Dean asked.

"This is tame," Daisy said. "Believe me. We're getting conversation out of them. That's a good thing."

"We're not that bad," Tabby said.

"Not right now, but give it a little time. They will be smacking on each other. It's gross," Daisy said.

"This coming from the girl who has never been kissed before."

"I am saving myself for the right guy. You of all people should know that. It's not my fault the right guy came to you when we were still in diapers." Daisy folded her arms. "Besides, it was a pleasure to meet you." She held her hand up and gave a little wave.

"What are you two losers doing back here?" Simon asked.

"Aw, and we thought you were sneaking out to find us," Eddie said, taking his seat back on the wall.

"I was, didn't actually think you boys would be here."

"My parents are ... being giant pains in the ass. I needed a break and so I came here."

"Shit, I'll talk to my dad. Is this about the whole marriage thing?" Simon asked.

"You got it. They've got my intended staying with me now. They've even put her in the same room. The sooner I get her pregnant, the quicker the wedding, and you guessed it." Dean shook his head. "I would have called you but you said you got this thing going."

"Am I missing something?" Tabby asked.

Simon looked to his friend.

For the next five minutes, Dean told them what was going on in his life.

"Wow, that is kind of fucked up," she said.

"Kind of fucked up? Nah, it *is* fucked up. It's not good." He shrugged. "I'm dealing with it."

"And Devil hasn't done anything yet?" Tabby asked.

"He's got shit going on with my mom. I promise. I'll talk to him tonight, and I'm going to say our door is always open if you need it."

"Thanks, man. That means a lot."

Thunder rolled through the air.

"Looks like we're heading back," Eddie said, jumping off the wall. "You want me to give you guys a ride?"

"Nah, we can walk," Simon said.

"Pleasure meeting the two of you."

"Damn, I hope I'm there when you meet Amber. I've got a feeling she's not going to like you."

Eddie and Dean left and Tabby turned to him. "This Amber girl sounds pretty interesting. Should I be worried?"

"Not at all." He kissed her lips.

"Let's head back," Anthony said.

Taking Tabby's hand, they walked back to his home. Daisy stood close to Anthony the entire time. When the heavens opened up, Anthony removed his jacket, placing it over her shoulders, and she sank into it, thanking him.

"I told you," Tabby said, whispering.

"Are they together?"

"No. She doesn't believe he sees her that way."

"Do you think she wants to be with him?"

She shrugged. "I don't know."

When they arrived at his home, Lash waited to take Anthony and Daisy to the motel where they were staying. Tabby hugged her friend close and then Anthony before they got into the car.

Entering his home, he took the jacket from her.

"I'm going to go and take a quick shower. Warm up. Go and talk to your dad. Your friend clearly needs something. The fact he'd rather hang out around the back of a library speaks for itself." She cupped his cheek, kissed him, and rushed off.

When The Skulls were in their home, they had always been told to treat it like their own. They rarely visited Piston County. Watching Tabby walk away, smelling her on his skin, damn, he felt at peace, which was the first time in a long time.

His mom and Eva were in the kitchen, cooking

and baking. Kids were everywhere. He checked the games rooms, the office, and the living room. Finally, he went outside onto the back porch. His dad had a thing for storms. He loved to watch the thunder and lightning as it lit up the sky and made so much noise.

Sure enough, that was where he found his dad with Tiny.

"Hey, Dad, can I talk to you for a minute?"

Tiny got to his feet. "I'm going to go and take a leak. Think about what I've said."

Devil laughed.

"Do I want to know what he said?" Simon asked.

"If you think boarding school is a good idea."

"It's not." Simon looked back at Tabby's dad, shaking his head.

"I won't send you to boarding school. Don't get me wrong, the idea of being a grandpa scares the shit out of me, but I won't send you away."

"Good to know you've got my back."

"You're my son. You can always come to me."

"Right, I want to talk to you about Dean. The emancipation. Have you had a chance to talk to a lawyer?"

Devil cursed, running a hand down his face. "Not recently, with everything going on. I've just, you know, I'll talk to him."

"Could you? It's getting worse for him."

"I'll handle it. I promise."

Simon nodded, thankful. "He's a good guy, you know, Dean. He wants to prospect for the club."

"Have you told him what that kind of shit means?" Devil asked.

"Not completely. I know I've got to get your permission to be able to talk about club stuff. He wants in. I think he wants to be part of a family, especially after his own has let him down."

"Prospecting isn't going to be easy, not even for you. The guys are going to want to test you. To put you through your paces."

"I'm ready for it."

"I know, but you can't come crying to me. When you're a prospect for the club, it's the club that rules you. You will always be my son."

"I don't expect you to hold back. I know I can hold my own."

Devil smiled. "I know you can."

"Dad, what is going on with mom? If it's not pregnancy, then what?" Simon asked.

His father's smile dropped. Sadness filled his face and Simon didn't know how much silence he could take. Devil blew out a breath and for a split second, he was sure he saw tears glistening in his eyes. "I … we don't know for sure. We're waiting for a couple more tests."

"But it's serious?"

"It could be."

"Is that why she's tired all the time? Pale?"

"Son, I don't want to spoil your Thanksgiving, and I don't want you to worry too much, but it could be serious. It's why I'm being careful with her. Why I'm taking my time."

Devil looked at his dad and said a word he hoped to never say.

"Cancer?"

Devil's lips thinned. The grip he had on the glass tightened until he put it down. The anger and rage simmering beneath the surface of his dad were very much real. "Possibly."

Simon gasped. "But you don't know for sure?"

"They're running tests. We're waiting for more results. Don't say anything, okay?"

Simon nodded.

"I'm doing the best I can, son."

He knew. Simon knew that if anything happened to his mother, something bad was going to happen, no doubt about it. He looked at his father and couldn't help but hug him. "It's going to be okay."

Devil patted him on the back. "I know. I refuse to believe anything different."

Tiny came out, and the mask was back in place on his father.

"Dean," he said.

"I'll go call the lawyer now," Devil said.

Simon didn't wait around to see. He made his way upstairs but before he did, he stopped at the kitchen.

His mom's head was thrown back and laughter filled the air. Eva was right with her as the two clearly had something fun to talk about.

Stepping back, he didn't go to his room, but to Tabby's. She still wasn't out of the shower, and he sat down on her bed. After kicking off his shoes, he slid back and stared at his socks. They were white but had some staining on them from his boots. Miles wasn't back yet, but he'd turn up when he wanted to.

Cancer.

It seemed … wrong.

He took a deep breath, rubbing at his chest.

Seconds passed, maybe even minutes and Tabby arrived.

Her smile vanished when she looked at him. "What's wrong?" she asked.

He licked his lips. "Close the door."

She closed the door.

Even in a towel, with her hair wet, cascading around her, she was the most beautiful person he'd ever seen.

"What is it?"

"What I'm about to tell you can't leave this room. Not to your parents, Daisy, anyone."

She nodded. "Okay."

"My mom may have cancer."

Tabby went to him. She wrapped her arms around him and held on to him. He took her comfort and couldn't let go. She ran her fingers through his hair. "What do you mean she may have cancer?"

"They're waiting on some tests."

"It might not be so bad," she said.

"I don't know. I've got a feeling it could be."

"You could be wrong," Tabby said, leaning back and cupping his face. "Look at me, they could be wrong."

He nodded and shook his head. "No, I don't think they have. Fuck, what am I going to do if anything happens to her?"

"Don't," Tabby said. "Don't ever think like that, okay?"

"My dad," he said.

"Nothing is going to happen." Tears were in her eyes. "You can't do that. I know this is scary, believe me, but I'm here. I'm always going to be here. I won't leave you."

"You're going back to Fort Wills."

"I know. That I can't control, but you know I'm just a phone call away when you need me. Always."

He nodded and pressed his face against her neck, breathing her in. "Fuck, I don't want to cry."

"Anthony killed Daisy's dad."

This made him pull away. Tabby bit her lip.

"For real?"

"Yeah, for real."

"Fuck. Does anyone know?"

"No. I wasn't supposed to tell you and it has been killing me. No one can know. This is between you and me."

He took her hand and agreed. "Always. We don't ever lie to each other. Ever."

"Of course not. We're the two people we can trust, forever." She put her hand on top of his. "I will always have your back, Simon, always."

He held her hand even tighter, wanting her comfort, needing it more than he liked to admit.

So long as he had Tabby, he could get through whatever life had to throw at him. Anything.

Chapter Nine

Lexie had cancer.

Tabitha heard the news a week later when she was back at Fort Wills.

The shock was felt between the two clubs.

Lexie was a wonderful, sweet, charming woman, and because of this, Tabitha begged to be able to go to Piston County to help out with her best friend.

Her dad was against it and her mother wasn't too thrilled. In the end, after some long conversations with Devil, she was able to do a small transfer to Simon's school, where she could pick up the school work with no issues. She wasn't staying in Piston County indefinitely, but between their fathers, and Lash, she was able to transition. She wouldn't be taking any of Simon's classes. Her work would be set for her at the school, and she'd work in the main office.

She had her own room, and when she arrived, Simon was there, hugging her tight. Devil patted her shoulder and Lexie hugged her close.

"Simon, go and deal with Tabitha's bags. I need to have a word with her," Devil said.

"Dad, come on, seriously?" Simon asked. "We both get it. You don't want us having sex under your roof. We can keep it in our pants."

"This is only happening because I agree to be in charge here. Believe me, I can send her ass right back to Fort Wills, in fact, I have a mind to if you keep giving me lip."

"It's fine," Tabitha said, smiling at Simon.

She couldn't believe she was actually in Piston County without her parents. They were trusting her to be sensible and to not break any rules, also to not get pregnant. Her dad had lectured her about that one. The not getting pregnant part. He didn't want her pregnant or in any way having a baby inside her. It was kind of scary how he kept saying no baby. No sex. No nothing.

As if she didn't know what led to a baby. She and Simon weren't going to do that to each other.

Simon took her bags and she followed Devil back to his office. She couldn't recall ever being in this room. Angel had originally offered to go as had Eva to help Lexie out. Tabitha had seen her chance. She was a good cook as she'd been the one to take care of herself and several of The Skulls kids when their parents had been way too busy. She'd also been taught a lot from Darcy as well. She had the ability to take care of herself. Angel and Eva were needed at home, while she was still a kid.

"Take a seat," he said.

"Do I have to sign some kind of contract?" She slid down into the chair and stared across the desk at Devil. He looked angry. She didn't look away. Growing up with Tiny as her dad, and well, most of The Skulls, the angered faces men often pulled didn't exactly affect her.

She put her hands on the arms of the chair and waited.

"I don't intimidate you, do I?" Devil asked.

"I'm guessing when I was small, it would work. I grew up with this. I know I'm safe and protected with you, unless, of course, I betray the club or clubs, then you'd kill me." She smiled widely at him, and he shook his head. "Sorry."

"Look, you being here, I'm not sure it's a good idea."

"I'm only here to help out. I promise. Simon told me that it was hard and I know how to babysit. I can help you, and I can be a sounding board for Simon. He's hurting too and I think I can be of better use to him while you're dealing with Lexie."

Devil ran his fingers through his hair. "Your dad has told me you've gotten into fights at school."

She licked her lips, nerves getting to her. "None of those have actually been proven."

"Two clubs fighting for dominance and to prove which one has the biggest balls. It's not the same here. There aren't two clubs. This town, Simon's school, is filled with a bunch of rich kids. Your fists won't be appreciated here."

"Devil, I only fight when I have to. For the longest time, I couldn't stand fighting. I don't do it for fun."

"What's the Quad?" he asked.

She winced. "Okay, it's still not for fun."

His brow went up.

"Simon does the exact same thing."

"You're avoiding."

"I'm not avoiding. I'm being, fine. Look, me and the guys know that we have a certain reputation to uphold. When we were in our happily separated towns with no interference, it was all fine. The Dogs go to the Quad. If we didn't turn up, it would look like we were cowards and we're not. We're fighters, through and through. The club will be in our hands one day. It's why we fight. Why I changed my mind and started to learn how to fight. It's not easy going up against people like that, you know?"

Devil kept on staring at her. "You don't enjoy it?"

"I've learned to just deal with it. Isn't that what most people do when they've got to do stuff that is expected of them? I'm a Skulls' kid. All of the trouble that's about to come our way because of me and Simon, put it aside. I've got to do what I can for the club," she said.

"You know, I sometimes forget you kids are only teenagers."

"We've all been through a lot. We're fighters. You can't take that away from us. We will do whatever we have to for the club. No questions asked."

"Then so long as you understand that I don't expect any fighting or trouble, you can stay. I have ground rules."

"I'm listening."

"No sex!" Devil snapped the words out.

"I can guarantee that."

"I was sixteen once. I know how this works."

"Clearly you don't know how Simon and I work. He knows I'm not ready and he's the perfect gentleman. Believe me, when I ask him to stop, he stops." Her face was going to be on fire by the time this was done.

"Good."

"I don't want you sleeping in his room," he said.

"What if he's upset?"

"No sleeping. Closeness and him being sad, I don't want you sleeping with my son out of pity."

"This is embarrassing."

"I was a boy once."

"And you keep saying that. It doesn't mean you can keep on telling me how this is going to be based on your experience, which was a completely different time. It's not right. Simon is not you, and I'm not some random sixteen-year-old girl. We're not that kind of couple." She put her hand to her chest, hoping he would realize that.

Devil took a deep breath.

"Please don't kill me," she said.

"I'm not going to kill you. It would start a war and Lash and I have a good relationship at best. Look, I just don't think I can handle whatever kid drama you can get yourself into. One step out of line, you're back with your parents, got it?"

"I'm only here to help out. Nothing bad, I promise."

"Fine. Go. I'm sure Simon's wearing out the carpet in your room."

She got to her feet. "Do I need to shake your hand?"

"Go!" Again, he snapped the word.

She left his office and went straight to her bedroom where, sure enough, Simon was there, pacing.

"You're okay?" he asked, pulling her into his arms.

"I'm fine."

"He didn't harm you?"

"He's not that bad. He's got a lot on his plate right now with your mom. He wants to make sure we keep it in our pants." She giggled. "What is it with our parents and thinking the moment we're together, we're having sex?"

"Because of our ages."

"I know a lot of people are having sex, like a lot, but I don't know, I mean, one day, I'm going to want to, but right now, I enjoy being with you."

He ran his hands down her arms, his touch setting her on fire. Even though she wanted to have sex to get it over with, and so she could have a reason to listen to their parents' warning, she wasn't ready.

"I enjoy being with you as well." He kissed her lips. "I can't believe you're here."

"I'm not going to be staying all the time. It's temporary."

"I know, but come on, this is … more than I could have hoped."

They sat down on her bed and she kicked her shoes off.

"Tell me how you're dealing," she said, reaching out and pushing some of his hair off his face. "Don't hide from me."

"I'm… It all kinds of feels like a blur right now. Like all of this is happening to someone else and I'm just along for the ride. I keep expecting someone to jump out and say it's a joke."

"It's not though," she said, softly.

"No, it's not."

She took his hand, kissing his knuckles.

"I, Tabby, cancer, it's not good."

"I know."

"I don't know how I'm going to deal. I know Darcy got through it, but she's not my mom."

Tears filled her eyes as she watched Simon slowly fall apart. This was why she had to come to him. She'd heard it in his voice. The confusion. The fear. His life was running too far too fast and he couldn't keep up. He was drowning in it.

"I'm here."

"I don't know what I'll do if anything happens to her. I don't want anything to happen to her. She's my mom." The tears fell down his cheeks.

She cried right along with him.

"Tabby, I don't know what to do. I feel, I feel angry."

She pulled him close and his face pressed against her chest. He cried harder and she held him, refusing to let him go. This was all she could do. This was how he needed her. Not back in Fort Wills, but so he could hold her, to have someone stable to make the world seem okay again.

The world was never going to be okay.

She knew that.

Lexie's life hung in the balance and with it, Simon's stability, even Devil's. The man downstairs hadn't scared her, but experience told her he was holding on by a thread. If this was an outside, physical force threatening them, they could all fight it together. There was nothing they could do. Only Lexie, and what her body was capable of.

Simon lifted up and pressed his thumb and finger to both of his eyes, which were closed tight. "I'm fine." His voice broke.

"You're not fine."

"I promised myself I wouldn't cry."

"I know. I did that with Darcy," she said. "It's not good to see people you love dying. It breaks you apart, piece by piece. You have to be strong for them. We've got to be strong for Lexie. It'll help her."

"I don't even know if this is an early diagnosis or not. Man, everything is so fucked up. I wish they'd just kept on having kids. This would have been so much easier."

They were shouted down for dinner and Tabby slid off the bed, taking Simon into the bathroom, and she helped him splash water on his face.

"It's going to be okay," she said.

"I know. I know you're just saying that."

"It may sound like it right now, but day by day, I'm going to be here."

He lifted his head. "Do I look like I've been crying?"

"No."

He took her hand and together, they walked downstairs. Devil was already in the dining room, dealing with the kids. Simon immediately went to help and she didn't take a seat but walked into the kitchen to see Lexie stirring up a large bowl.

"It's just garlic tomato pasta. I know it's Devil's favorite," Lexie said.

"I love it as well."

"Your mom told me that you've given up meat."

Tabitha laughed. "You should have heard my dad. He thought I was being a rebel and a giant pain in the ass."

"I bet. I remember you always running around, wanting sausages and burgers," Lexie said. "Wow, that seems like a lifetime ago. How are you handling it?"

"I'm doing fine."

"Dick and Martha went vegan as well," Lexie said. "I know the club thought they were crazy."

"I'm not vegan, just, you know, vegetarian. Daisy's going vegan, I think. She keeps on searching this stuff online, kind of scary. Do you want me to stir that?" she asked. Lexie was looking tired by the second.

"Yes, please, I would appreciate it. I still want to do everything. Nothing has changed, at least not yet."

Tabitha smiled and took over, stirring up the large bowl of pasta. Her stomach growled.

"Oh, I also made garlic bread," Lexie said. She went to bend down, but Tabitha quickly grabbed her and placed her on a chair. "Sorry, a little dizzy there."

"Don't worry about it. I'm here. I can help." She smiled at Lexie.

"You haven't asked," Lexie said after a couple of seconds had passed. The pasta was all combined with the intense sauce, and she was chopping the garlic bread into strips.

Tabitha paused and turned to the older woman. "I figure you've spent a lot of time talking about it. People, everyone you know is treating you differently, fragile. It only drills in that something is wrong. I know it can feel overwhelming."

"You helped Darcy," Lexie said.

"We're close. Most of the time. Not recently. What she went through was tough, you know. I remember feeling so helpless nearly all of the time. I know this is going to be hard on everyone. Darcy got tired of people treating her like she was sick." She laughed even as tears filled her eyes. "I never did. I always treated her the same and she needed that."

Lexie was crying now. "Thank you, Tabitha. I don't—this is going to be tough without everything. Simon is going to need you."

"And I'm going to be here for him and for you. I promise."

"You know, this brings back a memory, but not like you think." Lexie sighed.

"What kind of memory?" She was curious.

"Oh, it was when Simon was little. He wanted to learn how to bake chocolate chip cookies for you." Lexie chuckled. "I put out three whole cups of chocolate chips, and you know what, he ate them all. He had chocolate at the corners of his mouth. It was so cute." She laughed. "Wow, I haven't thought about that. I know this is of no relation to that time. Just one of those memories."

"I love it," Tabitha said.

She finished cutting the garlic bread and piled it high up on a plate. "Come on, let's get you and all of this to the table." She carried the tray to the table while also being ready to help Lexie.

"I think I'm going to enjoy having more help," Lexie said.

Returning to the kitchen, she swiped at her cheeks to make sure there were no tears. She wasn't here to cause more trouble.

Taking the pasta to the table, she offered a smile and left Devil to dish them all out some food. This was like being back at home. Already on the first day, she was missing home. The comfort of it.

Picking up her fork, she ate her food and tried not to think about everything happening around her. Devil took the time with each kid, asking them about school. This was the first time she'd seen him as a family man, especially this up close and personal.

Laughter filled the table.

Once the meal was finished, she helped clean the table and do the dishes before heading upstairs to shower and go to bed. Simon had whispered he'd be in as his dad wanted to have another talk with him.

With her hair wrapped up in a towel, she called Daisy. Her best friend's face appeared on the screen.

"It's about time you called me. I was starting to worry."

"Sorry. I was going to call."

"How is it?"

"It's ... fine."

"I know that voice."

"Really, it's fine. Everyone is happy and I think they're just trying to get through each day, you know?"

"I bet. It must suck with everything."

She nodded. "I miss you."

"I miss you too. How is Lexie?"

"She's fine. She had a dizzy spell while we were in the kitchen. I helped her the best way I can, but I don't even know if it's enough, you know? What am I doing here, Daisy?"

"You're being the best damn friend and girlfriend a person could be. You're not there for yourself, you're there to help Simon. Let's face it, we know you're only

153

there for him."

She chuckled. "I am, but I like Lexie as well. I want to help her."

"You will. You always know what to do."

"I hope so," Tabitha said. "You will not believe what happened when I got here. Devil took me to his office and he laid some ground rules down."

"He didn't?"

"Yep. He's worried Simon and I are having sex. I would love to know when our parents think we have the time to actually have sex. It must be nice to be a grownup."

Daisy laughed. "I miss you. School is going to suck royally without you."

"I know. I'll be back soon. This isn't permanent. Just helping out as best as I can."

"What if it is, you know, permanent?"

Tabitha shook her head. "Not happening. I know my parents wouldn't be happy about me staying here all the time." She sighed. "It's what I've got to do though."

"I'm sure Luke is missing you," Daisy said.

"Don't even start with all of that. How is Anthony?" Tabitha asked.

Daisy rolled her eyes.

"You're going to have to understand that you can't hide away from that for much longer."

"Nothing is going on and you keep on mentioning it."

"Seriously, Daisy, how can you not see that Anthony has the biggest crush on you? He has for as long as I've known him."

"I'm going to hang up now."

"Does it make you uncomfortable?" Tabitha asked.

"I … I think you're wrong. Look, I've got to go.

Dad's calling me."

"You're lying."

The line went dead and Tabitha blew out a breath. "I think she's uncomfortable."

She jumped and looked up to see Simon had snuck into her room.

"Do I need to put a bell on you?" she asked.

Simon laughed. "You were too busy telling your best friend how much Anthony has a crush on her."

"I'm not wrong. He does."

"Yeah, well, she clearly is afraid or doesn't want to see it."

"I know, which I don't get. Anthony dotes on her. He protects her all the time." Tabitha put her cell phone down, climbed off the bed, and unwrapped her hair. Running a brush through it, she looked over at Simon who was smiling widely at her. "What?"

"Nothing, I just can't believe you're here."

"I know. I meant what I said. I'm not going to break any one of his rules," she said.

Simon sighed and moved to her bed, climbing on in. "I'm not breaking any of his rules. I must be the most boring boyfriend on the planet." He lifted the blankets. "Are you coming in?"

She slid beneath the covers, snuggling up against him. "You're not boring. You're the best."

"The best kind of boyfriend would try to get a sneaky feel."

"No, he wouldn't. You respect me to not push my boundaries and like I've told you before and I will keep telling you, I love you even more for it." She gripped his face between her hands and kissed him, hard. "Love you so much."

"Love you too." His hand went to her back and she moaned a little. "We better get some sleep."

"Yes, a lot to do tomorrow." She switched off the light, snuggled in against him, and knew she would be here for him, no matter what.

****

Simon loved having his girl at school. She wasn't in any of his classes but walking into school with her on his arm felt fucking amazing. Of course his brother Josh, bless him, struggled with her presence.

Tabby hadn't said anything to Josh about his crush. She was too sweet to bring too much attention to it.

"This is your locker," Tabby asked, running her hand down the metal.

"You never seen a locker before?" Dean asked.

With the emancipation now going ahead, Dean was currently renting a motel room while he looked for a possible apartment. His dad and the lawyer were handling it. If he needed anything though, Simon was there for him.

"Yeah, we totally have them back home. I'm just basking in the moment."

"She's taking the piss, as I'm sure Adam would say," Simon said, referring to the British patched-in member of The Skulls.

"You got that right." She popped her gum, hands on hips. "Anyway, I've got to get to reception. If I in any way shirk my studies, my parents will kill me, and we all know they know how to hide a body. Walk me there?"

"You got it." He slammed his locker closed, fist-bumped his friends, and took off.

"It must be odd, being the oldest Chaos member," Tabby said. "I never thought about how lucky I am. For some of us, there are only a couple of months, and then there is always Miles." She wrinkled her nose. "I try not to think too much about that. Sharing a womb with him was way too much even for me."

Simon laughed. He walked down the corridor, his arm across her shoulder. People moved out of their way, all apart from Wayne, the douchebag football jock.

Tabby had her arm around Simon's waist.

"Move," Tabby said.

More of Wayne's jock friends stood at his back.

"Simon, you didn't tell me the people here didn't understand English."

"I don't think we've been introduced," Wayne said. "You're the new girl and you can do so much better than spending time with the likes of him." He offered out his hand.

Tabby stared at his hand and then burst out laughing. "Oh, that is a good one. Seriously, the likes of him?"

Simon kissed her head. He fucking loved this girl.

"Wow," Tabby said. She pulled out of Simon's hold and spun so they could see her leather jacket. Devil had agreed to allow her to wear her patched member jacket claiming her to be the property of The Skulls. "I am his kind, asshole, but thank you for clearing that up. Now, move, or I move you, simple as that."

Wayne looked a little startled but instantly masked it. "I see."

"Yeah, keep on throwing the names out. You think I don't hear them on a daily basis? Do they make guys like this in some kind of factory? For a jerk son, please apply?" Tabitha asked.

"Not a clue," Simon said. "I suggest you back off. She's not like your little groupies. She's more likely to cut your dick off than suck it."

He hadn't seen Tabitha fight in a long time, but he'd also promised his father. Stepping forward, he got in Wayne's face. "Or are you and I about to have a throw-down? I would kill to snap your leg right now." Thoughts of cancer, of his mom's pain, and of what his family was going through filled his head. He wanted to hurt someone. To do as much damage as possible.

Wayne laughed. "It looks like we're about to have a whole lot of fun." He backed off.

Simon looked at Tabby, who was frowning at their retreating backs. "They do know they've just labeled themselves as cowards, right?"

"It happens."

"Your school is way different from mine. If that would have been Luke, there would have been a fight. Of course, if a teacher turns up wanting to slap us all with suspensions or expulsions, it's the classic, we all slipped."

"I can't even imagine what it must be like at your school. I don't get into a lot of fights here. At least not anymore." They arrived at the reception and Tabby groaned.

"This is going to suck. I'll see you at lunch?" Tabby asked, putting a hand on his chest.

"Count on it." He kissed her head and turned, making his way to homeroom.

Throughout the morning, he heard the whispers and the rumors about the new girl. People were already curious about her. It wasn't like she was new. She didn't even attend their classes. The setup was that she'd complete her courses in the privacy of one of the offices near the principal. It had all been arranged between Tiny, Devil, and the school. Tabby wasn't part of the school, just continuing her education.

In History, Dean and Eddie sat in front of him, but leaned back.

"So have you heard?" Eddie asked.

"Heard what?"

"What people are saying about Tabitha?"

"Yeah, they're all curious about her. Who wouldn't be?" he asked. He was a little annoyed with the attention she was getting. Tabby belonged to him. He didn't like to share. Having her here was something he'd been wanting for a long time. Now that she was, he didn't like the idea of others getting to know her, of seeing how damn special she was. She belonged to him, only to him.

"He hasn't heard," Dean said.

"Amber's threatening to kick her ass at lunchtime."

"Really?"

"Yeah, it's what everyone is talking about." Eddie smiled.

Dean shrugged. "How does your girl fare in a fight?"

"Tabby can hold her own." Simon ran fingers through his hair.

"Why do you not look happy about this? Someone needs to put Amber in her place," Eddie said. "Come on, this could make for a good lunch."

"Tabby's here based on her being good. She's helping my family out. She causes more stress, she's heading back home. I don't want her to get into any kind of fucking fight." He threw down his pen. He sounded like a pussy.

"I also heard Wayne's got a hard-on for her," Dean said. "He believes he can take her from you."

Simon rolled his eyes. "I'd like to see him try."

No one took his girl away from him. Fucking no one. By the time lunch rolled around, he was as tense as he could be. He didn't want Tabby fighting, but if Amber got into her face, she was clearly asking for it.

Tabby waited for him by reception. He pulled her

159

to him and told her the rumors.

"Oh, please. You think I haven't heard stuff like this before? It happens all the time. Rumors are empty lies. Trust me. It's all going to be fine. You need to learn to relax. I don't know what has happened to you, but be calm."

"Is that an order?"

"Yes. Now, how were your classes, honey?"

"We're going domesticated?"

"Couples do it all the time and seeing as this is the first time I've been in school with my boyfriend, I thought I'd try it out."

"You sound sexy," he said, running a hand down her back to grab her ass. "I like it."

"You like me being all wifey?"

"Yeah, I do."

She giggled and kissed him. "Wait until I take you home and cook you dinner."

"Babe, none of this is bothering me. You're talking to the guy who actually wants to marry you. I'd have you as my old lady right now."

"Really?"

"Yeah. I'll ask my dad."

"As much as I'd like to, we both know our dads would pitch a giant fit if we let that happen."

"Let what happen? We're not pregnant."

"I know. Let's give them time."

He took her hand, rubbing the finger where an engagement and a wedding band would go. "When you're eighteen?" he asked.

"What?"

"We don't have to ask them for permission. When we're both eighteen, you'll be my wife."

She licked her lips. "What if you change your mind?"

He snorted. "You think after all this time I'm going to change my mind?"

"We don't know what is going to happen in the future," she said.

He cupped her face, tilting her head back. "I know what's going to happen. You and I are going to be a team, no matter what."

"The clubs?"

"We'll figure it out together. Tell me, make a pact with me right now. Both of us are eighteen, we're married. No doubt?"

Her smile lightened up his whole world.

"Yes. You can count on it."

He held her hand and they walked toward the cafeteria. Eddie and Dean, along with a couple of others, sat at the tables. He stood in the line with Tabby. She grabbed a salad, some pizza, and a pudding bowl. He loaded up with burgers, fries, and cake.

Simon didn't allow her to pay and carried her tray to their table, putting it down before his own. He couldn't help but think of when he was younger and telling his dad he intended to marry this girl.

"Hey, Dad, did you catch the bad guys?" Simon asked.

Devil entered the hospital room and pointed at him. "Why are you in Tabs's bed?"

"She has bad dreams."

"Oh, you do know that it stops when you get out of the hospital?" Devil asked.

"You sleep with Mom all the time."

"That's because your mom and I are married."

"Then I'll marry Tabitha. She's going to be my girl, anyway. It'll be cool."

"Son, you're not marrying. You're not even ten."

"That's not fair."

"Lucky for me, it doesn't have to be fair."

Before he could respond, Tabby had woken up.

"I'm sorry, Devil, the nightmares were bad. I dreamt of bullets and stuff. It was scary."

"It's okay, sweetie, I hope he chased the demons away." His dad had looked so tortured as he spoke.

"He did, and he told Gavin what for as well, which was really funny." Tabby looked toward him with a smile and he couldn't help but feel so proud. That big guy had been scary, but he hadn't been afraid. No one would come between him and Tabby.

Simon pulled out of the memory. That felt like a lifetime ago.

"You're the entire talk of the high school," Eddie said. "Wherever I go, you're there."

Tabby tucked her long hair behind her ears before sliding her jacket off. It was raining outside, otherwise, he would've taken their lunch out there to be more private.

"Yay, I'm miss popular at the moment. I won't be around long. I don't know what the big deal is. Don't you have new kids coming and going all the time?" Tabby asked, stealing one of his fries.

"You'd think so, but no. Piston County has got a lot going for it, but the whole MC element, they don't like it."

Tabby laughed. The sound filled his senses.

Simon watched her. She picked up her pizza and took a large bite, wiping some tomato sauce at the corner of her mouth.

"Believe me, they're wasting their time on me. I don't get involved in the little cliques."

"Babe, you're in your own clique, don't forget that."

"I guess you're right. I never thought of it like

that. We've got a couple of civilians on our squad as well."

"Civilians?" Dean asked.

"Non-MC kids. They're good people."

"Dean wants to prospect for the Chaos."

Tabby winced. "Good luck."

"Okay, you and Simon have both said stuff like that. He's got to prospect as well."

"Yeah, but he's like MC royalty. His dad's the prez, which is like a big deal. The same goes for my brother. My dad was the previous prez. My point being, they know what the deal is. They've grown up around all of it. They're not uncomfortable getting their hands dirty."

"And you think I am?" Dean asked.

Tabby reached across the table, taking hold of his hand. Simon didn't like her touching other people, but this was his own jealous, possessive personality, and he wasn't going to push it on Tabby.

"Look at these hands. They're soft. You can feel mine. I work hard. I will never prospect for the club because I'm a girl, but I will earn my place to be one of them. It's who I am. You need to know what you're getting yourself into. There's no crying about it, and there's certainly no trying again if you can't hack it the first time." She dropped Dean's hand.

"Okay."

"Not trying to scare you off. A couple of guys are thinking about doing it. I gave them the same warning, but they don't all have rich parents. It's second nature to them." She shrugged. "Want a bite?" Tabby asked, offering up her pizza.

Simon couldn't resist, watching her as he took a bite. She was going to be one hell of an old lady.

A girl cleared her voice and Simon tensed up as

he turned to see Amber standing there, a couple of her friends nearby. What was with the popular kids and having a little entourage?

"Hi, Simon. Don't think I don't see what you're doing. I do."

"Amber, I'd like you to meet my girlfriend," he said, wrapping his arm around Tabby and pulling her close. "Tabby. The love of my life." The cafeteria had gone silent and he slammed his lips down on hers, kissing her hard.

"Tabby, is that like a cat?" Amber asked. "Please, you can do so much better than that."

"Excuse me?" Tabby asked, getting to her feet. Simon stood, as did Dean and Eddie.

"You heard me. You're scum. Nothing but a fat, ugly cat. It's pathetic."

Tabby smiled. "Oh, you seem to mistake me for someone who gives a shit."

"Simon's mine. He and I are together."

"In your dreams," Simon said.

"You're so cute, but it's time for you to run along with your little whores."

"Do you have any idea who you're speaking to?" Amber asked, arms folded.

No one stood up to Amber, at least none of the girls Simon knew of.

Tabby got into Amber's face. "Do you know who *you're* dealing with? You may rule this school, but, girl, I'm not a coward. You and your little girls mean nothing to me. I've gone up against guys that are twice your size and they've gone squealing to mommy. Back off before I break your face and give your parents something they do need to spend their money on."

She took a step back and Simon thought he was going to have to protect her as Amber lashed out, but

Tabby saw it coming. As Amber went to claw at her, one punch to the face, and she was down, blood everywhere.

****

"What the fuck did I say?" Devil asked, slamming into the house. He couldn't believe on her first day of school he had to go and pick her up.

"You told me to not start fights. I didn't. She came at me. If you don't want me to defend myself, give me the update."

"Watch your lip, girl."

"You're not my dad. Seriously, if this was your daughter and she was about to get attacked, would you tell her to wait? What if this Amber had a good hit, or a disease, and she goes around scratching people? I don't care what she said to the principal, she was going to hit me."

"She was, Dad," Simon said.

"Enough, the both of you. You are both more than capable of handling shit without getting into a fight."

"Devil?" Lexie asked, coming out of the sitting room.

"It's fine, honey."

"No, it's not."

"I'm not having her here causing trouble."

"I know of this Amber girl. She's bad news. You and I both heard what she tried to threaten Simon with."

Devil gritted his teeth. Simon had come to them straight away with the recording of her voice and threats. He'd taken the device, gone to the girl's father, to make sure nothing came of it. It was a good thing he had. When he arrived at the house, Amber was acting like a victim, and the cops had already been there.

Nothing had come of it, not when he played the cell phone for Amber and her parents to hear.

What he didn't want right now was trouble. Every other day he could handle it, but not right now. Not with chemo around the corner, the possible operation, and all the medication. Not when he held his wife and knew there was a chance he was holding a ticking time bomb.

"Get out of my sight," he said.

Tabitha and Simon disappeared.

"You're both grounded!"

"You can't ground me."

"I can. Your father gave me plenty of permission and while you're under my roof, you will do as you're told."

He glared at both of them until they were out of his sight.

"That's not like you," Lexie said.

"They need to learn to do as they're told."

"I get that, I do, but come on, Devil, even you know that you've sometimes got to hit first. Tabitha is a Skull. I know from her mother that high school is not the easiest of places."

"They can't be starting shit. Not now."

"You mean because of me?" she asked.

He went to his wife. "I love you, Lexie. I don't want you to be under any more stress than you already are."

"You need to learn to relax, Devil. This isn't you. Don't push this. I trust Tabitha and Simon."

He pulled her close, breathing her in. Sinking his fingers into her hair, he allowed the silence to calm him.

"I'm here."

"I know."

"I'm going to keep fighting," she said. "And we're going to beat this thing."

"I know."

"Do you?"

He looked up and saw the tears in Lexie's eyes.

"When you asked me to trust you all these years, I have. You've been strong for me. Let me do this."

"This isn't some guy with a gun, Lexie. This is inside your body and I can't, I can't fucking kill it for you. I can't do anything." He gritted his teeth. Fuck! He wouldn't cry. Not now, he wouldn't allow himself to fucking cry. She needed him strong.

Lexie cupped his face.

He didn't know if it was in his mind or if her strength was disappearing. She felt weaker to him.

"I've got this, Devil. You make me strong. Every single day, you give me a reason to fight."

"It's not supposed to end like this. Not for us."

"It's not over. It will never be over, not with us. If I end up going first, then I expect you to pick up the pieces. To bring our kids up."

He shook his head.

"But that is the worst-case scenario. I know our kids need us both. Now stop, and hug me, and know you will help me every single day."

Devil held her close. He'd never considered himself a praying man, but whenever it came to Lexie, he always begged for her to live.

Chapter Ten

Lexie had been sick.

Tabitha was used to the vomit but each time, she caught Simon looking terrified. Like always, he'd help, make some excuse, and disappear. She'd wait for Devil to arrive home and then she'd go looking for him.

This had happened every single day this past week. Now, she found him on the edge of Piston County, right at the welcome sign.

"Shit, is he going to be okay?" Eddie asked.

She'd called Eddie as Dean was going through his emancipation and could no longer afford a car. He had to prove in the next month that he was capable of holding down a job and also taking care of himself. Devil had to make sure his family didn't interfere, and to guarantee it, Dean was working for Devil.

"Yeah, he'll be okay."

"I've never known him to be like this." He sighed, running a hand over his head and down to grip his neck.

"I know. Something like this, it can change a person. It's hard to explain."

"You've gone through this before?"

"Not me, but I have a friend back home. She struggled as well, but she got through it." Just thinking about Darcy always reminded her of home and how much she was missing it.

After climbing out of the car, she walked several steps. Simon was on the welcome side while she stood on the side that asked them to come back soon.

Gripping the cuffs of her jacket tightly, she stopped a foot away from him.

"Where are you going?"

Simon spun around, wiping at his face. "Tabby, what are you doing here?"

"You're here."

"I know. I'll be home soon." He turned his back on her.

"You know, I came here to help you. Not to do all of this for you." Devil had warned her she'd need to practice tough love with him. She hated the very idea of it, but if it would help, she'd do it.

Simon chuckled. "You're cute when you're trying to play a role."

"This isn't funny."

"I know it's not funny. You think I'm laughing?"

"Don't fucking yell at me."

"I don't mean to." He slammed his foot to the ground. A hand went to his mouth, and he shook his head. "I don't ... fuck, I don't know what to do."

"There's nothing you can do, Simon. This isn't something you can plan or rationalize. It happens. You move on. You get shit done." She shook her head. "You think Lexie wants this?"

"I know she doesn't."

"She's fighting every single day. For her kids, for you, for Devil. For the entire freaking club. I see it. What she doesn't need right now is this. If you can't handle this, then you need to come back to Fort Wills with me, and we will hang out, you'll go to school, and when it's all over, you come back, pick up the pieces."

Simon stared back at her, tears in his eyes. "You'll think less of me."

She pressed her lips together. Folding her arms, she glared at him. "You know what, yeah, I will. I was going to give you the pansy answer, telling you it would all be okay and I'd be fine with you walking away from your parents but you know what, that is a horrible idea, and I don't think you should do it."

"Tabby?"

"No!" She slashed her hand across the air. "No! You don't get to say my name as if I'm nagging, or if this is too much of a hard decision. Stop whining about it. It is what it is and we can't change it. What we can do is be strong. If you run away right now, I guarantee you'll regret it and not just because of me being pissed at you or whatever, but because for the first time in your life, you're being challenged and you can't take it. You talk to me all the time about wanting to take Devil's place when the time is right, then prove it. Be a man. Even now. Be a fucking man." Tears spilled down her eyes and Simon shook his head.

"Don't cry."

"I can't help it. I'm right here for you and you're there. You're on the opposite side of this sign."

"You don't know what this is like," he whispered.

"Are you crazy? You think I don't know what this is like? How this all feels?" She laughed. "You think I've never not wanted to run? That I've never not wanted to hide? To be as far away as possible?"

She licked her lips. spinning in a couple of circles, looking around them. "Simon, for a long time, I didn't even want to be an MC girl. I wanted nothing to do with The Skulls. My very future was about getting out until I talked to my grandpa and he convinced me, so yeah, I get that you're struggling. Really, I do. I probably understand you now more than ever."

"Then come with me," Simon said.

She shook her head. "No."

"Tabby."

"You will hate yourself for this. I can't stop you, but I'm not going to join you. Not here, not with this. If you're not home tonight, I'll pack a bag and go back to my family. I miss them so much, but I'm here for you." She went to him and cupped his face. "You're stronger than this, Simon. Stop fighting who you are."

She turned on her heel and got back into the car.

"What am I doing?" Eddie asked.

"Take me back to Devil's house." She ran her hands along her thighs, taking a deep breath.

"You okay?"

"I'll tell you later."

Eddie didn't ask any more questions. When they got back to Devil's house, she pulled out some cash, handing it to him. "Here you go."

"Don't. keep it. I would do anything for him, and he knows it."

She nodded. "Thanks."

"Don't mention it. If you need a ride anywhere, let me know, and there's nothing sexual in it."

She chuckled. "Thanks."

Heading indoors, she saw Sasha, Pussy's woman, was hanging out with the kids and Lexie.

She gave them a wave and headed upstairs to quickly change. After a shower, she pulled on some sweatpants and headed to the kitchen to cook something, anything. She'd helped her mother plenty of times. Angel, Lash's woman and old lady, was forever in the kitchen, and Tabitha always liked to watch. She settled on pasta. Devil tried to take over cooking as she'd been serving them up all-vegetable meals.

Tucking her hair behind her ear, she tried not to get her hopes up each time the door opened. No one back home knew she'd been sitting at the same welcome sign back home with a bag packed. Of course, she'd been younger as well. Daisy didn't know how she'd walked to the edge of town and held her bag. Every couple of cars had slowed down, asking her if she was okay. In the end, rather than hitchhiking it out of there, she'd gone back home, put her clothes away, and appeared at school the next day.

She got it.

But Simon was running from different things. He had to see that.

"This smells good," Simon said, drawing her out of her thoughts.

She spun around to find him right there, in front of her. "You came back."

"You think I'm going to do anything that would make you angry or sad to be near me on purpose?"

"I don't know. For all I know, my being here has made you stop caring about me." She shrugged, trying not to sound as broken as she felt at the very thought of him not wanting her.

Simon went to her, gripping the back of her neck, tilting her face up, and kissing her hard. Wrapping her arms around him, she held on for dear life, not wanting to let him go.

"You don't ever have to fear that," he said against her lips. "Tabby, what I feel for you isn't normal."

She laughed. "That's the way to a girl's heart."

"What can I say, you struck me when we were kids, and I can't move on. I love you way too much to ever be able to handle that."

"Damn, you say all the nicest things."

"Always."

****

"How is everything there?" Daisy asked.

"Fine, I guess. I don't know. It's tough."

"Yeah, I heard the parents talking. They think you should come home."

"I've already spoken to my dad. If it gets to be

too much, they want me home. I'm doing good. My schoolwork is on point so it's not like they can pull me away because of that."

Daisy pouted. "What about us?" She rolled over so now Tabitha looked at Daisy lying down.

"What about you guys?"

"We miss you."

"I know. I miss you guys so much."

"Don't sound so surprised." Daisy lifted and lowered the phone so Tabitha watched her face go distant then right up close.

"You're freaking me out doing that."

"I know. You know how much I hate these things. Does my double chin look bigger?"

Tabitha rolled her eyes. "Seriously?"

"I'll shut up."

"How's school?" Tabitha asked.

"You're sounding like a mom."

Tabitha glared at her and Daisy's brows went up. "Wow, all right, all right already. School is great, actually. Sure, we're not exactly in the open arms of the Dogs but there haven't been any fights. The Quad has been doing okay. Again, we've held up our end. I know Ryan wants a piece of Anthony but it seems a lot of people are pissed at him. With how quiet everything is, I'm starting to think you're the trouble causer."

"Don't start," she said.

"I'm only stating a fact," Daisy said, laughing. "In all seriousness, how are you holding up? I know this has to be bringing up some hard shit."

"It is. I'm doing okay. It's Simon I'm worried about. The club is always around. They have a reason to stop by. I think the strangest thing I've seen so far is Dick and Martha offering mediation with Lexie. It seems to help, though."

"I remember you telling me Dick's into holistic stuff now, right?"

"Yep. Seems that way. I asked about it, and he told me to have lived and survived through some of the crap he has, he has to believe in a higher power."

"Deep," Daisy said.

"Yeah, that's what I thought."

"So has this helped you to make a firm decision?"

"What do you mean?"

"Come on, Tabs. You and I both know that you're there for two reasons. To be there for Simon during this time, but to also figure out if you can become his old lady. I'm not an idiot. I know exactly what you're doing. I think all of us know what you're doing."

Tabitha groaned and sat up. "It wasn't my intention."

"But you're doing it?" Daisy asked.

"It's … hard." She wrinkled her nose.

"How?"

"I don't know." She glanced around her room. Simon was out with Devil doing some club stuff. Lexie was already in bed, and Tabitha had all the children monitors in her room in case anyone ever needed her. Josh asked if she wanted to watch a movie, but she'd refused, and he'd gone to bed in a sulk. "I guess because I miss you guys so much."

"Don't go blaming us. That's not fair."

"I'm not blaming you. Far from it."

"I hear blame in that voice."

She snorted. "You're being a bitch."

"You love me for it."

"You're right, I do. Any new developments with Anthony?"

Daisy's smile faded. "Don't start."

"Come on, don't be so obtuse about this."

"Obtuse?"

"I've decided to start using a new vocabulary. What do you think?"

"I think your vocabulary is certainly not obtuse." Daisy winked at her.

Tabitha scrunched up her nose and stuck her tongue out. "Bitch. I know you're trying to change the subject."

"I'm not. Me and Anthony, supposing he talks. If he likes a girl, wouldn't he talk?" she asked.

"He does talk."

"To you. Have you ever thought he has a crush on you?"

"Not at all. Believe me. He totally digs you. Don't you like that?"

"I don't know what I like," Daisy said. "It's easier to just see him as a friend."

"Why don't you ask him out on a date?" Tabitha asked.

"I'm not doing that." Daisy jerked back, shaking her head.

"Why not?" She moved to sit up against her bed.

"A girl doesn't ask. I mean, sure, I'm all for taking control of our lives, but come on, you can't be serious. What if he rejects me?"

"I guarantee he won't. Oh, and when you ask, have me there so I can watch."

"You're not even in the same town, weirdo," Daisy said.

Tabitha couldn't stop smiling. "That's what cell phones are for, nerd."

"I miss you. I miss this."

"Me too."

"I hate to say this, but I want you to come home."

"Soon," Tabitha said. She couldn't get away from

the fact she was getting homesick. Even though she got to see Simon every single day, she missed home.

"You've gone all sad and I feel like crying. We're not going to cry. What am I going to do if he turns me down flat?" Daisy asked. "I don't think I can handle that."

"How about this, if Anthony turns you down, I will totally freak out my parents in a bikini and dance. Maybe even do a striptease."

"Really?"

"Yep, I will make sure I get grounded for my entire life."

"You're that confident he's going to say yes?" Daisy asked.

"You know me. I won't make bets I won't win." Tabitha smiled. "Come on, you've got to ask him."

"And if he does say yes?"

"You go on a date and tell me all about it. Even if he kisses you, I want to know."

"But … I don't know. I've never been on a date."

"And you think I have?" Tabitha frowned. "Wow, I have never been on a date."

"You and Simon are always together."

"Exactly, we're never on a date. This sucks. Like big time. I'm going to force him to take me on a date." She nodded her head. "That's what I'm going to do."

Daisy giggled. "I have a feeling Simon is going to hate me."

"Not if he loves me he's not. I'm going on a date and there's going to be flowers."

****

Simon was nervous.

He hated to be this way, especially with Tabby. She wanted to go on a date. She'd been so freaking fierce about it that it had kind of concerned him. He figured they were living their lives as constant dates but according to Tabby, he was getting out of everything, and he didn't want to disappoint her. So, he'd done the only thing he could and went to his dad.

Devil had helped him to buy some flowers and even rented a suit. Now he felt like a fucking penguin, and he held a bouquet of flowers that cost a fortune. He stood in his dad's office.

"Don't laugh," Simon said.

"I'm not laughing."

"You're a terrible liar." He glared at his dad while trying not to wriggle in this suit. "How do men wear these things?"

"You look…"

"Just say it."

"You look smart. It does suit you."

"Ha ha. You're taking pictures for the guys."

Devil already had his phone in the air, snapping them. "I've got to keep these kinds of memories, son. You know that."

Simon rolled his eyes. "I hate you right now."

"That's your prerogative."

Lexie knocked on the door, gaining their attention. "She's ready and she's nervous."

"How can she possibly be nervous? This was her idea."

"I taught you better than that. Every girl will be nervous on her first date. Accept it." Lexie walked into the room and moved toward him. "You look handsome."

"Thanks, Mom."

Lexie sighed. "I can't … you make me so proud."

His stomach twisted. In the past few weeks, she'd been making comments that always made him think she believed she was going to die.

Wrapping his arms around her, he held on to her,

not squeezing too tightly when that was all he wanted to do.

Be a man. Don't be a pussy. She's your mom. She's going to fight this.

Simon pulled away. "Do you think the flowers are too much?"

"No, go and see her reaction," Lexie said. "She's waiting. Simon, she's special. Treat her right."

"Always."

Leaving his father's office, he found her sitting on the stairs, and she quickly stood. She wasn't wearing The Skulls' leather cut.

"Wow," she said.

"Wow." He pointed at her. "You look…"

"Like a dork?" She tugged at the bottom of the dress. It was a beautiful pink floral dress.

"No, you look beautiful."

She glanced down at herself. "You always say that."

"But you do, to me. You always are beautiful and I love it when you smile like that."

Devil cleared his throat. "We'll be waiting for your return." He dangled the car keys from his fingers. "Slow and steady. You've been taught."

"I will. I'll keep her safe."

"Have fun," Lexie said.

"We will." Simon looked at the flowers. "These are for you."

Tabby laughed. "They're beautiful."

Lexie took them. "I'll put them in some water for you."

"Thank you."

Putting a hand on her back, Simon walked out of the house and went to the car. He opened the passenger door and Tabby climbed in.

He took a deep breath, the nerves getting to him. He waved at his parents just as he got behind the wheel.

"They're still watching," Tabby said.

"I know." He pulled out of the driveway. "I booked us a seat at a restaurant in town. It's a cute little Italian place. They're the only ones who were willing to do vegetarian meals."

"Thank you, Simon."

"Anything for you." He took her hand, locking their fingers together.

"Your hand's a little sweaty."

"I'm nervous. I thought I was the best kind of boyfriend in the world."

"You are and don't let anyone else tell you any different. You're awesome." She rested her head on his shoulder. He could do this.

****

"Tabitha is going to keep him on his toes," Lexie said.

"Count on it. She has got that boy so twisted up, but at least it's keeping him out of trouble."

"She's struggling, though, Devil. You can see that."

Devil wrapped his arms around his wife. The headlights of the car had already faded in the distance. "I know."

"Do you think allowing her to come here and help was a mistake?" Lexie asked, turning to look at him.

"Do you want the truth?"

"Yeah."

"I do and I don't."

"That's one way of avoiding the answers," Lexie said, smiling.

He cupped her cheek. The love he had for this woman. "I don't think we made a mistake because she needs to realize what kind of future she has. Being with Simon means a choice has to be made. This is her one and only chance to realize that. She's a Skull. We all knew this day would come. We can't keep avoiding it. I expected Simon to move on. To find a girl in high school, or several girls, but it's Tabitha he wants, and the only person he seems to think about. We can't change that."

Lexie sighed. "I hate this. They are going to have such a hard time. We all know this and we're only now thinking about it."

He held her close. "Tell me what you want me to do."

"Nothing. There's nothing we can do. Unless there's a chance of you and Lash coming to some agreement."

"No."

"Then no, Devil. I know the club means the world to you, and I love you. This is the challenge they're going to have to face." She cupped his face. "Take me indoors. It's cold."

****

Twenty minutes later

"You hate this," Tabitha said, looking over her menu at her date.

"No, it's fine."

"It's not fine, you're wriggling." She looked at where his finger was digging into his neck. She pressed her lips together.

"You're finding this really funny."

"I'm sorry. I can't seem to help it."

"This isn't funny."

"It is a little funny." She lifted up the menu and then shook her head. "Let me." She leaned over the table and unbuttoned the top two, relieving his neck. "There, how is that?"

"Does it still look neat?"

"Simon, stop it. I wanted you to take me on a date, not dress up like someone I don't know. You look handsome, dashing. Stop worrying so much. Please. You're actually making me nervous."

"I am nervous. I thought we'd been on dates before."

"We have in a way, but nothing like this. Now, pick up your menu." She'd noticed the moment they entered the restaurant some of the couples had stopped eating to watch them. This was what she was used to. Even back home in a town that accepted them, there were a few people who didn't like to mingle with them.

Glancing over the menu, she went straight to the vegetarian section.

"I'm ready to order if you are."

Simon looked toward their waiter, who immediately came to their table. He gave his order and Tabitha asked for hers, offering up the menu. She settled on a chocolate pudding for dessert.

Linking her fingers together in her lap, she stared across the candlelit table. "This is nice."

"It is?" he asked.

"The suit aside, you and me, out to dinner. Come on, tell me you don't like this."

Simon reached across the table, taking her fingers. His touch made her ache all over. Locking their fingers together, he cleared his throat.

"I love this. I love being with you."

"But?"

"There's not a *but*."

"I know you. Come on, tell me."

Simon sighed. "Fine. To me, every single day is a date with you. I don't take a moment with you for granted. I mean, I know some people would think it's stupid, but with how we grew up, the danger, I know how precious it is to be with people you love. One moment they can be taken from you and you won't even see it coming. It's why I love being with you every chance I have. Eating barbeque is still being a date. Even at home, sitting opposite you, playing footsie, it's like a chance again. We only get so short a time, Tabby. Yeah, this makes me nervous, but I'm with you."

She lifted her glass of water, taking a sip.

"You're crying," Simon said.

She waved her hand in front of her face. Lexie had helped her to do her makeup. "These are not sad tears. I'm happy. Like really happy. I didn't realize you felt like that."

Simon ran his thumb across her knuckles. "I do. I'm not being cheap. If this is what you want, then I will give it to you every single week."

"I don't need it every single week. I just, I wanted to go on a real date, but now I see I've been an idiot."

"You're not."

"I am. Just being with you is enough. I don't need all of this."

"We've ordered and you're going to eat." He laughed. "We don't have our parents breathing down our necks, but I know for a fact Curse and Mia are eating somewhere in this restaurant."

Tabitha quickly looked around. "You're kidding. Where?"

"Not kidding. I heard Dad call them, asking if they could keep an eye, asking if they'd make sure we turned up."

"That is so rude."

"The whole grandpa thing. I feel your pain."

"It's not pain. I'm pissed. Why can't they trust

us?" she asked.

"We're kids."

She shook her head. "That excuse is getting old."

"Tell me about it."

Tabitha took his other hand. "I'm going to love you forever, you know that?"

"I do."

Staring across the table, she looked into his dark eyes and knew their life wasn't going to be easy, but she would make it work. For the both of them.

Chapter Eleven

After flicking through the book, Tabitha closed it and slid it back on the shelf. She went to the next one that was on her list that Daisy had sent her last night. Her best friend was helping her through some of the science she was struggling with. She was still being sent work from her old high school. She worked in one of the offices at reception, but right now, she was in the Piston County library as the main school one didn't have what she was looking for, trying to find everything she needed to get her work done.

There would come a point when they'd demand she enroll in a new school but until then, she was determined to have a connection to her old school. So long as she did the work, and didn't mess them around, she'd be good. She knew that. What she didn't want to do was enroll in Simon's school. It would be like her life at Fort Wills was officially over. The agreement, Lash and Devil made with both schools was temporary, which was why she worked in the office, rather than attend any classes. At least she didn't have to deal with Amber as she wasn't at school because Tabitha did break her nose. Rumors were running rife, but no one messed with her.

With the other book, she opened it up to the page Daisy suggested had a better description of reproduction and glanced through it.

She was scanning through the words as someone put their hands over her eyes. She dropped the book, grabbed the hand, and slammed them up against the wall. Her fist raised, she looked into Simon's smiling face.

"Simon, what the fuck?" She dropped her fist as someone threw a shush her way. She let him go, bending down to pick up her cell phone and book. The screen hadn't cracked, but she was pissed.

"What? Dad told me he dropped you off at the library again. Why don't you use the school library?"

"Besides the fact I don't have a card there, they didn't have what I needed. I want to do some extra studying this week." She pulled the text messages on her cell phone to check the other titles.

"You could just enroll."

"I can't. I've got my old high school, Simon, you understand that. Devil and Lash worked hard for this."

"I do, but I also know time is ticking. The longer you're here, you're going to have to enroll."

She looked up from her cell phone and glared at him. "Stop meddling. I will deal with that when the time comes." She rounded the bookshelf and Simon followed her. "Why are you here? Are you looking for a book?"

"Nope. I came to hang out with you but it seems your only focus is on work. I have to say I'm disappointed."

"Don't be like that. You know this is important to me. Normally, if I don't get anything, Daisy and I have a sleepover. We enjoy pizza, study, and finish with a movie, but she always makes sure I understand it. Even makes me have a test to make sure I understand it. Don't worry about it." She missed home, that wasn't a surprise.

Talking to her parents was hard. She listened to tales of her brother and other siblings, and it made her ache to be back in Fort Wills. She missed the salon and Lacey's experiments with hair color and nails. Her sleepovers with Daisy. Even Anthony's silent asshole ways. Even Miles, her twin, and his complete lack of respecting personal space. Michael, the irritating bastard, he could be with an attitude a mile long. All of it was hard, and now as she looked at Simon, the guilt hit her again, hard.

He loved her and she loved him so much. The thought of being without him was like a physical blow, but this wasn't home.

"I worry about you, Tabby, always."

"I know." She went to him, putting a hand on his chest. "It will be fine. I know it will. Let me get this book and head on out."

She didn't give Simon a chance to argue with her. The first thing she'd done when she arrived at Piston County was get a library card. After scanning the books, she shoved them into her backpack and turned to Simon. He flicked the keys in his finger.

"Dad let me have the car. You want to go for a drive?" he asked.

"Yes."

It wasn't a bike, which was what she felt she needed, but it was better than nothing. She threw her bag into the backseat, jumped in the front, and rolled the windows down. There was some light rain, but she didn't care.

Simon started the car and reeved the engine.

Driving out of the main town center, he went in the opposite direction. As soon as they were on the open road, he pressed his foot to the floor, and off they went.

Closing her eyes, she stuck her head out the window, feeling her hair in the wind. It was the next best thing. Sticking her hands out, she let out a whoop and heard Simon's chuckle.

After minutes passed and she felt more like herself, she opened her eyes and watched the passing world. This was her life. When she thought about leaving The Skulls, she wanted to hit the road, travel, and just be free.

Simon came to a stop, pulling up in the middle of

nowhere. No one was around.

"What are you doing?" she asked.

"No one is around. Come on." He turned the radio on and some heavy metal song came through. He turned it up then climbed out of the car.

She didn't follow him, and he rounded to her side, opening it up. "Come on."

"Simon?"

He took her hand, and she didn't argue, unbuckling her belt as he got her out of the car.

"You need to stop thinking," he said, tugging her close. Their hands rested at his chest. "I can see you're struggling and I get it. This isn't home and I wish there was something I could do to make this easier for you."

"Simon, it's not you."

"I know. I haven't been in Fort Wills for a long time without my parents. I don't know what you're going through."

"It's nothing."

"It is something and when it comes to you, I always want to make it right. Let me help you."

"I just miss home, Simon. It's nothing you can do." She ran her hands down his arms. "Nothing at all. Just being here helps."

He pulled her close and she rested her head on his chest. If she was like this after a few weeks, what would it be like after months, what about years? What about never being able to go home again because of some argument? The Skulls and Chaos Bleeds worked together, but there were times they had fall-outs. She and Simon were able to work their way around the last one, but what if something happened when they were older? If she was his wife, and Anthony took over from the club. She'd never be allowed back. That alone terrified her.

Daisy and home were there.

Don't think. Stop thinking.

She held him tightly, not wanting to let him go.

"I will always be here for you, Tabby. You need to know that."

"I do."

For several songs, they danced, and she loved it, feeling him around her. When another upbeat song came on, Tabitha pulled away, holding his hands, and she started to sway her hips. There was no way she was going to let either of them be pulled down into the darkness. All of that could come back later. They only had now and each other. She was going to work with that.

Tabitha slammed her foot down to the notes of the song, following the beat of a drum. Closing her eyes, she let the words fill her senses, and swinging her hips, she lifted her hands up. Simon put his hands on her waist, following her. He helped her dip back, and there was no doubt he'd catch her.

She could be herself with him. He'd catch her no matter what.

Spinning in his arms, she put her ass against him and he groaned, but she took his hands, locking their fingers together. She wasn't trying to tease him, just be close. Pulling his arms around her, she held on to him, not wanting to let go. This was everything to her.

Simon's lips caressed her neck, his tongue sliding across her pulse. She released a gasp.

"Promise me, Tabby."

"What?"

"That whenever you're missing home, you'll come to me."

She opened her eyes and turned her head to look at him. "I will." It was a lie and with the soft smile he offered her, she knew he knew. As she cupped his cheek, the moment was broken. She stopped dancing. "I think it's time we headed back."

****

"What do you think?" Dean asked.

Simon stared out of his friend's apartment window.

"Earth to Simon."

He frowned and looked up. Dean stood right in front of him. "Sorry, what?"

Dean laughed. "You came to check out my place and it's like you're not even here."

"I'm sorry."

"Don't be sorry, man. Don't worry about it. Tell me what's going on with you." Dean folded his arms.

"It's nothing."

"It's not nothing. I know you. Come on, let me have it."

Simon rubbed the back of his neck. "It's Tabby."

"What about her?"

He didn't want to talk about it. "So when will the furniture arrive?" Simon asked, stepping away from the window. There were a couple of old fruit crates, and through one of the doors, he spotted a mattress on the floor.

"Dude, don't do this."

"It's nothing. Believe me."

"I'm your friend. If you can't tell me, who can you tell?"

"It's club stuff."

Dean snorted. "Right and even though I have every intention of becoming a prospect, you can't talk to me about it."

"It's between Tabby and me."

"You think she doesn't talk to her own friends?"

"I don't know what she does." He looked around

the apartment. "She's missing home."

"And?"

"And if she's missing home, it means any chance of us being together, it starts to change our entire future."

"How does it?" Dean asked.

"It just does. We're club kids, okay? We know the deal. We know what we have to do. You wouldn't understand." He didn't want to fight with his friend.

Dean laughed. "I wouldn't understand. Simon, look around you. You think right now I don't miss home? Sure, I've got to do as I'm told with them, but it would beat sleeping on a used mattress on the floor. I'm sitting on fruit crates and I know Devil's leaving me food packages to help me get by. I've got rent to pay and bills are mounting up, but I know in the long term, this is better for me than home. Do I still miss it? Hell, yeah. Will I go back there? No. I don't know what the deal is between you and Tabby but I do know you love each other."

"I thought like that for a long time."

"What changed?"

"Reality? I don't know. I figured this was a done deal. I'm going to take over from my dad. It's all I ever wanted to do and now, I don't know, I can't become a Skull."

"But you want her to become a Chaos."

"I thought it was what she wanted." He scoffed. "Can you hear me?"

"I can and I do know that if you and Tabby want it to work, and you see all this trouble in front of you, one day you're going to work it out, and then it will be pretty damn awesome."

"Thanks, man. It's a great place."

"It's a shithole."

"My dad keeps leaving you packages?"

"Yep. Food stuff. I even have a microwave. I've got to save up for a stove. Takeout is too damn expensive." Dean dropped down onto a crate.

"And this is better than home?"

"It is, to me it is. I don't have to worry about an upcoming wedding or any of that shit. Taking over the family business." Dean offered up a can of soda. "It's not cold. I don't have a fridge."

Simon shook his head. "I could get my dad to adopt you."

"Not happening. I want to make this work and I'm not afraid of hard work."

Opening the soda, he took a large sip. He sat down on the opposite crate. "Have you had to deal with your parents?"

"Yep. They don't like any of this. As if that's a surprise to me. They don't like any part of my life." Dean shook his head. "To them, money makes the world go around."

"You're an idiot if you don't think it too. Money's not everything, but it makes life a hell of a lot easier."

"True. If I had money, I'd have cold sodas. I'm going to make this work. I know I can." Dean smiled. "You don't know what it was like, growing up with them. With their expectations."

"I have expectations back home, Dean. It's just different."

"True. So are you going to let Tabitha go, or are you going to fight for her?" he asked.

"I will always fight for her. No doubt about it. She's the love of my life."

"You know, Eddie and I, we teased the shit out of you, but one day, I hope I get a fraction of that kind of love with someone. What you've got with Tabs, dude, hang on to it."

"I will."

****

Today was a bad day.

Lexie had chemo and the moment she got home, the vomiting happened. She got a little dizzy on her feet. Devil was there, and Tabitha tried to keep the kids settled. Josh and Elizabeth helped, but seeing their mom so ill was taking its toll.

When the sounds of her spewing up could be heard throughout the house, Tabitha took them all out into the yard. It had been snowing. She wrapped them all up in jackets, scarves, and hats, and watched each one as they built snowmen and had fights.

Within no time at all, she had them laughing. After Simon arrived home from school, he did the same and helped out.

After a couple of hours, she left them with Simon as she went inside to go and make some dinner, coming to a stop when she saw Devil.

All her life, this man had been scary as fuck. Always in control. Never letting his guard down. She couldn't recall seeing him sad. Angry, sure. Pissed off, a given. She paused at the doorway of the kitchen, and he was crying.

They weren't giant sobs. If she hadn't stopped and looked at him, it could even be mistaken for him just sitting there, contemplating life.

"You can come in," he said. His voice hoarse as if he'd been screaming at something.

"Are you okay?"

"I'm fine."

She pressed her lips together. A smart comment was on the tip of her tongue, but she refused to spill it, not yet.

She stepped into the kitchen and looked into the fridge. There wasn't a lot to cook with.

"I didn't get a chance to go to the grocery store."

"I can go," she said. "Don't worry about it."

"I'll drive you," Devil said. "I need to … I need to."

"I'll let Simon know." She made her escape. She'd rather Simon drive her to the supermarket but she had a feeling Devil needed to get out of the house.

Simon kissed her, and she left the main house, finding Devil already in the car.

Climbing into the passenger side, she waited.

Silence was often a comfort. With Devil in the car, it made her uncomfortable.

Devil drove past the supermarket and she looked back. "We kind of need to go there."

She tensed up as he pressed his foot on the gas. He wouldn't try to kill her, would he? It wasn't her fault he was in pain.

Her heart raced. She felt sick to her stomach.

They cleared the town and the moment they got across the line, the worst sound she had ever heard came out of Devil's mouth. He screamed. His hand hit the steering wheel. The dashboard. Anything he could hurt was there in front of him. He didn't stop screaming or yelling.

They came to a stop near a beat-up-looking diner. Her lips were pressed together and she kept perfectly still.

Devil stilled. All the violence from a moment ago, gone, as if it never happened. She didn't dare look at him.

Waiting.

He took a deep breath, followed by another. Then another.

"Time to go back," he said.

Tabitha remained silent as he drove back, at the correct speed limit.

The music came on and Devil laughed. "Fuck, this hurts."

She vaguely recognized the tune.

"You know, in the first few weeks of me knowing Lexie, I pissed her off. I was so angry and I said some shit. She'd been working as a stripper to help ... with stuff, and, er, I said something mean, and she started dancing to this tune. Took her clothes off in front of the guys. I was so angry, but fuck, she was so full of life. So determined to show me how pissed off she was."

He coughed, clearing his throat. "I married her because I loved her. Because I couldn't live without her and I couldn't stand the thought of anyone else knowing that fire. With all the shit I caused in my past, I thought I'd be the one to die first. I deserve it. Not her. Yet, here I am. She's the one with cancer."

"She's not dead," Tabitha said. "She's fighting."

Devil breathed out. "I know."

"Is this how you deal?" Tabitha asked. "You drive off and scream like that?"

"Yeah. Sometimes I'm on my bike," he said.

"And it helps?"

"It does."

"Why are you telling me this?"

"Simon's going to piss you off. When you become a Chaos, you won't always be able to go home to daddy. You're going to need to learn to have an outlet. This is one of mine."

"I won't tell Lexie," Tabitha said.

"She knows. You're not keeping any great secret. She knows what I need to do to handle all of this."

"I'm sorry you're going through all of this. I wish

there was something I could do."

"There is. Treat my boy right. That's all I'm asking you, Tabitha, and be honest with him, he deserves it."

****

The days passed, as did the weeks.

Lexie had good days, bad days, worse ones, hopeful ones. Devil was always there. Christmas came and went by in a blur for everyone. When she was in Piston County, she decorated the house under Lexie's supervision. She went back home for a couple of days, leaving Simon behind. Being back at home reminded her of how much she missed life there, her parents, Daisy, the guys, the girls. All of them. She missed them even without returning but now, being back on the ground, she knew it was the one place she called home. Determined to help Lexie and Simon, she went back to them.

Back in Piston County, Lexie got sicker. The chemo took its toll and Tabitha was there when she shaved her head rather than allow any more hair to fall out. Lexie hadn't been able to cope, and so the decision had been quick. Lexie took the first cut, then Tabitha finished it for her.

Late at night, in Simon's arms, she would sometimes sob. The memories coming at her in full force of the time with Darcy. She had never allowed herself to let go, to show too much, but now, with Lexie, she felt it. The woman went from being strong to weak. But, and this was the part that made her feel the most guilt, she cried sometimes because of missing home. She never told Simon the truth about her tears and he never forced the issue.

Lexie's illness tore the club apart emotionally. Everyone felt it. Tabitha was there during New Year's, when they had their clubhouse get-together. All of the club members, their old ladies, kids, family, they were all there and at the table, Tabitha sensed the tension. Lexie was loved by all. She brought everyone together. Being Devil's old lady, she'd been the voice of reason to so many and helped make decisions as well.

Late January, Devil called her into his office and she knew why. Her bags were already packed. She'd helped out as much as she could, and even Lexie said it was time for her to go home to be with her family.

She sat down opposite him.

"You're going to be seventeen soon," he said.

Simon had already celebrated his birthday. They had a short age gap between them. Just a little over a year.

"I know. If I ask my dad, could I stay here?" she asked.

Devil rubbed the back of his head. "Look, Tabitha, having you here hasn't been a problem. You've followed most of the rules of my house."

"I followed all of them," she said, interrupting them.

"Simon shares your bed every single night. That is not following all of them."

"Oh, you knew?"

"This is my house. You think I don't know what's going on in it?"

She pressed her lips together, wishing the world could open up and allow her to sink right inside. "Of course."

"But I believe that you and he have stuck to your promises. I'm going to trust in that."

"Good. We didn't break any other rules."

"But I also know that with you guys getting closer to eighteen, you're going to have to make a choice. Staying here will make that choice easier for you."

"And you don't want me to have it easy?"

Devil shrugged. "I don't think you should cut off one part of your life just to make it easier for you. The Skulls is your family. Tiny and Eva are your parents. You have a life back in Fort Wills. The longer you stay here, you'll have to enroll in school. This wasn't supposed to be permanent. I've talked with Tiny. We're in agreement. We know you and Simon are together, but there's a path you both have to choose. We can't make that decision for you."

"So you're separating us, again?" Tabitha asked.

He sighed. "It doesn't matter what I say right now to you. I'll come across as the bad guy."

Tabitha ran her hands down the arms of the chair. "Is Lexie all clear?"

"We're waiting for the results but we know we've still got a long way to go."

Lexie had needed a mastectomy of both breasts. The cancer had spread.

"I came to help," she said. "I want you to understand that. I didn't come here to make my life easier."

"I know. You've helped me with the kids and with Simon. He's ... grown so much in the last couple of weeks. Thank you," he said.

Tears filled her eyes. "I ... I love my club," she said. "I know that Simon wants all of this. I can see why. I know you guys are amazing."

There was a sad smile on Devil's face. "But we're not The Skulls."

"You're not."

"And you miss them."

She nodded her head. "So much." She swiped at her eyes.

"Tabitha, if you stay here and you force this, one day, you're going to wake up, and I don't know, you're going to miss Daisy giving birth, or an event that they didn't think to invite you too because you're Chaos now. That will awaken a resentment so big you won't even begin to understand where it came from."

She sniffled. "So what you're saying is to get it out of my system?"

"We both know this choice isn't going to be easy for you or for Simon. It could tear you apart. I'm not going to deny that. You're not a Chaos girl. You never will be, not while you remain a Skull."

Tabitha got to her feet. "Does Simon know?"

"He's outside with Tiny."

"Oh," Tabitha said.

"We decided that it would be best if he comes and picks you up."

"It must be good to dictate how a person should live," Tabitha said.

Devil opened his hands before drawing the tips of his fingers together. He looked so calm. She knew the monster just beneath the surface. Why wouldn't he come out so she could scream and shout at him?

"Tiny and I knew this road you and Simon were determined to make together would become fraught."

"There is no reason for it to be. You guys work together all the time."

"Working together is different, Tabitha. Don't be an idiot or a fool. We're different clubs. You know that. There will never be any joining of our clubs. No matrimony or sharing of leadership. It's simple. The Skulls or Chaos Bleeds. One or the other. Never both. We're not mixing. We're not joining."

Tabitha nodded. She'd heard enough.

After leaving Devil's office, she grabbed her bags

and headed out to the car. Sure enough, Tiny was there waiting for her. He held his arms open. She wanted to punish him for making this even harder for her, but the truth was, she had been missing The Skulls. Piston County and Chaos Bleeds were fun. It was nice, but it wasn't home. There was no Quad, no gang. She missed them so much.

Simon went to her. "Hey," he said.

"Hey." She glanced over his shoulder at her dad who held up one finger letting her know she only had a short amount of time. "It seems we're always doing this."

"One day we won't have to."

"One day. This is happening so fast. I thought..."

"Tabby, I want you to stay. You know that, but I think for your sanity, you've got to go. You've got to go and do what you need to."

"You're being very understanding about this."

"I don't want to lose you," Simon said.

"You never will."

Tiny beeped the car. She rolled her eyes. "This is what I'm going home to."

"I'm going to miss all of those eye rolls."

Tabitha laughed. "They're not going to be directed at you."

"We'll talk every single night."

"You can count on it." She went up onto her toes, kissed his lips, and pulled away.

She didn't say anything as she climbed into the car, or as Tiny drove off, heading back home.

It was a long drive ahead, and they'd have no choice but to pit stop at a motel.

"Are you going to ignore me the entire drive home?"

"I'm not ignoring you."

"Do you hate me right now? More than an

average teenager would?"

She chuckled. "No, I don't hate you, Dad."

"But?"

"No buts. I get it. I do."

"Devil believed you were missing home."

"He's right. I was."

"Honey, talk to me."

"I honestly don't know what to say. Do you want me to say you're right, that you've been right from the start? You have. You know you have."

"I want you to be happy and to know that you can talk to me about anything, even stuff you don't think I can handle."

Tabitha licked her lips. "I thought…"

"What?"

"I thought I could do this. That it would be easy."

"Leaving home? Going to Piston County?"

"Both."

"And it wasn't?"

She shook her head. "No, it wasn't easy. I missed home a lot. All this time, I figured you and Devil were just being giant pains in the ass. Keeping us apart because of some dick-measuring contest, but it's not." She sighed. "You were right."

"I didn't want to be."

"Dad, I know there's a choice I'm going to have to make. Give up Simon or the club. It's one or the other. I can't have both."

Tiny didn't say anything.

"What would you have done?" Tabitha asked.

"I didn't have to make that choice. I've got my woman and the club."

"If you had to. If Mom made you choose between her and the club, what would you do?"

Tiny sighed. "I'd pick your mother, sweetheart,

but I'm not a leader anymore. If you want a true answer, talk to Lash. He'd give you an honest one."

She sat back. That wouldn't be helpful at all.

Chapter Twelve

A couple of days later

"Fancy meeting you here," Daisy said.

Tabitha held her hand up in a wave at her friend. She was out near the forest, sitting on a patch of earth she'd once snuggled up against Simon with. That seemed so far away right now. Of course, the moment had been lost when Luke and Ryan arrived, assholes.

Daisy dropped down onto her knees beside her. Her best friend wore a pair of jeans and a white shirt. Her brown hair was tied back in a ponytail. "I thought you'd be here."

"Yeah, I needed to think. I would have called you last night."

"It's fine. A lot's going on in your head right now, right?"

Tabitha nodded. "I guess." She tore out some grass, holding it within her grasp.

"So you spend all of this time with Simon and you're officially more miserable than ever. Want to tell me about that?" Daisy slid her legs out from beneath her and crossed them.

"I don't know if I can do it, Daisy," she said.

"Do what?"

"Be his old lady. Be what he needs me to be." Rubbing at her temple, she groaned. "Forget it."

"You mean leave Fort Wills indefinitely and go and live life as his old lady."

"Yeah, that's what I mean. You know, I'm so stupid."

"You're not stupid."

"Yeah, I am. All this time, I thought our parents

were just being jerks about this whole thing, and look what's happening."

"So you've had a bit of a reality check. That's not a bad thing."

"It is a bad thing." She looked away. "You wouldn't understand."

"Hey." Daisy put a hand over Tabitha's clenched fist. "I get that you've been away for some time, but don't shut me out. That's not fair. I don't do it to you, so don't do it to me."

"Oh, yeah, what about your dad?"

"We're not talking about that. Stop with being a bitch to me, okay? I get it. You've got to make this big tough decision but no one is forcing you to do that."

"Devil, my dad!"

"They're not telling you to make it now. They're making you aware of the decision you've got to make. They are trying to help you."

Tabitha pressed her face into her hands.

"You're making this a lot harder than it needs to be," Daisy said.

"Oh, that's easy for you to say. The love of your life is like a ten-minute walk away."

"First, I haven't even asked Anthony out, and don't think I've forgotten our little agreement there either. I haven't. If he turns me down, bikini dancing is in your future. Second, I don't even know if he feels that way about me. I know you keep on saying it but it doesn't mean it's actually true, does it?"

"Oh, please, I know what I'm talking about."

Tabitha screamed as Daisy suddenly launched herself at her, wrapping her arms around her.

"What the fuck are you doing?" Tabitha asked.

Daisy held her even tighter. "I'm holding on to you so you stay grounded. Remember, it's what you told me to do? If you ever feel like you can't cope, I can just hold on to you, and then all the bad stuff is going to go away."

Tabitha wanted to fight her. To let all of her anger and pain out, but Daisy wasn't the person she was angry at. No, she was mad at herself for thinking this would all be an easy choice for her. It wasn't. She was fighting everything and everyone.

Letting go, she cried and Daisy held her. Lying in the grass, she didn't let her friend go, not wanting to.

"I love you," Tabitha said.

"I love you too," Daisy said. "But I've got to know, how much did you want to hit me?"

"A lot. A whole lot." Tabitha laughed. "I don't hate you though."

"Come on, you can't hate me. I'm awesome."

"You really are. I'm sorry for being a bitch."

"I'm pretty sure I've covered the whole bitchy season myself. I may have been mean a time or two."

"Make it three or four," Tabitha said.

"Rude, totally rude." Daisy patted her arm. "It's good to have you back. I know you've got to make the 'big decision.'" She lifted her fingers up to make quotation marks. "But I'm glad you're here."

"I am too."

"Is that why you're so angry," Daisy asked. "You figured you would want to leave home and be with Simon?"

"You got it." Tabitha blew out a long breath. "I thought I would hate this place so much that it would just be me getting up, waving goodbye, and getting on with my life. Now, ugh, this is my home."

Daisy chuckled. "Try to say it without looking like you've given yourself a death sentence."

"I haven't. I missed you so much." Tabitha

hugged her friend close and they got to their feet. "Come on, it's getting way too cold out here."

"Angel's at the clubhouse. She's got a lot of leftovers she's making a pie with."

"Are you still going without meat?"

"Yep, so is my mom. You should see my dad. He keeps trying to tempt her." Daisy laughed.

"And if Anthony is there, you have to ask him on a date."

"I was thinking we'd save it 'til summer," Daisy said.

"Why summer?"

"You and a bikini. I don't expect you to wait around for me to forget. You are dancing." Daisy pointed a finger at her chest.

"I will dance and I'm so confident he'll say yes, I will dance in the cold."

"And get grounded your first couple of days back."

Tabitha opened her arms wide and took a little bow. "I'm that confident you will be eating your words."

"You know what, I'm just going to go ahead and do it. To hell with all of this waiting around."

Tabitha winked at her. They headed back to the clubhouse. For some reason, she felt like someone was watching her, and she turned back to see Luke coming out of the clearing. He'd been there all this time? She didn't let Daisy know. Turning away, she focused on going home to the clubhouse.

Linking her arms with Daisy, they walked through the town. A couple of people welcomed her back, which made her so happy. This was the life she loved. Back in Piston County, no one knew her. She'd been a stranger, and rather than love the freedom, she'd only been made aware of where she didn't belong.

Arriving at the clubhouse, she saw Lash out front, working on his bike. Nash, his brother, was there. Much to Tabitha's surprise, so was Anthony. He wore a short-sleeved black shirt over his jeans. His arms were folded.

"He's right there," Tabitha said.

"How about we do it tomorrow?" Daisy asked.

"I'm not going to wait around. Yo, Anthony, Daisy wants to talk to you." Her friend hit her in the chest. "Ouch."

"That serves you right."

Anthony approached.

"I hate you right now."

"You love me, Daisy."

He stopped.

"Hi," Daisy said, her voice high-pitched.

Tabitha tried to contain her laughter.

"You're back," he said.

"Yep, in the flesh. I am real." She offered him a wave.

Anthony's gaze turned back to Daisy. Her friend's hands shook.

"So, I wanted to talk to you. Right. Of course. Er, do you like food?"

"Yes."

"Good, I like food obviously, and when two people like food, they eat it."

A snort came out. Pressing a hand to her lips, Tabitha quickly apologized.

"This is stupid," Daisy said. She took a deep breath. "Would you like to go out with me?"

"Yes."

"See," Daisy said, looking victorious, and then she frowned. "Wait, what?"

"Yes, I'll go out with you. Tomorrow night, I'll take you to the diner. I know you like their garden burgers."

"Oh, er, oh, yes, of course."

Anthony nodded and walked off.

Daisy's mouth was open.

Reaching out, Tabitha placed a finger beneath her chin. "You might want to close that. It's catching flies."

"But what does that mean?"

"It means you have a date tomorrow night. What are you going to wear?" They headed inside the clubhouse.

Tabitha breathed in the familiar scents of leather, beer, food, and The Skulls. Home.

"But I've never been on a date." Daisy grabbed both of her arms. "I don't know what to do."

"Lucky for you, I've been on at least one. I also know how much Anthony has been crushing on you. If you turn up looking like a sack of potatoes, you won't have to worry. He'd dig you."

"Tabitha, this isn't funny," Daisy said.

They entered the kitchen and like most times, Angel was there.

"Hey, girls." Angel came over to Tabitha and within seconds, she was being pulled into a hug. "I'm so glad you're home."

Tabitha laughed, stepping back. "Of course, you are. What are you doing?"

"Ah, the guys have another mission to go on. It's going to be a tough one. I've got the hotel rooms ready, and some medics on standby. Lash told me it was going to be intense. I'm getting lunches ready for them to take. What's fun?" She turned her smile toward them.

Considering all the crap that had happened to Angel, she'd remained this sweet, nice person throughout it all.

"Anthony and Daisy are going on a date

tomorrow night."

"Oh," Angel said, her lips going into a perfect *O* before returning to a smile. "Are you excited?"

"I ... am, I think. I've never been on a date."

"What does Anthony like?" Tabitha asked.

"You know Anthony, he likes what he likes." Angel laughed. "I better get back to lunches. Help yourself to some sandwiches."

Anthony was such an anomaly, his own mother didn't understand him at times. Tabitha had to wonder if the hospital got it all wrong and accidentally swapped the wrong child at birth. That there was some sweet kid with weird parents.

After grabbing a couple of cheese and pickle sandwiches, she and Daisy headed out of the clubhouse again.

"Your house or mine?" Daisy asked.

"Let's go to yours. Mom keeps asking me constant questions. It's freaking me out."

"Why?"

"Because she wants so many answers. I think she's worried Simon and I had sex."

"Did you?" Daisy asked.

"Not you too."

"What? You think I don't know for a fact you keep things from me as well? I do."

"Daisy, you're my best friend."

"I know, but even BFFs have secrets. Don't worry, I'm not mad or sad, or anything. I accepted it long ago." Daisy finished her sandwich, brushing her hands. "I think my mom's working at the salon, and Dad is doing something. We've got the house to ourselves."

"No, we didn't have sex. In case you were wondering."

"I wasn't exactly thinking about it, you know,"

Daisy said. "It wasn't on my need-to-know basis."

"Shut up, nerd," Tabitha said, hitting her arm.

"What? You think it's impossible for me to go a day when I wasn't thinking about you or sex, or Simon?"

"That's a lot of someones," Tabitha said.

"Don't get me wrong, I love you and I missed you, but not enough to want to hear about all the nasty stuff you've got going on."

"Of course you want to hear about all my nasty stuff." She nudged Daisy's shoulder. "Let's stop talking about me and my love life. We've got to get you ready for your date tomorrow night."

Daisy groaned. "No, we don't."

"Yes, we do. You've got to look sexy and cute, and I can't wait to dress you up."

"No dresses."

"I wore a dress."

Daisy wrinkled her nose. "I don't think I should have asked Anthony out on a date."

"Why not?"

"Because, I mean, we're best friends. Isn't that going to be odd for the group?"

"You're asking me. The girl who is dating one of our own."

"But he's not one of our own, is he?"

Tabitha stopped.

"I'm sorry," Daisy said.

"No, you're right. Maybe I have been going about this all the wrong way. I didn't mean to, but think about it. I've been treating him as if he is a Skull. He's not. We're completely different."

"And that's a good thing," Daisy said.

"Is it? I mean, really?" Tabitha ran her fingers through her hair. They were outside Daisy's house.

Her best friend grabbed her hands. "Stop."

"But—"

Daisy covered her mouth with her hand. "No, stop. You are going to listen to me. Yes, you're going to have to make a decision. The club or Simon. I get it. It's going to be tough. You don't have to make that choice today, or tomorrow, or next week. Not even next year. If Simon loves you like you say he does, then he'll be happy to wait until you make that decision for yourself. Not a moment before. Got it?" Daisy asked. Her hand was still over Tabitha's mouth. "Got it?" she repeated more firmly.

She nodded her head. "When did you get all bossy?" she asked when her hand was gone.

"Since you were gone and I realized if I didn't, Miles was going to treat me like crap."

"My brother?"

"Yep. He seemed to think with you gone, it instantly put me and him on bestie terms. It didn't. I put him in his place. You would have been so proud of me."

"I am proud of you." Tabitha hugged her friend close. "Come on, let's go inside. We've got to prepare for your date and I'm going to have to give you some pointers in case he kisses you."

****

The following night

"I'm nervous. Is this normal?"

"Totally normal." Tabitha ran the brush down Daisy's hair as Lacey came in with some mascara.

Daisy wrinkled her nose. "No, Mom."

"They'll make your eyes pop."

"I think I'll be happy with them staying firmly in my head."

They all paused as the doorbell rang. "Holy crap, that's him. What do I do?"

"Don't worry, your dad will open the door,"

Lacey said.

"No, he'll give him the talk, won't he? The one he used when Sally started dating."

"And she's now happily married and has a couple of kids." Lacey cupped her cheek, smiling. "Your father's a matchmaker. You should be so happy."

"Why?"

"You and Anthony could be walking down the aisle in next to no time." Lacey kissed her cheek and left the room while Daisy turned wide eyes toward her.

"How the hell does one date become married? I don't know if I want to marry him."

"Don't worry about it. You think Lacey doesn't have a job to do? Her daughter is going out on a date and she's nervous."

"We're not going to do anything."

"I know that." She didn't. She knew a lot about Anthony but not necessarily all the good parts.

"Daisy, your date is here," Whizz said.

"I can't do this."

"You can."

"Why did I ask him out on a date?"

"I don't know. You wanted to?"

Daisy pressed her lips together and shook her head. "I don't know what the hell I'm doing."

"Breathe. It's a date. Nothing more. Nothing less."

"You're going to be here when I get back?"

"Count on it."

"Good. Okay. Good." Daisy looked toward the door and whimpered. "I guess we better get this show on the road."

Tabitha giggled and followed her friend downstairs to where Anthony stood by the door, waiting. Whizz was there, arms folded, all of his ink on display.

She tried to contain her amusement.

"Before midnight, clear?" Whizz said.

"Clear."

"Good. No funny business."

"Dad, you know him. Stop."

"And if you so much as touch her, I will break every single bone in your body."

"Dad, please stop."

"Have fun," Tabitha said.

Anthony actually smiled at Daisy. A real, lips lifted, showing teeth and not in a crazy serial killer way, smile.

She watched her friend tense up and then slowly relax.

They left after Daisy kissed her dad's cheek.

"She's all grown up. Why do they have to be so grown up?" Lacey hugged tight to Whizz's side. "I remember when I was enough of a date for Daisy and she'd just color and we'd eat meatballs and spaghetti."

"Do you mean you ordered them in?"

"Stop it," Lacey said.

"You want to come down?" Whizz asked, looking up at her.

"Nah, I'm going to go and study. Is that okay?"

"It's not a problem at all. We're down here if you need us."

Tabitha nodded and turned on her heel, heading back up into the bedroom. She didn't close the door. Pulling out her cell phone, she used the video app on her phone to call Simon.

"Hey," he said.

"Are you outside?" Tabitha asked, hearing the wind.

"Yep. I decided I needed to freeze my butt off. What about you?"

"I'm in Daisy's room. They went on their first official date today and get this, Anthony smiled."

"Get the fuck out. You're lying."

"Am not. It was an honest-to-god smile."

"Creepy?"

"No. I did wonder if he'd been practicing in the mirror."

"We're mean, aren't we?"

"The worst. So how are you?"

"You know, the same. Missing you."

"Your mom was getting some tests, right?

"They're going to do some more tests. She needs more chemo as well, just to be on the safe side. It sucks. It's draining her a lot more now."

"I'm sorry."

"How are things back there for you?" he asked.

"Odd. It's strange but good. I like being home." She nibbled on her lip.

"I get it," he said.

"You do?"

"Yeah."

Silence.

Tabitha licked her lips. "I do miss you as well."

"I know. Look, I've got to go. Dad's calling me." She heard his name being shouted in the distance.

"Okay, well, I'll be here if you need me. Don't forget that."

"I won't. Love you."

He'd already hung up by the time she went to say bye. Pressing her lips together, she turned the app off and leaned back against the bed. This was hard. Guilt filled her as she did love being home, but there was a giant hole.

Simon would never come to live here, not for any reason.

She reached for the necklace she always wore. This has been a gift from Simon so long ago. It meant a great deal to her.

"I got you something," Simon said.

She giggled at the same time she squeezed out her hair. "You don't have to get me anything, Simon. I'm fine." She pulled out the band keeping her other bunch of hair up, and then gave that a squeeze. The kids had totally lost this time with the water fight, but that was fine. They'd win one soon. No one beat The Skulls' kids. That was what they were. She glanced across the play area and saw Anthony brushing out Daisy's hair. Her best friend was trying to reach for the brush, but Anthony kept it out of reach.

"I wanted to give you something so that every time you saw it, you'd remember me."

"I'm not going to forget you. We talk all the time." She rested her damp head on his shoulder.

"Please, take it." He held out a box that she saw had been hand-created with a card. Taking it, she opened the lid as she knew he wanted her to do this. She saw a silver chain, and there in the center was the insignia of Chaos Bleeds. "I know you're part of The Skulls, but you're always going to be my girl."

She stared at the necklace. It was delicate, and as she lifted it over her head to rest on her chest, she looked at it. He was right. It did remind her of him. "It's really pretty."

"Do you think you could wear that for me all the time?"

"Yeah. My dad will pitch a fit, but I love it." The Skulls was the only club she was ever going to be part of, and she knew there was going to come a time when she'd have to make a choice. The Skulls were her family. Simon took the box and then her hand.

"We're only here for a couple of days."

She rested her chin on his shoulder.

"It's hard leaving," he said.

They were nearly twelve years old now, and she knew that he loved her without a doubt. Whenever he did come to visit, he'd always get moody because he'd have to leave her again.

"We'll write all the time like always. I love reading what you're doing, and I do think it's great that you kick ass with bullies." She stared down at their hands and snuggled against him. "You're going to be my big bear."

He turned and stroked a curl behind her ear. This time, he lingered, caressing her cheek.

"What's wrong?" she asked.

"Nothing. I just like being with you."

She laughed. "I'd drive you crazy in school. Daisy's always having to remind me to keep my head down and focus. I'm always looking out the window, thinking of other things. School is so boring. Now they're talking about what you want to be when you grow up. I don't know. Older, I guess."

"I'm going to take my dad's place. Chaos Bleeds is going to need a hero someday." Simon pushed his chest out. "That's going to be me. Total badass."

She couldn't stop laughing. Pulling out of his hold, she stared at him, popping the gum she'd been chewing. "You're not a badass."

He stood up, and she took a step back. "I am."

Tabitha shook her head. He was finally smiling again, and she liked that. She hated it when he was sad.

"What are you two doing?" her father, Tiny, asked.

"Nothing," Tabitha said. "But The Skulls rule, Chaos Bleeds ... drool." She winked at Simon, letting

him know she was doing this on purpose.

"That's my girl!" Eva, her mother, called out.

While Simon looked toward where their parents were, Tabitha took a step toward him and placed a hand on his chest. She didn't know if he felt that spark or whatever it was when she touched him, but she felt it all the time. It was like a constant hum between them. Moving toward his ear, she whispered the words. "Tag, you're it."

Reluctantly, she pulled away and began running away from Simon. He gave her a couple of seconds, and she ran around the swings, watching as several of The Skulls were now facing off with the Chaos Bleeds. Simon wasn't interested in anyone else though. He was on the other side of the swings, and she smiled at him. "You're not going to chase anyone else?"

"No one else I want to chase." This just made her smile at him. She couldn't help it. Simon made her feel even more alive. As she rushed one way, Simon followed, and she quickly changed direction, running across the park and heading toward the small garden that Angel liked to maintain while she was there. She didn't get far as Simon grabbed her and spun her around. They both collapsed on the ground, and she was laughing as he landed beside her.

"Tag."

"You caught me."

Simon stared into her eyes, and it almost made her forget to breathe. "I'll always catch you, Tabby. You'll never have to fall again, and if you ever do, I'll be there with you."

Silence fell between them, and she was breathing hard as she stared at him. Simon always offered her the world, and her mother had told her to be careful. There was only so much that she could do. She was a Skull, and

Simon a Chaos Bleeds, but she loved him. She didn't care what her parents said. She knew she was in love with Simon, and no matter what, she belonged to him.

"Food!" The spell was broken. Simon stood and held his hand out. She took it, knowing she always would, no matter what.

Pulling out of the memory, she felt an equal measure of happiness and sadness. Even then, she'd known a choice needed to be made and it would have to be her to make it. Running a hand down her face, she decided to take Daisy's advice and not think about it. Instead, she opened up the books Daisy had left for her and got some studying in. After an hour of looking through all of Daisy's notes, she headed downstairs to get a drink. Lacey was in the kitchen, attempting to make a sandwich.

"You want one?"

Seeing the amount of mustard on one slice of bread, she shook her head.

"I know I can't cook, but I can order takeout. I think that is what Whizz and John are getting."

"It's fine." John was Daisy's adoptive brother. Whizz and Lacey had taken him in a couple of years ago. Where Sally and Daisy had been older and knew they weren't their real parents, John didn't know the truth. There were a few times she'd babysat with Daisy, but Lacey liked to do everything herself, or at least as much of it as possible. Tabitha took a sip and watched as lettuce was placed on the bread, along with large slices of tomato.

"I know it's tough, this thing you have going with Simon. It's a hard decision to make."

Lacey was once part of a different MC that was completely wiped out, burned to the ground. Their name ceased to exist.

"I know."

"I picked Whizz," she said.

"You're telling me to pick Simon?" Tabitha asked. "Over the club?"

"I know it was easy for me. I didn't have any family and the club died, and I'm not going to delve into that. What I'm trying to say is even before all of that, I did pick Whizz. I know you're supposed to be loyal to the club, but what is loyalty if after a time you become so resentful of them?"

Lacey stopped making a sandwich. "We're your family and I get that there will possibly be a chance that trouble will fall between all of us at some point. You've got two hard-assed Presidents. It's going to happen, but that doesn't mean between Chaos Bleeds and The Skulls, they can't work it out at some point. Don't give up on him just yet."

"I won't," Tabitha said.

"I figured you've had your mom and the men telling you their point of views. I figured an outsider perspective would help."

"There is no way you're an outsider."

Lacey laughed. "I was once. Don't forget that. I've got a wealth of knowledge that doesn't include any of The Skulls."

"Thank you."

"No, thank you. For helping Daisy. I know she's had a tough time of it and I'm just so happy to see her smile again. It means a lot to me."

"She loves you, you know. You and Whizz. She loves you both."

Lacey's eyes filled with tears. "Well, thank you."

She walked past Lacey and gripped her arm, hugging her. "Also, the bread is off. There's mold on it."

"Wait, you can eat that stuff on cheese."

"It's completely different on bread."

Poor Daisy. Lacey didn't know the first thing about food and cooking.

After making her way back upstairs, she got down to studying. The time ticked on by and before she knew it, Daisy was back.

She stood at the top of the stairs. Daisy looked fine. There was nothing off about her. Whizz and Lacey bombarded her with questions.

"I'm fine. The date went well. It's school tomorrow. I'm going to take a shower and get ready for bed. Goodnight." She kissed Whizz, then Lacey before heading upstairs.

Tabitha followed her back to her room. "Well?"

"Let me shower first." Daisy removed her jacket, looking at the bed. "Did they help?"

"I don't care about them right now. Come on, tell me."

Daisy rolled her eyes. "Okay, okay, let me get a shower, okay?"

She disappeared to the bathroom.

Cleaning up the books, Tabitha changed into her own pajamas and climbed into the bed.

She waited. Twiddling her thumbs.

Daisy finally entered. Her hair was curled up in a towel but she wore a pair of flannel pajamas.

"So, how was it?" Tabitha asked.

She sat on the edge of the bed and smiled. "It was good."

"Did he sit in silence? Did he speak? Did he even eat? Did he stare at you? Come on. A girl needs to know answers right now." She reached out and touched her arm. "Please."

"We talked about everything and nothing. He was … totally different." Daisy frowned.

"He was? Good different? Bad?"

"I ... it was nice," she said. "Yeah, I was nervous and he held my hand and we talked about school. He asked me about my plans once we graduate. Where I want to go to college. What I want to do. We laughed about Miles and his antics. He had the same spaghetti as me."

"Did he kiss you?" Tabitha asked.

Daisy's face heated up and Tabitha gasped. "He did!"

She covered her face and Tabitha reached out. "Come on, tell me."

"You're going to think it's stupid."

"No, I'm not. Nothing about this is stupid. My best friend got her first kiss."

"It wasn't exactly a first kiss." She winced. "Okay. His lips went right here." She touched the corner of her mouth. "He cupped my face, gently, told me that I had no idea how precious I was, and kissed me there."

"Oh," Tabitha said. "Are we happy about that?"

"I ... he was sweet. Like crazy sweet. I can't, this is crazy. I'm so happy right now."

"So we're putting this in the awesome pile?"

"We're putting this in the hell yeah and I want to go out with him again." Daisy climbed off the bed, removed the towel, and left to put it in the laundry basket. She returned, grabbed the brush, and started to comb through her hair.

"Will you go on a second date?"

"I don't know. We didn't say anything. I don't want to push. Tonight's date was so amazing. I can't even tell you how amazing. He's a great guy. I know that he's a little strange, but people don't know him, at all."

"He doesn't give people the chance to get to know him, Daisy."

"I guess, but even I wasn't expecting what I got. Wow." She dropped the brush and flopped to the bed. "Tonight was amazing. Thank you for helping me get ready."

"It was my pleasure. We always made each other promises when we were little to always be there for each other. Do you realize if you marry Anthony and he does become President of The Skulls, you'd be his old lady?"

"And you'd be Simon's old lady for Chaos Bleeds. I suppose if we look at it like that, two besties besides their men, we could make it work for each other and for them."

"Not through manipulation or anything."

Daisy shook her head. "No. I don't mean anything like that. I meant, reminding them of who they were. The fact we're friends." Daisy reached out to stroke some hair back behind her ear. "Did you think about it tonight?"

"I called him. I think he's pissed at me."

"Because you're back home?"

She nodded. "And I'm happy to be back home."

"If I know Simon, he won't stay mad at you for long. It's impossible to do."

"You promise to never stay mad at me for too long?"

"Promise."

Chapter Thirteen

Time didn't stand still. Not even for Tabitha.

Seventeen came and went without any real event. There was cake and a party. Simon wasn't able to make it due to a bad turn Lexie had taken. Daisy was by her side throughout.

School finished for another term and she passed all the necessary exams she'd needed to take.

Chaos Bleeds visited Fort Wills.

Simon came and it was like there was no elephant in the room whenever they were together. He held her, told her how beautiful she was, and when the time came for him to leave, she hated it.

The only way she'd come to deal with the pain was by going to the Quad, regularly, much to her parents' annoyance.

A busted lip and eyebrow started to annoy them. She would sometimes let the opponent get a shot in just so she could feel the pain on the outside. Of course there were people from the Dogs who also liked to challenge her, especially the girls. In the past six months alone, she'd gotten into more fights at school than she could ever know to think about.

Another fight that had her sitting outside the principal's office, nibbling on the edge of her nails and waiting for her parents to arrive.

The chick in question was one of Daniella's posse. Another Dogs kid, Rebecca.

"Hey," Daisy said, coming to sit with her.

"What are you doing here?"

"I figured I'd be here as some backup."

"You don't need to worry about it."

"I do. I'm not having that bitch say you attacked her."

"We all know she had it coming to her," Miles said, climbing on top of the desk.

Anthony had also joined, but he sat beside her and patted her hand. "He takes one of us in, he deals with us all."

Her throat felt thick as her people surrounded her.

"Gotta say, Tabs, loved how you handled this one," Constance said.

She laughed.

"I think the head slam was the best," Rachel said. "Didn't it, like, hurt?"

She'd head-butted Rebecca after slamming Daniella into a wall.

"It did." She rubbed at her head. She had a throbbing headache.

John sat down on the floor. "It was badass."

Markus nibbled on an apple and nodded.

"You know there's a risk I could get suspended and he could do the same to all of you," Tabitha said. "That could mean grounded for all of you."

"Don't care," Blaise said. "The bitches deserved it."

Tabitha sighed, running her hands down her thighs.

The door opened and the principal came out. Daniella's nose was covered in dried blood. Tear tracks were already down her face.

She was ready to go again with the bitch, but the principal merely escorted the two girls away from them.

Tabitha turned as her mother arrived. The moment Eva caught sight of her and the crew, she stopped. "Okay, am I even needed here?"

"You're Tabitha's mother?" the principal asked.

Tabitha stood.

"I am."

"We need to talk. Tabitha, join us please."

All of her friends got up.

The principal stopped in the doorway. "No. I only need Tabitha and her parents. You are all children and should be back to class."

"Not happening," Miles said.

"Miles, go back to class."

"Sorry, Mom, you didn't see what happened back there. We all did and there's no way we're letting that kind of shit slide."

"Miles!" Eva snapped.

"Why didn't those other bitches have their parents here?" Daisy asked. "You're going to suspend Tabs for protecting herself, is that it?"

"If you don't all leave this instant and allow me to deal with this, I will suspend you all."

Tabitha looked at her friends and saw them all staring at each other.

"Kids, think about how annoyed your parents are going to be," Eva said.

"You know what? Fuck this school," Anthony said. "We'll be back after suspension." He picked up a chair and launched it across the room. The receptionist had to duck as it took out the computer on her desk.

"Rock-fucking-on," Miles said.

Tabitha watched as her friends turned on the school, banging on lockers, screaming at the top of their lungs. She looked at her mom, mouthed the word *sorry*, stuck her middle fingers up at the principal, and followed right along with them. They busted out of school.

Daisy had already passed her driver's license and for her seventeenth birthday, she'd gotten a car. She went with her friend, climbing in the front seat as Constance climbed in with Rachel.

"Any idea what the hell we're doing?" Rachel asked.

"We're being rebels. They can all go and fuck themselves. This is my girl right here."

Daisy turned the radio up and music filled the air as they took off, heading to the only place she knew they'd be left alone, the lake.

Anthony was driving the guys. They drove through town and she spotted several of their parents.

"Oh, this is going to be so bad," Rachel said. "Dad's going to so give me the lecture on what it means to be doing the right thing."

"This coming from your dad who also used to be a drug addict?" Constance asked.

"Damn, rumors are hard to kill, aren't they?"

"Yep!" Daisy yelled and laughed.

It had been several months since her date with Anthony. Tabitha didn't even know if they were going steady or not. There were moments she caught them together. They always looked like they were on the verge of making out or even fucking, but again, nothing.

"Come on, Tabs, how did it feel to smash that girl's face in?" Daisy asked. "She called you a Skull whore."

"It was pretty damn good." She'd been so angry at this other girl getting in her face. The same girl she'd noticed at the Quad a few times but had never given her the time of day. Now, because of her, she was suspended, which also meant as soon as she got home, she'd be grounded. Like that stuck for long.

Daisy pulled into the parking space near the lake. After climbing out, Tabitha didn't wait around. She headed to the lake, removed her clothes, not caring who saw, and dove right on in the water.

"There could be sharks in there," Rachel said.

"So, if they even take a chunk right out of me, they know I'm going to be pissed. Also, you watch way too many shark movies." Tabitha leaned back in the water. The guys finally arrived. "What do you say, Daisy? Are you coming in?"

Daisy shook her head but kicked off her shoes.

Tabitha couldn't resist glancing over at Anthony. Of course, his gaze was right on her. Smiling, Daisy wriggled out of her jeans and removed her sweater but kept on her shirt that had several buttons open.

She ran to the edge and jumped right on in. In the past few months, her best friend had come out of her shell. Daisy broke the surface, gasping and pushing her hair out of her face, laughing. "Shit, this is fucking cold."

"Come on, do you think our parents are going to let us out after today? We're going to be confined to our rooms."

"Speak for yourself," Anthony said.

"Yeah, Tabs, like that's going to stop us going to the Quad. Our parents are going to be pissed, but they can't control us. Not anymore," Miles said.

"You know what, that looks like fun. I'll deal with everything later." Constance stripped down to her underwear, silencing Miles, and like the others, she jumped right on in.

"How are you feeling?" Daisy asked.

"I'm fine."

"Are you sure? It looked to me when you were beating the crap out of that girl that you were having a few more issues than you were letting on."

"Are you analyzing me now?" Tabitha asked, but she smiled so her friend knew she wasn't pissed off.

"A little." Daisy held her thumb and finger apart in front of her face.

Everyone joined them in the lake, including Anthony. She could only imagine why he needed to cool off.

"I guess she pissed me off." The girl had reminded her of Amber. Even though Amber hadn't been part of an MC, the two girls had that air of authority around them that they were going to get what they wanted. Daisy already knew she'd broken Amber's nose.

"You know there's going to be retaliation, right? They're not going to have a choice?" Miles said.

"Like I care," Tabitha said. "I can handle them."

"Not if they jump you. We're going to have to make sure Tabs is never alone," Miles said.

"Agreed."

"Are you all freaking kidding me right now? I mean, seriously?"

"It's important you don't let your guard down," Anthony said. "You know this."

"I've got your back," Daisy said.

"I know." She kissed her friend's cheek. "Love you."

"I love you too."

"Out of the lake, now!"

Tabitha gasped as she looked toward the edge and saw pretty much all of their parents. Holy shit. Lash stood, glaring. "Out now!" He snapped each word.

Tabitha looked toward Anthony.

Lash looked at them all as they didn't move. It was a standoff. Lash didn't look away, he glanced at each of them in turn. For the first time for her, he actually looked freaking scary.

"One more chance!" His voice seemed to echo around the lake.

No one moved.

"Right, we figured this was how it was going to

go." Lash bent down and retrieved her phone. Tabitha frowned as he also got Anthony's, then Daisy's.

"No!" She screamed out the word as he put them on the ground and stomped on each of the three phones.

"I'm not joking around. Out now, all of you." He snapped his fingers, searching for other phones.

Tiny was there with his arms folded, Nash, Killer, holy shit, even Whizz.

She scrambled out of the lake, quickly rushing to get her clothes.

"No, get in the fucking car," Lash said, retrieving their clothes.

Whizz had Daisy's car keys in her hand and there was already a tow truck.

"What's going on?" Daisy asked.

"Your friends are being taken back home and I've got Sandy talking to them. You're all coming back to the clubhouse right the fuck now!" He snapped his fingers.

Tabitha walked past in her underwear and climbed into her father's car. She folded her arms, pissed off as Lash picked up the necessary clothes and had Anthony in his car.

"Are we going home?" she asked as they pulled away from the lake and headed back to town.

"You heard Lash."

"You're going to follow his orders?"

"Yep. Don't even start with me."

"You don't want to hear my side of things?"

"I'm pretty sure I know your side of things."

"You don't, but like always, you're just going to assume." She slammed her back against the seat and stomped her foot. She was cold and this was humiliating as they had to wait at a traffic light and she sat in her father's car, in her underwear. Lash knew how to punish them, there was no doubt about that. She was so fucking angry at him, at all of them.

Actually, anger didn't even begin to cover what she felt. She was so pissed off.

They arrived at the clubhouse. There were some of the prospects outside, smoking and chatting with some of the club girls. The club didn't have a lot of free pussy, but there were occasionally women who liked to hang around for whatever they could get.

After she slammed the car door closed, Lash arrived seconds later, and with her friends, they were marched into the room where the club always had church.

"Take a fucking seat. You all might as well get used to it because clearly you all don't seem to understand what hard work means."

"That's out of line," Miles said.

"Don't start with me," Lash said. "You think I don't know a fucking punk-ass when I see one? I was one many years ago. You don't fucking scare me. None of you do."

Folding her arms, Tabitha stared down at the table. She hated this.

"So you all think it's funny to be suspended?" Lash asked. "You think it's good to break noses?"

His fists went to the table and he leaned on them.

"I don't think it's fun or good." She glared at him. "You're all accusing us and you don't even know the facts."

"Let's see, she had it coming to her!"

"Yes, she did. She got in my face."

"She did," Daisy said.

"Since when did The Skulls want us to start taking shit?" Miles asked. "You think we don't get enough crap from the Dogs as it is? They're breathing down our neck all the fucking time. None of us can breathe because of it. We're watching our backs and now you're telling us to what, not fight at all? We'll be the laughing stock of the entire school."

Lash slammed his hand down. "Is that what it is with you kids today? You like to assume what I'm going to say before I say it? Your presence is no longer at that school for the next three weeks. That may sound like time to you, but it means you're going to have to take your place once again. A whole load of shit can happen in three weeks. Your mom could have handled this but as usual, you all had to open your mouths and think you know what's best for you."

He moved away but she saw the tension in his body and had no doubt, if they were the enemy, he'd have killed them all already. "Not only are you guys suspended, but you also got your little buddies done too. You may think this is going to be fun and games for you, but you've all got another thing coming. Take a look around you. This is where you're going to be learning. I've already got everything ready. You think lockdown was over, well, for you kids, it has only just fucking begun. You will stay here. Eat here. Sleep here. Study here. Your friends will come here and study right alongside you. You want to start badmouthing me, I've just given my prospects three weeks' grace. You can clean toilets and I will make my boys take the biggest fucking shits so you guys are sick of it. That's not the worst I can do either. You want to try me, bring it on. You think you're such rebels, none of you saw men when I was younger. Tiny doesn't even know the kind of shit I got up to. You will all follow my orders. Do I make myself clear?"

"Do all of our parents agree?" Tabitha asked.

"If they didn't agree, you wouldn't be fucking sitting here."

"You broke my phone."

"I know and guess what, you're not getting a new one for the next three weeks. You're now in The Skulls' jail. Congratulations. I hope you all feel so damn good about yourselves."

****

"The Skulls' jail?" Simon asked.

He sat at the dinner table as his mom served out some more food to everyone.

"That's what Eva said. They all just went a little crazy at the school and left. They broke some windows and computers and stuff like that."

"Sounds like fun," Josh said.

"Yeah, and look where that fun has gotten them," Devil said.

Lexie chuckled. "Yes, please, kids, don't take after The Skulls."

"So I can't talk to her?"

"No, honey. Eva said that Lash won't accept it."

"But he's not her dad. Why is he being given the responsibility of saying what she can and cannot do?" He didn't understand it.

"I guess because it is all The Skulls' kids, sweetie."

"So, aside from our BFFs at The Skulls, we have some news." Devil touched Lexie's hands and smiled at her.

Simon watched and he had a feeling he knew what it was. He stayed silent, waiting.

"Your mother got the news today," Devil said. "She's cancer-free."

They all cheered. Simon got to his feet and rushed toward her, hugging her tightly. "Congratulations. I'm so happy."

"We all are."

Lexie laughed and tears streamed down her face. "Thank you. Thank you all for everything. I know you've been put through a great deal these past few months, but there is an end in sight."

They finished their meal and it was a relief to know that she would be on a road to recovery. There would always be a risk she'd get it again, but they were going to test for it regularly.

He helped with the dishes and then his dad asked him to drop something off at the clubhouse that Ripper needed. It was a file. Devil would have gone himself, but he wanted to stay home to keep an eye on Lexie.

Simon was more than happy to go. He'd gotten a new bike for his seventeenth birthday and he used any excuse to ride it. He also hated using a helmet and so he rode all the way to the Chaos Bleeds clubhouse.

There wasn't a lot of activity even though it was night. He imagined they were going to have a party to celebrate Lexie's good news. It was what the club did, all the time, celebrated good news.

He headed indoors and found Ripper sitting at Devil's desk.

"Thanks, man," Ripper said, flicking open the file.

"No problem."

"Good news about Lexie."

"Yeah, who's organizing the party?"

Ripper laughed. "We've become so predictable of late, haven't we?"

"Pretty much."

"Judi's handling this one. She's excited."

"If you need anything, you know where I am." He left the office, feeling good, feeling alive. He took several deep breaths, happy and content.

He stood outside the clubhouse and breathed in

the fresh air. His mom was going to be okay. The past year was finally going to be behind them. So many nights he'd lain awake, waiting for the bad news to come in that she hadn't been able to fight it.

"You heard the good news about Lexie?"

Simon recognized Curse's voice.

"Yeah, I did," Mia said. Simon didn't move from where he stood. The couple hadn't heard him there. "I'm so glad she was able to fight it. Leaving all of those kids behind."

"I know."

"I mean, I know the truth about Simon, but still, he's hers."

Simon tensed up.

"I know, she's been more of a mother to him than her sister ever was."

Simon's heart raced. What the fuck? What were they talking about?

"What was her name again? The sister?"

"Kayla. She got knocked up by Devil and dumped Simon on Lexie's lap. She ended up stripping to take care of them both. Devil, of course, took one look at Lexie, and well, the rest is history. Devil never wants Simon to know the truth."

There was no way he could unhear this shit.

Stepping away from the wall, he rounded it to look at Curse.

"Oh, shit," Curse said.

"What the fuck are you talking about?"

"Simon, man, we're talking about someone else."

"No, you don't get to lie. Lexie's not my mom? I had a different mom?"

"You don't know what you heard."

"Oh, I know what I heard all right." He turned on his heel and got on his bike. He heard Curse and Mia screaming at him. There was no way he was stopping.

The pictures.

He recalled his question about the pictures. How could he have been so damn stupid? Coming to the edge of the driveway, he looked at his home.

All of his life had been one big fat lie.

Devil opened the door, a phone to his ear.

Rain started to pour.

After climbing off his bike, he stormed into his home.

Lexie was a few feet away from Devil. His father put a hand on his shoulder.

"Don't fucking touch me."

"Son, I don't know what—"

"You were never pregnant with me. That's why there are no pictures."

"This is not the time or the place," Devil said.

Tears fell down her cheeks, but Lexie didn't say anything. "You were never supposed to find out this way."

"I was never supposed to find out at all." He turned to his dad. "All this time you've been lying to me. You fucked her sister and what, she wasn't good enough, so you moved onto the next one?"

"Do not even demean what is between your mother and me."

"Which one? Lexie or Kayla?"

Devil's hand clenched into a fist. "Kayla was never your mother. The moment she could, she dumped your ass and Lexie had to pick up the pieces."

"Do you two even care about each other or is that a lie too?"

"Be careful," Devil said.

"Of what? You're my dad but she's not my fucking mother. You both lied to me. I'm not part of this family. I don't have a place. There are no pictures, no memories, nothing." He shook his head. "Fuck you both."

He took off.

Devil chased after him as Lexie's cry of his name echoed in the air.

"Son, don't do anything stupid."

"You lied to me. Not once did you tell me the truth. I shouldn't have had to find out this way. You should have always trusted me. Given me a chance to understand, but you didn't." He pulled out of his father's arms. "Stay the fuck away from me."

Climbing onto his bike, he took off, knowing there was only one place he was going to go.

****

"Devil, what are we going to do?"

"You're going to go back inside, call Lash."

"Why?"

"We both know there is only one place that boy is going and I need to make sure Lash can handle him. He's going to Tabitha. The only person he feels hasn't lied to him."

Lexie's hand went to her mouth as she tried to contain her sob. "I can't believe he found out this way."

"Don't worry about it. I'll fix it," Devil said.

"Did you see the look in his eyes, Devil? He's angry."

"Of course he's angry, but don't you feel any kind of guilt."

"We lied to him."

"I lied to him. I was the one who told you what to do. None of this is your fault and I won't let you take the blame, not for any of it. This is all on me and I'll deal with it." He went to her, cupping her cheeks and kissing her lips. "I've got to go and take care of this. I'll be back.

You rest."

"Devil, don't do anything stupid."

"I won't. Call Lash."

Devil left the house, being careful not to slam the door. After climbing onto his bike, he took off, going right to the clubhouse. No one was around. The moment Curse called him, he'd known shit was going to hit the fan. His boy, he'd asked about Lexie's pregnancy and shit like that. Whenever they talked to Elizabeth, Josh, their kids, Lexie would say what she was craving, or how tired she was. Devil always changed the subject when it came to Simon's memories. Lexie had nothing to give because she'd never been pregnant with him. She wouldn't just make shit up either as she hated lying to him. Devil always said he'd deal with this.

He'd hoped to never have to as his men knew to keep their shit to themselves.

Entering the clubhouse, he saw Curse sitting with Mia.

"Devil, I'm so sorry."

Devil slammed his fist against the bastard's face. He didn't care how sorry Curse was. He didn't give a shit about anything. At that moment, he didn't see a club brother, but a man who'd fucked up.

Mia cried out.

Ripper was there but he made no move to stop him. Curse didn't even defend himself.

"Please, stop. We didn't know he was there. We promise. We never wanted to hurt anyone."

"You should have fucking looked. That shit is private. You had no fucking right to be saying anything." Devil threw Curse across the room. "Simon's gone. Any plans you had at celebrating, stop them." He pointed a finger at Curse. "Right now, until this shit is right, you're dead to me. I don't want to see your face."

"Devil?" Ripper asked.

"You can wear your patch but if anything happens to my son, you better start running because I will fucking end you."

Chapter Fourteen

"What was that all about?" Angel asked, rubbing cream into her hands.

Lash looked back at his beautiful, sweet, perfect wife, and sighed. "It would appear we're going to have a Chaos living with us for a short time."

"We are?"

"Simon."

"He's coming here? Don't tell me he got expelled from school?" Angel asked.

"No, he found out about his parentage."

Angel's hands dropped. "Oh."

"Yeah, oh. So not only do I have a bunch of pissed-off teenagers I'm playing principal to, I've now got another one who is going to be volatile. Yay."

Angel giggled. She got to her knees and crawled across the bed. She put her hands on his shoulders and began to knead them. "You're doing fine."

"Really? I've had the Billionaires calling me. A shipment of girls is heading in and they're getting the necessary details. Some of them are missing girls, others appear to be street kids. We're talking between the fifteen to twenty-five range, about fifty of them." He ran a hand down his face.

"This one dangerous?"

"You know they're all dangerous, babe," he said.

"I know, but I also know you don't like to leave anyone behind. You know about these girls and so now you're going to have to protect them, it's what you do." Angel kissed his cheek. "You've got this. You can handle all of this."

"You think so? One more pissed-off teen that

even Devil couldn't handle?"

"You've got something he doesn't have," Angel said.

He grabbed his wife around the waist and pulled her close. "What's that?"

"The key to his heart."

He frowned.

"You've got Tabitha. Simon will do anything for her. You should know that considering you're a man in love as well."

"My wife is so clever," he said.

"The best, and now I think I should get my reward."

****

The following day

Tabitha stood near the clubhouse doorway. Lash was just in front of her. He hadn't been wrong about them all being punished and forced to live in lockdown at the clubhouse. It wasn't so bad. There was a tutor, and someone was there at all times. Even when they went to the bathroom so there was no chance of escape either.

"You're not sharing a room," Lash said.

"I know."

"And there won't be any sex in my clubhouse, do you understand?"

"Everyone is always assuming we're having sex."

"Understood?"

"Yes."

"I don't want any kids getting pregnant in my school." He shook his head. "My clubhouse. Fucking kids."

She smiled and couldn't believe what she was hearing from Lash. There was a time this guy was supposed to be fun. His brother and a few others still talked about the time he snapped a guy's neck with his bare hands. She couldn't see it herself, but according to everyone here, she was just a kid.

Tabitha was pulled out of her thoughts by the roar of a bike. She watched Tiny, along with Adam, Nash, and Alex, as they escorted Simon into the clubhouse parking lot.

He got off his bike. He hadn't been wearing a helmet.

"Tabby," he said, rushing toward her.

Lash put a hand out and stopped him. Simon glared at him and she tensed up seeing the anger in his eyes. The rage simmering beneath the surface threatening to come out. "I don't give a fuck who your father is. This is my club, you will abide by my rules. For the next two weeks, you're going to study in this clubhouse, and if you're still here, you will enroll in the high school. Got it?"

There was a short silence. Tabitha wondered if Simon was going to start something. She waited, hoping he'd just accept Lash's rules. There was no other way he'd be allowed to stay.

"Got it."

No one moved.

Tabitha smiled at Simon.

"Go," Lash said.

Simon pulled her into his arms, pressing his face against her neck.

"You two aren't allowed alone together. You can talk out here." Lash clicked his fingers and one of the newer prospects she didn't know the name of stepped forward.

"Come on." She took Simon's hands and they walked over to the swings. With all the kids being born, the small park that had been installed in the clubhouse had never gotten old. As she sat on one of the swings,

Simon lowered himself down on the other.

"Do you know what's going on?"

"I know what happened. You can tell me."

She listened as he told her what he'd heard and what he knew.

"I'm so sorry," she said.

"Do you know what is worse?" he asked.

"No."

"I feel guilty because my mom…" He stopped, shaking his head and rubbing at his eyes. "No, Lexie. I'm angry because Lexie was given the all-clear and I can't be there to celebrate it. Everything I know is one big, giant, fat lie."

She rested her head against the chains. "It's not a complete and total lie."

"It is." He pressed his lips together. "My mom was another woman. Lexie's sister."

"Simon, it doesn't stop the fact that Lexie is your mom."

"You're going to take her side?"

"I'm going to make sure you don't jumble this mess up inside your head. I know you're hurting right now and I get it. I really, really do, but she's not the bad guy." She took Simon's hand. She expected him to pull back, but he didn't.

"I'm so fucking angry."

"I can tell."

"I'm sorry."

"Don't apologize to me."

"I just, I can't stand the fact I've been lied to all these years. I thought she was my mom."

"She is. Please, Simon, no matter what, you've got to give her credit there. She loves you so much. She even sacrificed a great deal to be with you. Your dad, he does love her."

"I don't know who I am anymore."

She got to her feet and stepped toward him. "You're Simon. My very crazy boyfriend." She tucked some of his hair behind his ear. It had grown out since the last time she saw him. "What's your plan, anyway? You ride all the way here and what?"

"I had to see you. You're the only person I have."

"That's not true. You've got all of your brothers and sisters, Dean, Eddie, the Chaos crew. Your parents."

He snorted.

She gripped his chin, forcing him to look at her. "Hey, don't ever do that. Look at Daisy. Her real parents never wanted her and there is no way she would ever think less of Lacey and Whizz. They are her real parents and she loves them. Don't ever act like that."

"Wow, you really are bossy."

"I learned from the best."

He put his hands on her hips. The prospect cleared his throat.

Tabitha rolled her eyes. "Seriously, get a life. You see what I'm having to put up with here?"

"Lash broke your phone?"

"Yep. Stepped on it, crushed it. He did the same to Anthony's and Daisy's, and the others'. We're on a complete lockdown ban."

"You haven't left the clubhouse."

She looked behind her to see the prospect was still paying attention to them. She leaned down, her lips close to Simon's ear. "I didn't say we didn't get out." She pulled away. "We have our ways. I think I know a good place we can go. It might help you to get whatever this is out of your system."

He nodded. "I'm sticking around for a while."

"You think your dad will let you?"

"If he knows me, he'll let me cool off."

"Come on, I'll take you inside. Miles is the guy we see to make our escape tonight." She took Simon's hand, and all of the guys rushed to hug him and shake his hand. Daisy even kissed his cheek. They were all happy to see him.

Lash came in, clearing his throat. "All of you back to work. You as well, Simon. There's space."

Tabitha sat down at her desk while Simon lowered himself down.

"In silence."

They all shut up. Staring down at her book, she knew they only had half an hour to go. The time went by way too slowly. Each time she looked up, she caught Simon watching her.

"Work." She mouthed the word, not making a sound.

"Okay." He lifted up his book and she couldn't help but laugh. He was being a total goofball.

She loved him so much and just having him here, well, it reminded her of all that she'd been missing for too long.

Their time was up. Lash came back and ordered them to their rooms. Simon was escorted by Nash.

"Wow, this is like an actual prison, isn't it?" Simon asked.

She chuckled. Daisy rushed to her side. "How are you?"

"I'm fine."

"How is he?"

"I don't know. We need to go to the Quad. I think it will help."

Even if Simon was keeping his shit together, she knew it wouldn't last long before he exploded again, and she didn't want him to have to go through that alone.

After heading upstairs, she closed her door and

sat down on her bed. As she ran her fingers through her hair, it was a matter of minutes before Miles was there, opening the door.

"So the prospect on duty tonight has a girl coming around at nine. We sneak out past the back door, from the kitchen and out. We go to the Quad for a couple of hours. No fighting. We observe only."

"Thanks. Let Simon know. Angel's coming with the food."

Miles tipped an imaginary hat to her.

Seconds later, Angel was there.

"Hey, sweetie."

"Hey, Angel," she said.

"I know this is all seeming a little much," she said.

"Nah, it's fine. I mean, what more can I do? I did break a girl's nose and hurt another one."

"I know, sweetie. Do you think violence is the answer, though?" Angel asked.

"Sometimes the only vocabulary people know is violence, that and sex."

"Enjoy your food." Angel left.

Fries and a garden burger, her favorite. Angel had embraced her, Daisy's, and Lacey's vegetarian diet. Picking up the burger, she took a large bite and closed her eyes, enjoying it. After dinner, they were expected to get changed for bed, read, and then there were lights out.

There was no way Lash could believe they were following his protocol. If he did, she felt a little sorry for him. It wasn't like they went out of their way to disrespect them. That was a lie. They totally did.

Lash came for the dishes and their doors were closed.

Checking the time, she showered, changed into her pajamas, sat, and read for ten minutes before the allotted escape time. Then she quickly pulled on a pair of jeans, a shirt, and her leather jacket.

At exactly nine, she opened her door, just as the others did.

Simon moved down the hall, going to her.

Miles was in front, Anthony right behind him. She didn't know how her brother was able to find out all of this information, but he was a master at getting what he wanted.

They made their way down the stairs, past the prospect who was moaning as the girl gasped at how big he was.

Seriously?

Simon snickered and held her hand tightly. They were out of the kitchen, past the wall, and running like the hounds of hell were chasing after them.

No one stopped them as they made it clear to the Quad.

"We can escape but we don't have any cars. We're walking the entire way," Miles said. "It is damn good to have you here." He shook Simon's hand.

"Why are you guys putting up with this?" Simon asked. "Why not just overrule them?"

"He's my dad, dickface," Anthony said.

"We did kind of deserve it. He has a point," Daisy said. "We fucked up and now we're paying the price."

"Yeah, but we've got to get our shit back when we're in school again. There's no telling what the Dogs have been up to," Markus said.

"It's why we're determined to keep showing our face at the Quad," Rachel said. "You want to come?"

"Hell, yeah. I'm not breaking out for the fun of it. I need to hit something or someone." Simon pulled her in tightly against him.

"Then we're going to the right place for you," Miles said.

****

"They snuck off again," Angel said, wrapping her arms around Lash's stomach as she stared past his shoulder.

"Yep."

"And you're not going to stop them?"

"No."

"Then why are you forcing them into lockdown and doing their schooling? They're not even allowed to eat dinner with each other." Angel kissed his shoulder.

He groaned. "Do you want to talk about the kids?"

"I want to understand your mind better."

"You've been trying to do that for years, and you still don't understand me."

She giggled. "Come on, tell me."

"They were hotheads who thought they knew best. They're all going to need to learn restraint."

"And this is the best way to teach them?"

"It's the only way I know how to teach them. One day, this is all going to be theirs. If they screw it up, this could be gone." He tugged her around so she stood in front of him. "You remember what it was like before. All the trouble we had." He pushed some of her hair out of the way. "I don't want to go through that again."

"I get it."

"And we're never leaving the club, so we're going to be at their mercy."

"Putting them on lockdown during the day is okay, but at night, they can do whatever they want?"

"They're going to the Quad. As much as I want to keep them contained here and doing as they're told, I can't. There is only so much I can do." He shrugged.

"Besides, they need to protect the Skull name at all costs and because of the Dogs, they're in the thick of it."

"Did you and Nash have to ever deal with something like that?"

"No. We didn't. Not really. We got into a whole lot of fights, but you know how it is."

"I do. Will you be staying up all night for them to return?"

"I will, but they'll be gone long enough for me to make love, or fuck my wife, if she needs it."

****

Simon had his arm wrapped around Tabby's shoulders, and he pulled her in close, kissing her head as they paid their admission to the club.

He wanted to hit something.

I've been lied to my whole life.

People were screaming, laughing, cheering. He looked up toward the stadium and there was a bloodbath going on.

"You're telling me these are all kids? Students?" he asked.

"We have college guys as well. It's a variety. I figured you'd like that," Tabitha said.

"And you've all fought here?" Simon asked.

"Hell, yeah, it's what we do," Miles said. "You want to make a name for yourself and not get beaten up in school, this is the place to come to."

"And you've all been here?"

"Apart from Daisy," Rachel said.

"Daisy doesn't fight," Tabby said.

"Why?"

His girl slammed her lips on his, kissing him deeply. Running a hand down her back, he cupped her ass and bit her lip. She chuckled. "She just doesn't, so drop it."

"Dude, stop smacking on my sister, it's gross. I'm wishing you'd gone back home or something."

Daisy laughed.

"Fuck you."

"What are you going to do?" Daisy asked. "Are you going to stick around here forever?"

"I hadn't decided. You think Lash is going to send me back home?"

"I don't know what's going to happen," Tabby said.

"I don't care, to be honest. For now, I'm thinking of enrolling in your school. If I can show that I'm willing to not cause trouble, he might let me stay."

"And that's what you want to do?" Tabby asked.

"For now, yeah. I can't go back there. Not yet. I'm too fucking confused."

"But you're going to go back there?" Daisy asked.

"Why does it matter?" He glared at his girl's best friend.

"No reason."

"Well, well, look what hell spat back out," Miles said.

Tabby tensed up and turned, so they all stood in a cluster. He glanced over to see two guys he recognized. They were both wearing leather jackets.

"You shouldn't be here."

"Ask Daniella how her nose is for me," Tabby said. "And next time, tell her I'll make sure no doctor can repair her face."

"You're a fucking slut, you are," the one on the leader's right said.

"Who the fuck are you talking to?" Simon asked, stepping in front of his girl. No one talked to his girl like that and got away with it. Tabby gripped his arm.

"You heard me. I can see why you like her. She's got a big enough mouth and I bet she doesn't even have a gag reflex. That's what all Skull girls are for, getting their face fucked sucking cock."

He slammed his fist into the guy's face, and grabbed him again, hitting him. He didn't stop until he was suddenly restrained and pulled off. Anthony had a hold of him, and fuck, he was strong. No words were spoken and he glanced behind him. Anthony looked bored. Everything had gone blank in those few seconds of attack. Simon's heart raced. His blood pumped. He wanted to do more destruction.

"In the ring, now," the man who'd rushed over said. "I don't give a fuck if you were fighting in the ring."

He was taken from Anthony and marched over toward the stadium. Thrown inside, he stood up. Tabby rushed to the edge and patted the concrete floor. He smiled down at her.

"What the hell are you doing?"

"I need to do this. No one talks to my girl like she's a piece of shit."

"Si, it's the Dogs. That was Ryan. He's always talking to me that way. Believe me, I don't care."

He crouched down. "You scared?"

"No, I know you're a vicious motherfucker when you fight, but I also know you've got some serious problems right now. You're angry."

"Damn right, I'm angry."

"Not about this. You're angry about what your parents have done."

"Don't go there, Tabby."

"I will go there. It's what we promised each other. We will go there. We'll talk about it. Deal with it."

"I'm going to fight this prick."

"Si, you started that fight out there. Ryan may not even enter the fucking fight."

He shrugged. "I'll get to fight someone." He gripped the back of her neck and kissed her hard. "Love you. Are you rooting for me?"

She rolled her eyes. "As if I'd root for anyone else. Don't die on me, asshole."

"Not going to. We've got a wedding to be alive for. Do you still have the bouquet from Natalie's wedding?"

"You remember that?" she asked.

"It's a day I won't ever forget." He winked at her. "It was the fates' way of telling us both we're getting married."

"It's time to throw the bouquet," Lexie said.

"We're still doing that?" Natalie asked.

"Yes, of course. There's single women here too, and it's a lot of fun."

"Two seconds," she said, kissing Simon on the lips. She'd run onto the floor as she'd been keeping a close eye on Natalie all day. The flowers were so beautiful and Simon had already proposed to her. If she caught the bouquet, their parents couldn't argue about it. Natalie turned her back to the group and threw the bouquet over her head. Tabitha watched and moved into position as it flew right into her arms. Simon fist-pumped and rushed toward her.

"We've got to get married now," Simon said. Tabitha laughed, and they both ran to their fathers, holding up the roses. "We've got to. We've got to."

She shook her head and stepped back right next to Daisy.

"We all know the rules about fighting in the Quad," the man said who'd marched him right across to this little stadium.

He looked out across the audience.

"It seems we have a new pretty face to mess up, but I warn you, he's with The Skulls, so I'm guessing you're one fierce motherfucker."

"I'm a Chaos."

"Pardon?"

"I'm part of Chaos Bleeds, I'm not a Skull. My girl is though and anyone who calls her a slut deals with me."

"So, you heard the man. Who would like to give this punk a lesson? No fighting unless it's earning money."

There were cheers from the audience.

Movement across the way caught his eye, and he saw the other guy who'd been the leader back there but hadn't stopped his boy.

"Well, well, well, this is exciting. Our very own Luke from the Monster Dogs. You guys better get your bets going. This is going to be one fierce fucking fight."

Luke climbed into the ring and started to remove his jacket and shirt.

"You want to fuck me, is that it?"

"Are you braindead? It's how the fights are." Luke glared at him.

"Your jacket and shirt," Tabby said, drawing his attention.

"Hey, beautiful."

"Hey."

"Kiss me for good luck?" he asked.

She climbed up, wrapped her arms around his neck, and kissed him hard. Cheers and more dirty talk were spewed their way.

"Okay, enough," the guy said. "If we start shooting a gang bang, we'll let you up, but we're not shooting porn, we're fighting."

Simon stepped away from his woman and took a step toward his opponent. He looked at Luke but he hadn't covered his expression. The fucker watched Tabby and Simon understood his look more than anything. This piece of shit wanted his girl. Oh, he was in for a rude awakening. No fucking way was he ever going to allow him.

"You stare at me. Not at my girl."

"Your girl's got a pretty ass."

"Don't kill each other," the guy said.

Simon rammed Luke, throwing him to the floor. "She doesn't even look at you." He raised his fist, about to land a blow, but Luke blocked it.

Climbing off him, he stood, tense, waiting for the next hit, but Luke just smiled. Back on their feet, the humor was still on his opponent's face, and he didn't like it. He wanted to completely rub it out, get rid of it.

"Are you worried that she'll stray? A little curious to see if she'd rather have me than you?"

"Fucker." He attacked. Luke blocked him and even as Luke tried to take a shot at him, he dodged it.

As he stepped back, the crowd went silent.

They were equally matched.

"I know my girl. I've known her since we were kids. You think I'm going to fuck that up? She'll be my old lady, by my side, carrying my kids. Not you. Never you." He lashed out, finally landing a blow.

Luke got a shot into his lower ribs.

It was on.

Hit for hit.

They didn't kick.

A face blow.

A kidney shot. Neither of them admitted defeat and they blocked each other with equal shots.

The guy who'd been leading the fight came back

onto the stadium as they were circling each other.

"It looks to me like we are equally matched and I don't know about you guys, but I find this all boring. We'll call this a draw."

The crowd cheered, especially those who would have earned money from it.

He wanted to kill.

"Come in, boys, show great sportsmanship."

Simon stepped in close, holding out his hand. Luke took it. They squeezed hard.

"I guess I'll be seeing you in school," Simon said, winking at him.

"I can't wait."

Stepping out of the stadium, he moved toward his girl's side, taking her into his arms. He kissed her hard, driving it home that she belonged to him.

Rather than accept his kisses, she stepped back. "Don't ever do that," she said.

"What?"

"Use me like that to mark your territory. I belong to you, Simon. Have for a long time, but don't ever make me feel cheap." She went to Daisy. "Come on, let's get out of here."

"Tabby," he said.

She held up her middle finger in a fuck you.

Pulling on his shirt and jacket, he followed The Skulls out into the night. He didn't realize he and Luke had been fighting for a good half an hour. No wonder the crowd was bored.

"Aren't you guys going to fight?" he asked, following Miles, Markus, Simon, and Anthony.

"You fought for us." Miles spoke up when no one else did.

"I'm not a Skull."

"Coming to the Quad with us, you are. You want

to keep saying that shit how you're a Chaos, go back home. When you're here hanging with us, you're one of us. End of discussion. You should be lucky we're not sending your ass right on back home," Miles said.

"Are you all fucking serious?" he asked.

Anthony stopped and moved into his space. "Do we look serious? You're not one of us but while you've got your little mommy complex, you will be. You got a problem with that, fuck off."

Simon stood, watching his friends walk away.

It was the first time in his life that he finally understood his father. They were two different clubs. Sure, they were friends, but that didn't for a second mean it was going to last. He caught up with them, following them back to the clubhouse.

He wasn't a Skull, nor would he ever be one. Going back home wasn't an option. For now, he was just going to have to deal with what he'd done.

When they got back to the clubhouse, they snuck inside. Tabby was already in her room and had closed the door.

He quickly went to his room, showered, changed into a pair of shorts, and snuck down the hall. He tried her door, rather than knock.

It was open.

Her light was still on and she rolled over, looking at him. "What are you doing here?"

"I came to apologize."

"I don't want to hear it."

"I shouldn't have done what I did."

"I know that. The entire club knows that." She glared at him. "I don't want to talk to you."

He stepped into the room. "I want to talk to you."

She threw her blanket off and stood. "You want to talk. So because you want to talk, I've got to listen."

"I'm sorry."

"Fuck you. You don't ever get to treat me like a piece of property and think a little thank you is all I deserve."

"Do you like him?"

She frowned. "What? Who?"

"Luke. The Dog I was fighting tonight."

"No, why?"

He shrugged.

"Oh, come on. That's what this is about?" she asked. "I don't fucking believe you. Get out."

"I'm sorry."

"No. You don't get to throw accusations like that around. I never once questioned you with that Amber chick, did I? I believed in you, and now you're asking me if I've got feelings for one of our enemies. Are you crazy?"

He didn't think he was but now he had an idea.

"I'm sorry."

"Get out. If you have any regard for me at all, but I'm starting to think you don't, get the fuck out. Now."

He looked at her as she climbed back into bed and he stepped out of her room. This wasn't where he wanted to be. He needed to learn to keep his big mouth shut. He had no doubt she wouldn't stray. None. She loved him just as much as he loved her. He'd fucked up.

Daisy was coming back from the bathroom and stopped. "You want to gloat?" he asked.

"Someone is in a pissy mood, but I can tell you deserve it."

"Thanks, that's just what every single guy wants to hear."

Daisy tilted her head to the side. "You are a big dick, aren't you?" She chuckled. "You are so going to have to make up for it with her."

"And I take it I'm not going to get any help from you?"

"Not a single one." She stepped past him. "Oh, and yes, everyone at the club knows that Luke has the hots for Tabs. It has been that way for a long time. I don't know if she sees it, or if she has simply chosen to ignore it, because to her, it's not important. None of us have ever brought it up as we all know it's pointless. Luke and Tabs will never happen, unless of course you're a big enough of a dick to send her on her way."

Daisy patted his shoulder. "Whatever's going on inside that head of yours, get over it, or you're going to lose the only person who has ever liked you."

She stepped into her bedroom and Simon shook his head.

He'd fucked up big time.

Chapter Fifteen

"Are you okay?" Daisy asked.

Tabitha looked up from the swing to see her best friend approaching. It had been a week since her argument with Simon and she hadn't forgiven him. She was still pissed at him and didn't want to give in too soon. It seemed wrong to do so.

"Yeah, I'm okay. You?"

"I figured I'd ask you. See how you're feeling." Daisy lowered herself into the swing.

"I'm fine. I think. Can you believe we're heading back to school today?" Tabitha asked, wanting to change the subject.

"Don't do that," Daisy said. "I'm not Simon or one of your other friends. I'm here with you. For you."

"I know. I just, I find it hard to talk about, you know?"

"Yeah. Simon's a dick. We can keep on talking about the dick." Daisy's lips pressed together as she looked past her shoulder. Tabitha glanced back and saw Anthony heading toward them.

Their parents were dealing with something urgent with the Billionaires and once that was done, they were all going to school. There was of course a little meeting with the principal to get through, yay.

Anthony stepped behind Daisy, taking the chains and pulling her back. Her best friend held on as he started to help her to swing. She smiled.

"What were you talking about?" Anthony asked.

Raising a brow at his question, she looked at Daisy. "Dicks. We were talking about them. Do you have anything to add about them?"

"Tabs?" Daisy asked.

"What? I'm keeping it real."

"We weren't talking about actual … penises."

Tabitha smiled at her friend, who looked a nice darker shade of pink. So cute.

"Please tell me why we're talking about a penis," Miles said, walking over.

"Ugh, I don't need to hear about your penis."

"Likewise, I never want to hear about your vagina. Nasty."

They all burst out laughing.

"Tabby," Simon said.

The laughter died as she turned toward Simon.

"Can we talk?" he asked.

"You can talk anywhere. You don't need my sister's permission, unless of course she has you by the balls?" Miles held his hand out as if he was holding a pair of balls.

"This conversation has gone far enough. I'm over it." She climbed off the swing. "You want to talk?"

Simon nodded and they walked toward the edge of the gate, not stepping outside.

"You okay?" he asked.

"Yeah, you?"

"I'm not fine."

She looked at him, waiting.

He glanced past her shoulder, looking everywhere but at her.

"You've got to be kidding me. You want me to start this conversation?"

"I don't know where to begin, babe," he said.

"First, don't call me babe. Second, you tell me what it is you want to say. I've got nothing to say to you."

"I was an asshole. I don't—I was angry and I

took it out on you. I shouldn't have. This whole thing with Lexie, and then to see Luke and the way he watched you."

"I don't care about the way he watches me, Simon. I don't see it. The only person I ever see is you, but don't ever, and I mean this, don't ever for a second try to put this blame on me. I didn't do anything wrong."

"I know that. I'm an asshole and I hate myself."

"Good," she said with a smile. "The roses yesterday were a nice touch."

"You liked them?" he asked.

"Yeah, I loved them."

"Good. I didn't mean to fuck this up."

"Don't ever do it again."

"I won't."

She stepped into his arms. "I mean it. Next time, I'll cut your dick off and you haven't had a chance to use it."

"I won't fuck up again. I love you."

She kissed him, smiling.

"Enough of that," Tiny said. "Get in the fucking car."

She turned to see the rest of her friends were already getting in the car. "It looks like the school is ready."

"Simon, you're with Lash," Tiny said.

"Why can't I drive in your car?"

Tiny didn't answer.

"I wouldn't push my luck with my dad if I was you." She patted his chest. "It looks like he's pissed."

She climbed into the back of her dad's car. Miles was in the front. Her mom was clearly taking her little brother to school.

"Are we about to have the serious talk?" Miles asked.

"I don't have the head for you taking the piss, Miles. I suggest you reel that shit in."

"Consider it done."

"Good." Tiny drove slowly.

She stared out of the window.

"I get why you did what you did, sweetheart, but from now on, don't get caught."

She turned to look at her dad. "You do realize in an off-the-cuff way, you've given me permission to beat the shit out of people?"

"I've given you permission to stand up for yourself. If that is what you need to do, I'm going to stand by you."

"Cool," she said.

"Make sure you don't get caught and they can't prove it's you."

"You were a badass when you were prez, weren't you?"

Tiny sighed. "I did my job well, but the one thing I will always tell you is you've got to know when to take a step back or a step down. I don't have any regrets about Lash taking over. I know he didn't want it, but he has proven to be one hell of a president. One I'm more than proud to serve under. You guys should be as well."

"Aren't you pissed that you don't get a chance at being president?" Tabitha asked, leaning forward, pulling on Miles's hair.

"Ouch, stop it."

"Come on, doesn't it bother you?"

"No, it doesn't."

"Why not?"

"I'm a hothead. I've got no place being at the top. We all know that and besides, it means I can keep on being a hothead with no repercussions." Miles swatted at her hands. "I don't care if you're a girl."

She giggled. Teasing her twin brother was fun.

Sitting back, they arrived at school. She glanced out and saw people had stopped to watch. It was a rare occurrence for their parents to arrive at school. She found the Dogs standing near the edge of the parking lot, their leather jackets a neon sign.

She climbed out of the car and any teasing was long gone.

Joining up with their buddies, including Blaise, Constance, Damien, and John, who had all been suspended along with them, they headed into school.

Now, normal kids may be slightly embarrassed to have their parents escort them into school to deal with the principal. Their parents, the leather cuts, the scars, all of them looking fierce as fuck, Tabitha was proud. Holding her head high, they entered the school and walked down to the main reception.

First were Constance, Blaise, John, Damien, and their parents. They were the civilians. Taking one of the now-vacant seats next to Simon, they were all silent as they waited.

"Fuck me," Lash said, the first to speak up. "Damn, could you imagine me and you here?" He nudged Nash's shoulder.

"Hell, no." Nash whistled. "We would've burned this place down to the ground."

Tabitha smiled. Lash and Nash were brothers. Their parents had been killed, which put them in Tiny's care.

"I don't even want to imagine you boys here." Tiny shook his head. "I've already got a son here."

"Don't worry, pop, I'm keeping the family name alive." Miles spread his arms wide as if he was talking with real passion.

She tapped her foot on the floor, waiting.

Their friends came out looking bored while their parents were pale.

The principal had done a number on them. Clearly stating what would happen if they continued to hang out with this unsavory crowd.

Tucking her hair behind her ear, she got to her feet as the principal cleared his throat. It was their turn. The seats were available for the parents. She stood behind her father's chair.

"I hope you all understand and appreciate this school from this day forward," the principal said. "I will not have fights or bullying."

"Hold the fuck up. We don't bully."

"Son!"

"We don't bully," Miles said, repeating himself.

"If they don't bully, don't put them in the same league as some of your other kids," Lash said. "In fact, let's not pretend here. I donate a lot of money to this school." He leaned forward. "I accepted this suspension as a healthy teaching opportunity, but let's cut the shit. A couple of girls got into Tabitha's face. She defended herself. The next time she defends herself, this will not swing your way. Understood? Our kids are entitled to an education. You can spew your little rules and laws, but let's face it, I bet the first chance you get, a hot little piece of ass comes in here, you'd be all over it, so don't even think of trying to test me or my family. Every single kid, even those little fuckers you just had in and tried to scare their parents, they are my family. They are my responsibility, and if you want to go down that path, bring it. You will not punish them without coming to me first."

"You don't seem to know how this works."

"I know how this works. I was a kid and now I'm a fucking adult. I know the hypocrisy dripping from you and I don't like it. Next time you got a problem, you call me. Don't ever make this kind of decision without me." Lash slammed his hand against the table. "I think that is all that needs to be said."

They got to their feet and left the principal's office.

"Remember what I said," Tiny said. He kissed her head and ruffled Miles's hair, who backed away, groaning.

"I'm not six anymore."

"You'll always be my baby," Tiny said.

"Dad, stop. It's gross."

Lash whistled. "Be good. That threat, it was a real one, but I can still only protect you so far."

"Got it," they all said in unison.

"Simon, I enrolled you for the time being. I've also pulled some strings. The teachers know you're a year ahead but I arranged for you to be in classes with these guys," Lash said. "Your shit is at the main reception. You will all be picked up at the end of the day."

Their parents left and they stood there staring at each other.

"Looks like I'm in school with you guys," Simon said.

"I'll help him," Tabitha said. "Catch you all at lunch."

Daisy pulled her close, kissing her cheek.

They all left, heading toward their first class of the day, while she went to the main reception with Simon. The woman at the counter was so nervous. Her hand shook as she passed over his schedule, which was set out in a two-week set of classes. They took a seat and she pulled her schedule out of her back pocket.

"We've got a couple of classes together. I can't

believe he managed to arrange that."

"I have biology now."

"I'll walk you to class," she said. Standing up, she took his hand and they walked side by side toward his biology class. "Daisy's in here, so she'll help you to your next class."

"When do I see you again?" he asked.

"At lunch."

"Are you still my girl?"

"Simon, I will always be your girl, even when you piss me off." She went onto her toes and kissed him. "See you at lunch."

****

"And we just sit here?" Simon asked.

"It's what we do," Miles said. "Don't worry, Tabs will be here before you know it."

The first part of his day had been uneventful. From Daisy, he ended up in a class with Anthony, from there, Miles, and now lunch.

He always had this ideology of school with Tabby. Where he'd get to be in every single class. Of course he knew it would never happen as he was one year older than her. He was actually due to graduate in a few months. It was kind of corny, but he'd also love to carry her books. The kind of shit he saw in movies. Only, he hadn't seen her since this morning and he did want to make it up to her.

He'd pissed her off and that hadn't been his intention, far from it.

The Dogs' leader wasn't there, which, to him, meant Luke was in the same class as Tabby. He didn't like that.

"So you're the elusive Simon," Constance said.

"Yep, that's me."

"I didn't think you were real," John said.

The Skulls had people like his Dean and Eddie. Thinking about his boys always made him a little sad. He'd left them and he knew he was going to have to call them soon. They'd been blowing up his phone so he'd turned it off. His dad and mom had also been trying to reach him and he hadn't wanted to speak to them.

Neither had arrived in Fort Wills so far, so at least they were giving him space. It was what he needed, even though since his argument with Tabby, he'd been more focused on making it right with her than dealing with the revelation about his parents.

"I'm very real. Have been for a lot of years." He took a bite out of his burger and relaxed as Tabby and Daisy walked into the room. They were hand in hand, and he spotted Luke checking out Tabby's ass.

He tensed up.

"Don't," Anthony said.

Glaring at his friend, he didn't like being told no.

"You're not my boss," Simon said.

"I am while you're at this school. Don't. Not today."

"And you would just let anyone stare at Daisy's ass?"

Anthony finally turned his gaze to Simon's. "Look around you. Does it look like anyone is willing to look at her ass?"

Simon stared at him. Anthony's face was blank, as if they were talking about the weather.

"You're either implying that you only see Daisy's potential, or you've scared every single date she might have so the only person she has is you."

Anthony's face didn't change.

Simon shook his head. "I can't do that."

"True, but making a scene isn't the answer."

"Did you have your coffee this morning?" Miles

asked. "You're using big words. Ouch." Miles winced and rubbed at his leg.

Tabitha and Daisy came over, as did Markus and Rachel.

She leaned over the table. "How was your first morning?" she asked.

He kissed her back, trying not to look in the direction of Luke or the Dogs. He'd upset her last time, and it wasn't his intention to do it again. Even with Luke following them, Tabby hadn't looked back or even acknowledged his existence. He couldn't imagine having a crush on someone and them not returning it, let alone even showing any sign it was there. How long had Luke been that way?

"Earth to Simon. Hello?" she asked, giggling. She waved a hand in front of his face.

"It was good. Anthony is thrilling company."

"I bet, there's just something about the silent treatment that is so hot," Tabby asked. "Right, Daisy?"

Anthony lifted his head and Daisy went bright red.

"The pizza is good."

"It is, huh?" Tabby asked. "So is everyone fight-free so far? No sign of causing any trouble?"

"We're all clear," Rachel and Markus said.

John, Blaise, Constance, and Damien all nodded.

Anthony lifted his fingers as if in surrender, so did her brother.

"Awesome. We can get through this entire day without any shit," Anthony said.

"What does it mean our parents are picking us up?" Daisy asked. "You think Lash is going to keep on punishing us?"

"Nah, I think it's because they had to drive us in, so they can take us all the way back home," Miles said.

Simon finished off his cheeseburger and turned to watch Tabby as she ate. Some cheese dribbled down her chin and she wiped it off.

"What are you staring at?" she asked.

"You."

"Aw, you love to watch me eat?"

"You got it."

"You're a weirdo."

"I'm your weirdo."

She leaned in to kiss him and he relished it. This was what he'd been hoping for. He hated fighting with her. Gripping the back of her neck, he held her close, tracing his tongue across her lips.

"You two need to get a room," Damien said.

Tabby giggled. "If you can't handle it, close your eyes."

She finished off her food and lunch ended. Tabby escorted him to his next class which was physical education, yay.

"Have fun. I'll be at the library." She kissed him again, and he entered the main hall.

Heading toward the changing rooms, he went to the teacher who handed him a uniform to change into.

A bunch of guys were already changed when he entered the locker room.

Anthony was there and he went to him, standing beside him. The silence was welcome, and he pulled his clothes off, put them into the locker, and pulled on the gym shorts and shirt. They were too tight, but he didn't care. Anthony had already left and as he turned around, there was Luke. He should have known the Dog couldn't resist a confrontation.

"Do you want me to rearrange your face?" Simon asked.

"Last time we tried that, it didn't exactly go to

plan."

"I can get the job done without an audience." He took a step toward him. "You better start averting your eyes from my woman."

Luke smirked. "You're laying claim to that piece of ass?" he asked.

"That piece of ass belongs to me. She has for a long time. You should count your blessings that you only get to look. She will never belong to you. She doesn't even give a shit about you. Your gaze, your attention, it means nothing to her because she is mine, and always will be."

Luke smiled, licked his lips, and stepped up close. "Yeah, but one day, you're going to have to go home, and I'm still going to be here. I wonder which one she will prefer. The absentee boyfriend, or the guy who is there every single time she turns around."

"Simon," Anthony said, calling his attention.

He wanted to hit Luke, to wipe that smile off his face, but he saw his game. If he fought him, Lash would have no choice but to pull him from the school.

"Looks like I'll be sticking around a long time." He slapped Luke on the shoulder and left. He wasn't going to get drawn into any fight. If Luke wanted to keep on looking at her ass, he'd let him, and each chance he got, Simon would be sure to squeeze that sweet ass because it belonged to him.

Chapter Sixteen

A couple of weeks later at the clubhouse, Simon had Tabby on his lap and she was giggling like crazy as he tickled her. Some romance movie was playing on the screen in the cinema room that Lash had installed at the clubhouse.

"Sh," Daisy said, laughing along with them.

"Stop it. Stop it. I mean it, stop it." She couldn't stop laughing and he loved to hear the sound spilling from her lips.

Pulling her close, he kissed her lips and those giggles turned to moans. "I love having you on my lap," he said.

"I love being on your lap." She gave a little wriggle.

Resting his hand on her stomach, his cock stirred, hardening. Tabby's gaze turned heated.

As quickly as the arousal came and he wanted to be alone in a room with her, Lash cleared his throat.

"Simon, you're needed."

"Can I just finish watching the movie?" he asked.

"Now." Lash was already leaving.

As he got to his feet, Tabby slipped off his lap and waved him goodbye.

He headed out of the cinema room and came to a stop when he caught sight of his dad with his crew. Devil looked angry, which changed as soon as he saw him.

"Hello, Simon," he said.

"Dad."

Silence fell and he looked at the bikers who'd been his family the entire time. He noticed Curse wasn't with them.

"Can we talk?" he asked.

Simon wanted to tell him to fuck off. To get the hell out, but he couldn't do it. Devil was still his father and telling him to leave just didn't feel right.

Nodding his head, they left The Skulls' clubhouse and walked outside. There were a couple of The Skulls, prospects, and a few of the old ladies. Folding his arms, he looked all around, then down at his shoes, not knowing where to pay attention.

"You don't have to avoid me," Devil said.

"What are you doing here?"

"Work. We've got another call that's going to require both clubs. We're going to be working together."

"That's good." No matter the danger, his father was doing good and he respected that.

"Do you want to join us?" Devil asked.

"No. I've got stuff going on."

"Lash told me he enrolled you in school. Dean and Eddie told me you're doing well."

"Yeah," he said.

"Look, Simon, I get that you're pissed, but you don't have a right to be."

"I don't have a right to be? If I don't, where is Curse? You think I don't notice that he's gone?" he asked, glaring.

Devil ran his fingers through his hair. "You had no right to find out that way."

"Why did I have to find out that way? Why the fuck didn't you tell me?" he asked.

"You want to know the truth? That I met Kayla on the road, fucked her, and she stole from the club. I didn't even know about your existence. I followed her all the way to Piston County to discover she'd dumped you with Lexie. You know what she did to keep you in diapers and formula, clothes, toys? She turned to stripping. She could have fucking left you."

Devil's voice got louder. "A lot of women would have dumped your ass at a hospital. Not Lexie. No, she took care of you." He ran a hand down her face. "From the first moment I met that woman, and yes, it was her getting her clothes off for money, I didn't even know who she was, or that you were born."

Simon felt sick to his stomach.

"From the moment I met that woman, she has always … surprised me. Even when she didn't need to take care of you, she did. You know all about Kayla, Simon. Damn it, you've visited her fucking gravestone with her. Lexie may not be your birth mother, but she is your mother in every single right. She has been willing to die for you. Kayla, she dumped you. She put Lexie in danger."

"You'd never kill her."

"No, but in putting you in her arms, I came looking, and from that first look, I wanted her. Every single day since then, her life is at risk. Now that her cancer is … she's winning. Look, I know you're angry, but you don't get to be angry at her. I was the one who said you would never find out the truth. Kayla isn't worth your time. She was a fucking whore. The only good thing about her was she gave you to Lexie. That was all."

"You don't regret it at all. Sleeping with one sister and making a life with another."

Devil cursed, hands on hips. "How can I regret what happened for a single moment, Simon? If I hadn't fucked Kayla, you wouldn't be here and I'd never have met Lexie. Am I proud of what I did? No. Do I regret it? Hell no. I love my life. I love my son. I love my woman. I've got a family, a place in this world. There's nothing to regret. I'm the happiest motherfucker around. Hate me all you want. This was my decision, not Lexie's, but don't wait around too long to talk to her. She misses you. I miss you."

"I can't come back. Not yet."

"Fine. You've got stuff you need to do, I get it. Don't make her suffer for my decisions. That I can never accept."

Simon nodded.

"I made any sense to you?" Devil asked.

"Yeah."

"A lot?"

"Some."

"Good. That's all I needed to know. I can't convince you to come back with me?" Devil asked.

"You can order me back."

"No, I'm not going to do that. You know where your home is. I can wait. I don't like you being here but at least I know you're in good hands." Devil rubbed at his brow.

"I'm shocked," Simon said. "I expected you to order me back home."

Devil blew out a breath. "Sometimes we've got to get a shitload of stuff out of our system. Whatever you need to do here, I'll respect that decision, so long as you talk to your mother."

Simon pulled out his cell phone. He found his mom's number and called. Part of him wanted it to go to voicemail. Of course, he wasn't that lucky and she answered right away.

"Hey … Mom," he said, hesitating just slightly. "It's me."

"Oh, honey. It's you. I bet your dad is there, isn't he?"

He chuckled. "Yeah, he's here. He's watching me right now."

"You tell him that I've told him to leave you

alone." He repeated it and Devil just stared.

"He's giving me the evils."

She chuckled. "I've missed you."

"I've missed you too, Mom," he said.

"You have?"

"Yes."

"I wish ... oh, Simon, I wish a lot of things could have gone differently. I hope you know that."

"I know it."

"Good. I never wanted to hurt you."

"I know. I get it."

"I do have some pictures of Kayla, not a lot, and they are old. None of her pregnant. You see, I didn't know she was pregnant with you until she came. You were such a beautiful baby. I loved you so much."

Tears filled his eyes as he imagined a young Lexie. There were plenty of pictures of her younger, and she'd always looked so sweet and kind.

"Thank you," he said.

"What for?"

"For taking me in."

"Of course I would, silly. You're my son. I mean, nephew. I'm not good at this."

"No, you're my mom. You will always be my mom. I've been stupid. That's all. I was so confused and hearing Curse, I made a mistake."

"We can talk about it anytime. I'm a phone call away unless you're coming home soon?" she asked.

He heard the hope in her voice and he hated the thought of disappointing her.

"No, I can't. Not yet. There are a few things I've got to do first." He ran a hand down his face, clearing his eyes from the tears.

"O-okay, well, I'm here, always. Go easy on your father. He misses you, and he was only ever making the right decision for you."

He said his goodbyes and hung up.

"You can hate me all you want to, son, I don't mind. Never, ever take it out on her."

He nodded his agreement.

"How are things going with Tabitha?" Devil asked.

"You're not going to be a grandpa yet."

Devil laughed. "So long as it stays that way."

"It will."

"I'm going to head back. You sure you don't want to come?"

In his mind, he saw Tabby, Luke, and what he hoped to do come her eighteenth birthday.

"Not yet."

"You're sure?" Devil asked.

"I'm sure. I've got things I need to do."

"You're still wearing the colors," he said.

"Because there is no other club I could ever want."

"Good answer." Devil stepped toward him and Simon was surprised as he hugged him. "Thank you."

He slapped his dad's back, feeling the emotion clog his throat. He didn't want to cry and he felt like such a fucking loser for it.

Tabby came to join him as he saw his father and the crew off. She wrapped her arms around his waist as he held up his hand, waving them goodbye.

"You okay?" she asked.

"I will be."

"You didn't go back with them."

"I'm not ready to leave."

"Good," she said, kissing his neck. "I don't want you to leave."

****

"I can't believe you've been on dates and you haven't told me about them," Tabitha said, flopping down on the grass beside her best friend.

Daisy sighed. "Just be silent and enjoy the sunshine while it lasts."

"That is your way of not getting me to talk," she said. "I see your game. I do."

"Tabs, it hasn't been a big deal. It's been ice cream and not a lot else." Daisy rolled onto her side. "What is it you want to know?"

"Have you kissed?"

Daisy's face gave the game away.

"You have. Was it good?"

"Tabs, you kiss Simon like all the time." In the past couple of months, Simon had gone back home a couple of times. She always expected a call from him to say that he was staying at home, but he continued to surprise her by returning each and every time. She loved him being around.

Of course, it meant a lot of sneaking. He stayed with Lash most of the time. They'd set him up in a bedroom as a permanent feature for him. Of course, he didn't always stay in his bed as he snuck out all the time to come and sleep with her.

"Yeah, I know, and now we can talk about our boys' kissing."

"I don't know if Anthony is mine."

"He is totally yours. Now, tell me, is he a good kisser?"

"You tell me, is Simon?"

"Hell, yeah, of course he is. I love it when he starts at the corner of my mouth. His tongue tracing, and okay, I can go into graphic detail."

"No thanks. I don't want to hear about him. Hearing about Simon is kind of like a brother."

"Simon is no brother, believe me. Anthony is kind of like it but I need some material to tease him with. Is he good? Bad?"

"Anthony is awesome," Daisy said.

"You're only saying that so I don't tease him."

Daisy shrugged. "You can't tease him. He's like amazing. I don't think there is anyone in the world who is going to beat him in the kissing department. I'm sorry. But I can officially say I got the best boyfriend in the world."

"Not possible," she said, laughing.

Daisy joined in and they collapsed to the ground, chuckling. "Damn, this is so much fun."

"Yeah, we've got to do this more often." Tabitha took her friend's hand. "Can we make a pact or a promise to each other?"

"What kind?"

"The kind that says no matter what choices we make in life, or if we hate each other, we'll always be best friends and it means we can hate each other for a little while but we've always got to stick together?"

"You're going to follow Simon to Piston County, aren't you?" Daisy asked. "It's why you want to make this pact."

"I love him, Daisy. I know he would give up the club for me and I'm not going to do that."

"What about you and this club?" Daisy asked. "We're your family."

"And I will always be your family no matter what. It's not like I'm ever going to be a patched-in member, is it? I'll wear the property patch of my dad and then onto my husband, even if I was to stay here. I love Simon. He is my entire world and I know that now. I see it. It's all clear."

"It took him having to come here for you to

realize it?" Daisy asked.

"Yeah, I just, I don't want us to ever fight, you know? I love you so much and I don't want to lose you."

"You'll never lose me," Daisy said. "It will always be me and you, no matter what the guys say. They can go and suck it."

Tabitha laughed, hugging her friend close. They sat up now and she closed her eyes, happy with her decision. Of course, she still had to tell Simon, but that would come in time. She had no intention of moving away soon.

"Well, lookie what we got here."

Tabitha tensed up. She and Daisy got to her feet as they looked across the field to see Ryan and Luke. They weren't alone either. It looked like a couple of guys from their crew were with them. They were in Fort Wills territory.

"You need to leave," Tabitha said.

"Why? We're on open land."

"Skulls' land," Daisy said. "You're in Fort Wills. The Skulls could see this as an act of war and you don't want that."

"Maybe we do."

She looked at Luke. He was glaring right at her and she did the same right back. There was no way these guys were going to intimidate her.

"I've got to say. We were out for a stroll and I didn't expect to come across two whores begging for it," Ryan said, stepping away from the group.

"Ryan," Luke said. His voice was firm.

Tabitha kept Ryan in her sight. Now if she knew Anthony, he wouldn't allow Daisy to go anywhere without some form of protection. So long as they waited this out, he'd come to her rescue. She had no doubt.

She was tense, waiting for the impending fight.

If Anthony was close, Simon wouldn't be far. He'd been dealing with something with Lash about his upcoming birthday.

Ryan was getting closer and Tabitha stepped in front of her friend. She wasn't going to show fear. Rather than back down or try not to fight, she got into Ryan's face.

"Fuck off!" she snarled at him.

He grabbed her arms and she went to knee him between the thighs, but he shoved her away hard.

Just as he was about to kick her, a rock hit Ryan in the head.

Anthony was already making his way across the field. He tossed another rock. This one hitting Ryan in the face. Tabitha scrambled back. She remembered as kids that Anthony would spend hours tossing rocks or balls. He didn't stop until he'd mastered the perfect aim to hit every single target.

Ryan stumbled back and Luke came forward.

"I suggest you take your boys and get the hell away," Anthony said.

Fear ran down Tabitha's back. Anthony kept on walking toward them. The stones were gone but the intention was there.

Luke held his hands up. "We were just walking."

"Then walk elsewhere. You want to start a fight, you come to me. Stop cornering our women like a bunch of pussies." Anthony stood, hands on his hips, waiting.

Tabitha's heart raced.

Luke looked at her, turned, and left.

"I don't get him," she said, hugging Daisy. "You okay?"

"I should be asking you if you're okay. I don't know what their game is."

"Luke wants to fuck with Simon. He likes you,"

Anthony said. "Be careful there. Ryan's unhinged."

"And you're sane."

"I'm not pissed at my leader's infatuation. Ryan is." Anthony turned toward her.

"I don't encourage any of that shit! We were here first." Her anger built.

Anthony held his hand up. "I didn't say you did. What I'm saying is what I'm seeing. I'm making you aware. That's all."

"Did you follow us?" Daisy asked.

"You don't go anywhere where I can't guarantee your protection," he said.

"What does that mean?" she asked.

"It means I will always be there if you need me."

Okay, she was starting to feel like she'd invaded a private moment. "I think it's time we headed back."

Daisy kept staring at Anthony.

Tabitha tugged her arm.

"Right, heading back. Yes. Let's head back."

"Is Simon free yet?" Tabitha asked.

"They're negotiating his party," Anthony said. "Chaos Bleeds are coming to town."

"Oh, joy," Daisy said. "When they come to town, there's always a chance they could argue. I hate it."

"They've been on good terms for a long time," Tabitha said. "Don't worry about it."

"I can't help it. It feels like something big is going to happen and that scares me. Doesn't it scare you?" Daisy asked wrapping her arms around herself.

"I'm starting to believe you're a little paranoid."

"Again, I don't know why that's a problem. I get this horrible feeling something bad is going to happen and each time I do, something does," Daisy said. "You should heed my warning. I don't make them every single day."

"Have I told you lately how much I love you?" Tabitha asked.

"Don't mock me."

****

Eighteen.

He was at that age he could get married without his parents' consent.

He just needed to wait until Tabby was of age and then she'd belong to him. Glancing down at the woman in question, he smiled. Her head rested on his chest. Her hair fanned out. She was so beautiful. He glanced at the clock and saw it was a little after six. His parents had already arrived yesterday, as had the club.

Running a hand down his face, he didn't want to move. Tiny and Eva hadn't given any sign of movement yet. He'd have no choice but to sneak out and pretend to be there for breakfast. He didn't know if they'd fooled her parents yet, or if they were very much aware of his presence at night.

Tabitha let out a moan and stretched.

"Morning, beautiful," he said.

"Happy Birthday."

"Ah, so you remembered my birthday?" he asked.

"Of course, I remembered." She sat up, stretching, pushing her hair off her face. "I even got you a present." She leaned over him and he got a good look at her shapely ass. Seconds later, she sat back and held out a slim box for him. She pushed some hair out of her face and smiled. "Open it."

"Open it?"

"Please, it's your present. You're going to have so many later. You're eighteen. Legally an adult." She ran a hand down her face. "Open it."

He reached out, grabbed her neck, and pulled her close.

"I have morning breath," she said.

"I don't care." He kissed her hard. She wrapped her arms around his neck, moaning, and he swallowed it. Still holding the present, he didn't let go of her.

She pulled away breathless. "Open it."

"Okay, okay, I'll open it." He wanted to keep on kissing her.

He untied the ribbon and slid the box open. Inside was a locket.

"I got it 'specially designed. There's a jeweler who was willing to put your Chaos Bleeds symbol on the front. You can put any picture inside you want. I had to make sure you had one of me."

He opened the locket and inside was his woman.

"You can change it of course."

"I wouldn't change it." The chain was big enough it slid over his neck. "I love it."

Wrapping his arm around her, he tackled her to the bed, capturing her hands. He locked them above her head and kissed her. As he slid between her thighs, his cock hardened and he pressed against her core.

She got one of her hands free and it ran down his body, cupping his dick.

As much as he wanted to let her continue, he captured her wrist and shook his head.

"You don't want to?"

"No."

Tabby frowned. "Why not?"

He leaned back, putting some space between them. Holding the hand that had been on his cock, he released a breath.

"I'm a little confused right now, Simon. I thought you would've wanted to."

He kissed her hard. "I do. I want to. I want to have sex with you, Tabby. You've got to know that some days I watch you and it's all I think about."

"I'm ready. I want this."

"Not today."

"Why not? It's your birthday."

"No, on our wedding night."

"What?"

"You heard me. When we have sex for the first time, I want it to be with you as my wife."

She groaned. "Don't you think that's a little old-fashioned?"

"Not to me. You'll be eighteen and we'll be married. It's not about God or any of that. We will belong to each other completely. You're not just some girl, Tabby, and I'm not going to treat us, this, as some kind of quickie. Your parents are going to wake up soon. I'm not going to rush. I want to take my time. To make love to you."

"Do you think our first time is going to be great?" she asked.

"Yeah, I do, because it's going to be with you." He kissed her.

"You know, you never fail to surprise me," she said, cupping his face. "I love you so much."

"I love you too. My gift is perfect and there is only one woman I'll ever want close to my heart, and that is you."

"You say all the right things."

"Good." He kissed her hard and pulled away as they heard a door opening and closing.

Simon dived off the bed and rolled beneath it as Tabby's door opened.

"Hey, sweetie. Are you ready for breakfast?" Eva asked.

"I'm starved. Simon's, er, he's coming over as well. I had a text from him."

He stayed perfectly still.

"Honey, I'm not stupid. Simon, you can come out and just come downstairs. We know he's been sneaking into your room."

He crawled out from under the bed.

"How did you know?" Tabby asked.

"You're not silent when you climb in through the window. Now your dad wants to kill him, but I convinced him that you two are sensible. Am I right?"

"Yes, we are," Tabby said. "We're perfectly safe."

"Good. I can't guarantee you won't get glared at. Tiny's not happy." Eva closed the door and Tabby turned to look at him.

"Wow," she said, covering her face. "I wasn't expecting that."

Simon climbed onto the bed, moved her hands out of the way, and cupped her face. "You know I love you, right?" He couldn't stop saying it.

"Simon?" she asked.

"You do?"

"Yes, I know you love me."

"Good. I want to be with you. This is not a rejection."

"I know. You don't have to keep saying that. I'm starving. Let's go and get some breakfast. I want to keep you all to myself all day, but others want to wish you a happy birthday as well."

Tabby moved off the bed, grabbing some clothes and going to the bathroom. He pulled on his jeans and shirt. They weren't creased. After running her brush through his hair, he made her bed for her and sat on the edge, waiting.

She arrived seconds later, complete in a cute dress that fell to her knees and only enhanced her curves.

"You're doing this to torture me?" he asked.

"Just a little. I think it's only fair."

He groaned. "Come on. I better see your dad eventually. He's going to be pissed at me anyway."

"Of course, he is."

Tabby took his hand and they made their way downstairs. Miles was at the table, smirking, as was her other brother. Tiny was at the head of the table glaring.

"Wish him happy birthday," Eva said.

Tiny continued to glare and Miles laughed.

"Seeing as she's having boys in her room, can I at least bring a girl home? Like a different one every night? I'll kick her out when I'm done with her," Miles said.

Eva slapped him around the back of the head.

"Ouch. What was that for?"

"I taught you to respect women a lot better than that."

"And I will. I'll call them a cab." When Eva went to hit him again, he ducked, laughing. "Look at this, out there in the world it's double standards against women. In my own home, it's against boys."

"Get used to it, son," Tiny said.

"You should be on my side," Eva said.

"I am. It's why I've agreed with you. He can't have a girl in the house."

****

"Are you having fun?" Tabitha asked.

She held on to Simon and smiled up at him. His family was here even though he hadn't gone and spent much time with them, with any of them.

"Yeah, I'm having fun."

"More fun than if you were going to have sex?" she asked. His rejection hadn't hurt as it wasn't him telling her to stop.

He groaned. "Please, don't. I'm going to have

nightmares about stopping for a long time to come."

"So you're waiting until we're married?" she asked.

"Yes, and if my memory serves me well, I don't have long to wait."

She tilted her head to the side. "Huh?"

"Have you forgotten already?" He leaned forward and kissed her head. "You promised me you'd married me when you became eighteen. I'm going to hold it to you."

"Really?"

"Yeah, really. You and me, and we're going to have a whole lot of fun." He ran his hand down to the curve of her ass.

She giggled when he stopped. Since this morning, she'd noticed her dad had been keeping a closer eye on Simon. If only he knew she'd offered herself up to him and Simon wanted to wait. She doubted he'd be proud of the reasons he wanted to wait.

Lexie came across the room and seeing as the relationship with his parents was tense, she took a step back and went to the edge of the dancefloor.

"How are you?" Daisy asked, handing her a soda.

"I'm good. You?"

"Yeah, I'm good. Are you happy?"

Tabitha chuckled. "Can't you tell that I am?"

"I can tell but, you know, with you I can't always tell. You laugh in the face of your enemies, remember?"

Tabitha nudged her friend's shoulder. "I love having him here."

"You do."

"Yeah, but, I've made my decision." She turned to Daisy. "I'm going to be with him."

"You're going to become a Chaos?" Daisy asked.

Tabitha nodded. "Yeah, I think I am. Don't get

me wrong, I love being here. I love being a Skull, but I know my life is with him. This has only proven it even more so. I love him. My life is with him."

She glanced back at the dance floor. Lexie's head was tilted back as she laughed at something he said. She smiled, more pleased than anything to see the two finally getting along. She ran fingers through her hair. "Did you know I was going to have sex with him today?"

"You were? Wait, you still haven't?"

She shoved her friend's shoulder. "Get your head out of the gutter."

Daisy chuckled. "Sorry. Just the two of you alone in a room, you'd expect fireworks."

"There are fireworks, but he wants to wait until we're married. How can I not go with him? He's right for me on so many levels."

Daisy wrapped an arm around her waist. "Well, I hope nothing bad ever happens between the two clubs."

"Me neither. I don't think I'd ever want to give you or anyone else up."

She held on to her best friend, watching as Simon then took Angel onto the dance floor and started to dance with her.

It wasn't long before he came back for her.

She went right into his arms.

"Please, tell me this isn't me," he said. "You can feel it too?"

She pressed her head against his chest, breathing him in. His arms were around her, and she felt safe and loved. "It's not you. I can feel it too."

For as long as she could remember, when it came to Simon, he'd made her feel this way. Loved, protected, safe, and it was a feeling she was going to take with her. Grandpa Ned had once said to her if you can find someone who makes your heart race and each time they step into the room, you just want to go and be with them, they're the kind of person you want to keep around for a lifetime.

Simon was that person.

He was hers, just as she was his.

Nothing was ever going to take him away from her. Nothing.

Chapter Seventeen

Simon never went back home to live, he only ever went to visit. Each time he left on a Friday, he was back by the Monday, and Tabitha would wake up to him in her bed. Time went by as it did. The days turning to weeks, the weeks to months. His graduation was nearing as they all got closer to their end of the term. She didn't know what he was going to do while she had one year to go at school.

Daisy had already decided on a local college and Tabitha had picked the one closest to Piston County. She'd already told her dad and Lash of her intentions after next summer, to leave Fort Wills and go with Simon. Of course, her parents were upset, but that was to be expected.

Time passed. School came and went. Simon was part of her life, but he did spend a little longer at home. At school, tensions still ran high but for the longest time, she hadn't started a single fight with any of the Dogs. She'd taken Anthony's warning seriously. She wasn't going to let down her guard, not for a single moment.

Before too long, which was a huge surprise to her, her birthday approached. Rather than dread it, she looked forward to it. She would become Simon's old lady, or more importantly, his wife. This was a moment they'd been planning for years. Even before she caught Natalie's bouquet all those years ago.

On the day of her eighteenth birthday, Simon was there in the morning. She'd fallen asleep in his arms and woken up right where she belonged.

Tilting her head back, she saw he was already awake, watching her. "You know, that's a little scary."

He chuckled. "I love to watch you sleep."

"How long have you been watching me?" she asked.

"Long enough." He stroked a finger down her nose. "You're eighteen."

"I am." He hadn't made any more comments about them getting married. She didn't think it was possible for her to be married to him, at least not without a church and a few other details.

"I've got a dress I'd like you to wear for me."

"Is it slutty?"

"No, it's not slutty." He kissed the top of her head and moved toward the wardrobe. He came out holding a white floral summer dress. "Would you wear this for me?"

"I will wear anything for you," she said. Climbing out of bed, she went into his arms. "I love you."

"I love you too."

Her door was knocked and her mother appeared. "Breakfast is downstairs, waiting."

"We'll be right down," she said, looking behind her. "Why do I feel you've got something planned today?"

"I have. When your parents ask, tell them you're meeting up with Daisy."

"Okay," she said. "I know there's a big party. Miles told me about it the other day."

"Of course there would be a big party, but trust me, okay?"

"I'm trusting you. Can't you see? Full of trust."

"Good. Wear the dress." He tilted her head back, kissing her lips. "I love you."

She smiled, watching him leave her room. It was still crazy to her that he joined them all for breakfast, even after her father persistently gave him death stares. She knew without a doubt Tiny was plotting his death.

After heading into the bathroom, she took a quick shower, brushed her teeth, and then blow-dried her hair before going back to the bedroom and stepping into the dress. There was a little catch at the back and she was able to reach it. Brushing her hands down her body, she stared at her reflection. The dress fell to her ankles, skimmed over her curves, and there were two slits along each side.

"This is going to have to do," she said.

She headed downstairs to find her parents waiting. Her present was a car, which she loved instantly and decided to call Ned. It was her father's old car that he rarely used, five seater, but she could tell it had been cleaned up nicely. Tiny demanded she take it out for a spin with him in the car. Simon stayed back, and as they got to the edge of town, they took a turn, and she came right on back. She'd been learning to drive for a few months and had finally passed her test, not long after Daisy had. Lash had told them all that they needed to learn to ride or drive. She liked being a passenger on a motorcycle but not riding one. There were way too many bends and curves.

As she arrived back home, Simon stood next to his bike, waiting for her.

"Tabitha, I want to say that I'm so proud of you."

"But?"

"No buts. There were days when you were growing up that I didn't think either of us would live to this moment."

She took her dad's hand. "We got through it. All of us did. I love you."

"I love you too. Simon, he's a good kid, and considering he's related to Devil, well, that's saying something."

She giggled. "Is that you giving my boyfriend a compliment?"

"It is."

"I love you, Daddy."

"I love you too, sweetheart. I never wanted you to grow up but you've gone and done it anyway."

She hugged him tightly before climbing out of her car. "What do you think?"

"I think you look sexy as hell. You want to come with me for a ride?" Simon asked.

"I'd love to."

She rushed toward him, putting on a helmet since her father was watching. She worked the dress between her thighs so it wouldn't blow up in her face, and wrapped her arms around Simon. This was how it was supposed to be.

"Ride me anywhere," she said.

"You do realize how dirty that sounded."

She kissed his neck.

Simon took off and she closed her eyes, giving herself up to the moment as well as the speed of the machine. It felt good, exhilarating. Every now and then, she opened her eyes and didn't have a clue where they were going, but she didn't care. She gave herself completely to Simon, knowing he'd never hurt her.

They'd been doing this for so long. He was the only person in the world who loved her unconditionally. Her parents loved her, so did her friends, but they weren't even close to Simon.

He started to slow down and they came to a stop. She frowned as she caught sight of Miles, Anthony, and Daisy, but also another man, older, wearing priest robes.

Simon stopped his bike and she climbed off.

"What's going on?"

"I told you I was going to marry you. I got your brother and Anthony's help to find a priest willing to do the ceremony, taking into account we're eighteen and we're legally adults."

"And you found someone."

"Yes. Of course. Don't underestimate me."

"I don't."

She put her hands on his chest.

"What do you say, Tabby?" he asked. "Will you be my wife?"

She never…. it was all a little surreal. Daisy stood with some flowers in her hair, holding a bouquet of roses and a smile.

Her best friend had known about this and hadn't told her.

She didn't care.

"Yes," she said. "I'll marry you."

Simon took her hand and stepped up to the priest.

"I haven't made any vows," she said. "This is crazy."

"I'm just going to speak my heart."

The priest waited for her to nod her head for him to begin. She took a deep breath and listened as he read from his book. When it came time to do the vows, Simon started.

"Tabby, I love you more than anything else in the world. From the moment you gave me shit, I knew you were the one for me. You don't let me walk all over you. You give as good as you get. Above all else, every single day, you give me a reason to love you more. I can't guarantee I'll make you happy every single day, but I sure know I'm going to try. You're the only person I want, all I've ever wanted. I don't want to waste a single moment of my life where you're not in it."

Tears filled her eyes.

It was now her turn.

"Er, I love you so much, Simon. I know there have been times that I haven't been as forthcoming or open, but you own my heart. Always have. Whenever something good or bad happened, you were always and will always be the first person I turn to. You're the love of my life. The man I want to spend all of my time with. It's why after next summer, I'm going to follow you back to Piston County. I'll be your old lady, and this is my choice. I want to be with you, 'til death takes us away."

"You know I won't ever fucking allow that to happen. Even in death I'd find you."

She giggled. "See, my stubborn man."

They turned to the priest who said the magical words, and then Simon pulled her into his arms, kissing her. They were now married.

Miles, Anthony, and Daisy all cheered for them.

Breaking from the kiss, she looked at her friends. She wished their family could have been there, but there was no way they would've agreed to this, not so soon. She was married. Simon was now her husband.

"So, we're going to let you guys, you know," Miles said. "We're going to handle the parental front. You two do your bit and we'll do ours." Miles hugged her close. "I'm happy for you, sis. I don't want you to leave, but I'm also not going to stop you. I know you and Simon have always been meant for each other."

"I love you too. Happy birthday."

"And to you."

She kissed his cheek. He stepped back and Daisy held her close. "I can't wait to hear all the details."

Tabitha laughed and Anthony merely nodded at her before leaving. She watched as Daisy climbed on the back of Anthony's bike and took off.

"I ... er, got us a room," Simon said. "You

know."

"To have sex?"

"We don't have to."

"Simon." She stepped toward him so their bodies were flush against each other. "I've been trying to have sex with you for some time. Now I'm legal." She kissed him. "I'm ready. Are you?"

****

The hotel was nice.

Simon closed the door and pulled the curtains so they were in complete privacy. He'd spared no expense in the room and if she didn't want to leave, she didn't have to.

His cock was hard as fucking rock and as Tabby turned toward him, there was a glint in her eye no one could deny.

"I watched a lot of porn," he said. "And instruction videos."

Tabby giggled and was once again flush against him. "You have?"

"Yeah."

"Me too. I mean, our first time, it's not going to be great. There could be pain and it might not take that long either." She put her hands on his chest.

He kept his hands by his sides.

"Simon, touch me. You're not rushing me, I promise."

He put his hands at her waist.

She sighed, taking his hands and placing them over her breasts. "Touch me. I trust you." She went onto her tiptoes and brushed her lips across his.

Fuck, he didn't want to rush and he certainly didn't want to hurt her. Sex with a virgin was painful for a woman. At the thought of causing her any kind of pain, he didn't want to do it.

Just this first time.

Deepening the kiss, he heard her moan as he cupped her tits, feeling the hard buds against his palm. She ran her hands down toward his stomach, and she stopped, her fingers grazing across the band of his pants. He was already hard but as she slid inside and touched him, he broke the kiss, resting his head against hers as he cried out.

"Does it hurt?"

"No, it feels good. So fucking good."

She suddenly stepped back and he watched as she reached behind her. Slowly, she wriggled out of the dress. He'd found it with the sole intention of marrying her in it and taking it off. The perfect disguise so her parents wouldn't know what he had planned.

White lace sat on her body beneath the dress, enhancing her red nipples and thatch of hair between her thighs.

He pulled his shirt off, unbuttoned his jeans, and kicked off his boots. Tabby had already removed her shoes.

When she went for the catch of her bra, he shook his head. "Let me." He stepped up toward her and flicked the catch. Her bra opened and her tits spilled forward. Cupping them in his palm, he teased the nipple. As he stared into her eyes, he leaned down and flicked each bud with his tongue.

She cried out, arching up.

Her hand moved between his thighs as she cupped him. He let out a curse, especially as she moved his pants out of the way and stroked his rock-hard erection.

Skimming his fingers down her body, he touched her pussy, stroking across her panties, sliding a finger between her slit, and using the friction of her panties to create some pleasure.

"Simon, that feels so good."

He moved her toward the bed, sitting her down on the edge of it. Pulling her panties down, he spread her thighs.

"Simon?"

"Trust me?"

"Of course. Always."

He leaned in close and flicked her clit, touching his tongue to her pussy. "Relax."

She lay back and he worked her pussy, teasing his tongue across her nub, then down to her entrance and back up again. Sucking her into his mouth, he heard her moans. She tasted so good and feeling her move her pussy over his face felt good.

It didn't take her long to come and as she screamed his name, he swallowed her down. Drawing her down to earth, he leaned back, wiping his face.

"Wow," she said. "Where did you learn that?"

"I want to give you the world, baby," he said.

He reached into his jeans, grabbed his wallet, and removed the condom. After tearing into it, he slid it down his length and Tabby moved toward the center of the bed.

"Tell me if you want me to stop?"

"Are you crazy? Hell, no," she said.

"Good." He took possession of her lips, pressing the tip of his cock to her entrance. He paused. Waiting. The seconds passed, and then, he slammed deep inside her, tearing through her virginity, finally claiming his girl all for himself.

She cried out, tensing up, and he swallowed down her pain, staying perfectly still as she got accustomed to the length of his cock.

"Simon," she said.

"I know. Please, don't hate me."

She chuckled, the sound rushing through his body. He pulled back to see tears in her eyes, but he had some in his own as well. She cupped his cheek. "You have no reason to cry."

"I can't stand the thought of hurting you."

"I'm the luckiest woman in the world," she said. "I don't know what I did to get you."

"You were yourself, and I will always be with you."

"Make love to me, Simon."

"I don't want to hurt you."

"You won't. I'm ready."

He pulled out of her, watching for any sign of discomfort. When there was none, he slowly began to rock inside her. She felt so good, and the pleasure, it was already building. She was tight, warm, and it was so good.

She cried out as he went harder but she didn't allow him to slow down. He tried to make it last, but it was too much. He came, hard, filling her as he wrapped his arms around her.

"It will get better," he said.

"I don't know, I thought that was pretty damn perfect."

Chapter Eighteen

Present Day

They kept their marriage private. Only Miles, Anthony, and Daisy knew. She also confided in her sister Tate, who was also in agreement about keeping the marriage on the down-low. She believed their parents would pitch a fit, which would cause trouble. She wasn't interested in causing trouble.

"I'm going to miss you," Tabitha said to Simon in the cafeteria. He'd already told her he was heading back to Piston County to see his parents and his friends. Simon had already started to prospect for the club. As he was only eighteen, there hadn't been a big initiation yet, and he was testing the waters at home. He didn't want to leave her for long periods of time. She knew he was nervous about her getting too comfortable being back in Fort Wills. She smiled when she thought of how he made a fuss whenever he returned home. Thinking about him, she touched her chest where her ring currently lay. They both wore their wedding rings around their necks. She had hers on the necklace he gave her when they were younger that she rarely took off, while Simon had placed his on the locket. So far, they'd been able to keep their marriage a secret. They'd also gotten better at sex. It had been a week and already Tabitha enjoyed it a lot more than the first time. Of course, there was nothing better than when Simon went down on her, and they'd even tried it the other way around, but he'd asked her to stop as he'd enjoyed it too much. Being with him was better than she could have imagined.

After lunch, Simon headed out of the school while she went to English. Taking a seat in the back, she stared out of the window, ignoring her companion who'd been sitting next to her for months. Luke hadn't tried to talk to her for a while now, which she was happy about. He was still the enemy, even if he did try to play nice.

Holding on to the wedding band, she twirled it in her fingers, smiling as she recalled the moment Simon became hers.

"What are your plans for the summer?" Luke asked.

She turned to her right. "Huh?"

"The summer. After graduation."

"Oh, wouldn't you like to know?"

"I would, actually."

"It's good to want things." She offered him a smile.

"I don't think that loser you're dating is good for you."

She rolled her eyes. "You don't know the first thing about Simon or me. Don't even think you can talk to me about him." She didn't want to talk to this guy.

"Look, I get that you've been together since you were kids—"

"How did you know that?" she asked, glaring at him.

"I asked around. People know shit as well, even about my club."

"They shouldn't be telling you anything." Her anger grew.

"I'm not trying to cause an argument here, Tabs. I'm just letting you know there are guys here for you. Who want you."

This was the closest he'd come to even hinting at his attraction.

"Don't," she said.

"Tabs, please," he said.

She shook her head. "I know what you're getting at, but stop. Okay? I'm Simon's. I've always belonged to him. There is no way on earth I would ever pick you. You're the enemy. I don't want you at all."

"What seems to be the problem there?" the teacher asked.

Tabitha looked up to see she and Luke had caught the attention of the entire class. Grabbing her books, she got to her feet.

"Tabitha, wait," Luke said.

She ignored him. Leaving the classroom, she ignored the teacher and told her she was heading to the library. Instead, she made her way outside and went to go and watch the football team play as she sat on the bleachers. Luke didn't follow her.

After opening up her notebook, she doodled as she waited for the time to pass so she could go to her next class.

"You okay?" Daisy asked, coming out to her.

"Let me guess, even you have people keeping an eye on me?" she asked.

"You're my best friend and it was pretty big news. You and Luke drawing the attention of the entire class."

"He tried to tell me I had options. Plenty of them open." She shook her head, touching the ring. "He's never done anything like that."

"Are you tempted?" Daisy asked.

"Hell, no. I'm sorry, but Luke? Please. You know I only belong to Simon."

Daisy sat beside her. "I'm sorry, just making conversation."

"He waited until Simon wasn't here today. You know that, don't you?"

"Simon's going to beat the shit out of him when

he finds out."

"He probably already knows," Tabitha said, groaning.

They sat until the football team headed inside. After going to her next class, she didn't see Luke for the rest of the day, and she promised to meet up with Daisy after school. Everyone gave her a wide berth as she left the grounds that day. Daisy was already waiting by her car. As she climbed in, Tabitha looked through her bag and groaned.

"Shit, I forgot something," Tabitha said.

"What do you mean you forgot something?" Daisy asked. "You keep that bag on you at all times."

"I know. I'll be right back."

"Okay, fine." Daisy opened her book. "I'll be waiting."

Heading back into the eerily quiet school, she went to her locker and suddenly needed to pee as well. Groaning, she opened her locker, found the two books she'd forgotten, and shoved them in her bag. Before heading out, she took a quick detour to the bathroom.

She'd finished and was washing her hands as Daniella and her posse of Dogs came into the bathroom. She was surprised to see Ryan there as well.

Drying her hands on some towel, she turned to look at Daniella. "Seriously, you want this to go down?"

"You think you can get away with breaking my nose and hurting one of our own."

She looked at the four girls. Ryan's arms were folded.

"Wow, I should be happy that it takes you, three other girls, and a pussy to take me on," Tabitha said. "You couldn't come at me face-to-face."

She was going to get her ass kicked. There were five to one, and those odds were dangerous. She clenched her hands into fists, ready.

"Oh, don't worry, Tabby, we're going to enjoy this."

Daniella struck first.

Tabitha hit out, swinging for the second girl, followed by the third. Daniella got up first, pulling her hair. It was so hard she felt some actually rip out of her head. Kicking out to the third girl, she knocked her back. Daniella threw her back and she hit the door of a stall. She hit her head as she fell down, but stopped her fall.

The fall was her undoing as she was pulled out.

Hands punched, shoes kicked, and she felt a bone crack.

Someone pulled her head back and smacked it against the floor. She didn't beg them to stop. She didn't do anything but take the beating.

Daisy would come.

"That's it, girls," Ryan said.

Tabitha moaned and tried to get up. Someone stomped on her back and she collapsed. Stars played out in front of her eyes, the pain consuming her. She was going to pass out, she just knew it.

Someone gripped her hair. "You know, I don't see the attraction. Luke has had the hots for you from the first moment he saw you. I wonder if he'll like you when you're all broken and bloody. Until next time, beautiful," he said.

He hit her hard and everything went black.

****

"Come on, Tabby, baby, open your eyes."

Simon's voice sounded distant, as did the sound of hospital machines. Tabitha had spent way too much time on hospital machines.

Pain.

She felt it. Burning its way up and down her

body.

She needed to stop the pain. There was no way for her to.

She gritted her teeth as she felt it.

Finally, she opened her eyes. The attack, all of it came back to her, along with Ryan's threat.

Fuck. She hurt everywhere and she winced.

"Oh, fuck, let me get a doctor," Simon said. "Of course you'd wake up when your parents went to go and get a coffee."

"Don't go," she said. She went to sit up and winced. "Fuck, this hurts. What happened?"

"Daisy found you. You were passed out, unresponsive. She called an ambulance. You've been beaten fucking bloody. You don't remember it?"

The four girls, Ryan.

"Oh, I remember it. Don't get the doctor. I don't want to stay here."

"You have to. You've got a cut on your head, baby. It's so deep. They need to keep you here for observation."

"Not happening."

"Don't argue, please."

"I'm not arguing. I'm stating a fact. I'm not staying." Fucking bitch was going to pay. "I've got to get out of here. I'm not letting those Dog bitches get away with this."

"I get that you're fucking hot as shit when you're angry, but I'm not going to let you go and hurt yourself. Besides, Daisy is taking care of it."

"What?" Tabitha asked, freezing up.

"Daisy, she's at the Quad right now. She's going after Daniella. We got word they were bragging about what happened to you. Daisy's pissed she didn't follow you inside."

"Daisy's going to fight?"

"I know. I don't think it's going to go well."

Any pain she felt, she ignored it as she started to remove the machines that were hooked up to her.

"Baby, seriously, stop this."

"I've got to go to Daisy. She can't fight them."

"She wants to. I know she's going to get her ass kicked."

"You don't understand," Tabitha said. "I promised Daisy she would never have to fight. I fight, not her."

"You're in no position to fight."

"Simon, I swear to God, you act like my husband right now, and you get me to the Quad."

"I don't see what the big deal is. Daisy's going to need to fight."

"It's not Daisy I'm worried about." Tabitha groaned as she stepped off of the bed.

"Shit, what the fuck do you mean?"

"Daisy can fight, Simon. She always has been able to, but it's like a switch goes off in her brain. Once they trigger it, she can't stop it. She just keeps fighting. She can kill someone." And there was no way Anthony would stop her either. "Get me to the Quad. Please."

"But—"

"Now!"

"Shit, okay. Fine."

Simon helped her get into some clothes. It took a great deal of time, which she didn't have if she was going to help her friend. Her parents hadn't returned and Simon snuck her down the back stairs toward the parking lot.

"I've got my car," he said.

"Oh, good." She was breaking out of the hospital in so much pain.

She slid into the passenger seat as Simon got behind the wheel. "I think this is a big mistake."

"I don't care, Simon. Daisy isn't going to fight."

"I've never seen her fight."

"And you don't want to either. It's not pretty. It's not pretty at all."

She cried out when he drove over speed bumps. "How long ago were they at The Quad?" she asked.

"I don't know. An hour, but they have to drive there," he said. "I don't like this."

"I don't care what you like right now," she said. "What are you doing back?"

"When I heard what happened, I was already on my way back. Daisy called me immediately after the ambulance. Why were you alone?" he asked.

"I needed to use the toilet and I forgot."

"You forgot?"

"Yeah, I guess I've been so happy lately, I didn't even think of all the people that want to see me dead, you know?" She took a deep breath and winced. "Fuck. They beat the shit out of me. Kicking me when I was down. Fucking cowards."

Her heart raced. If she was too late, Daisy would never forgive herself.

They arrived at the Quad, and of course, there was a shit load of cars around. She climbed out and Simon helped her. They headed toward the main gate and Simon paid their fees.

"What the fuck happened to you?" the man asked.

Ignoring him, they stumbled inside. The stadium was lit up and Tabitha froze. The crowd was huge. Daniella was in the ring and she'd just hit Daisy.

"I don't see the big deal," Simon said. "She's getting her ass kicked."

Tabitha's heart raced as she watched her friend.

Daisy could take a lot of hits, but it was the right one that finally pushed.

She knew what she was looking for and saw it happen. Daniella hit Daisy, who stumbled back. Whatever Daniella had said, it turned Daisy. With her stumbling, Daniella thought she was the better opponent. Daisy always played fair, but the moment she pressed that button, this was like a completely different person.

"Holy shit," Simon said.

With Daniella's hands in the air, playing the crowd, Daisy had struck. She pulled Daniella back by the hair. The girl's screams rang out. A fist to Daniella's face had her going down but Daisy lifted her back up by her hair, hitting her again, and again. The punches rang down, and Daisy stomped on her as well.

At some point, Daniella was able to break free, but Daisy wasn't allowing her to escape. She wrapped her fingers around her throat and pinned her to the ground.

"Get me to the ring."

Anthony was there, looking so fucking proud.

"You've got to stop this," Tabitha said.

"No, Daniella deserves what's coming to her."

She cried out as someone knocked into her. She looked toward Miles and the rest of the gang.

None of them would stop it.

Tabitha knew she had to break the rules. Once a fight started, no one intervened.

"Get me in the ring," she said.

"Tabby, no."

"I don't care. I promised Daisy and I'm not going to let her down."

Simon helped her into the ring and even as each step made her hurt, Daniella's face was already a mess.

If she wasn't careful, Daisy would turn on her.

Remembering the one and only time this had happened, their little secret, she rushed to her friend, and wrapped her arms around Daisy, trapping her arms at her sides.

"Let me fucking go. That slut needs to die," Daisy said.

"I've got you."

"I mean it, Tabs. Let me the fuck go."

"Not happening." She held on even as pain exploded in her body. "If you don't stop, you're going to hurt me," she said. "Please, Daisy, stop. You don't need to fight. You shouldn't fight."

Daniella whimpered and moved as far away from Daisy as she could get.

Daisy laughed. "You fucking coward. How many of you were there?" she asked. "I know it wasn't just you."

Tabitha looked past Daisy's shoulder and saw Luke staring back at her. He didn't know. She saw that in the way he looked at her.

Daisy took several deep breaths.

"You shouldn't be in the ring," Ryan said, climbing on in.

One by one, Anthony, Miles, Simon, her crew climbed into the ring. She still held on to Daisy, not letting her go.

The Dogs joined him, Luke staring at her.

"You should look for a better crew," she said. "This one likes to hit a woman when she's down. Did you feel like a big tough man, huh? Is that it? You feel all hot."

"I'm fine," Daisy said.

Tabitha felt the change in her friend and slowly let her go.

The crowd was getting nervous, but she didn't care. Staring at their enemies, she did something she thought she would never do.

"Is this what the Dogs are capable of?" she asked, lifting her shirt up over her head, letting them see the bruises, the cuts. Her ribs had been bound up. "I don't even know all the damage but this is what your people do. You're nothing but weak and as for you"—she looked at Ryan—"you shouldn't wear a leather cut, you piece of shit."

Simon charged forward, landing a blow to Ryan.

"Stop," Tabitha said, moving forward. Simon went crazy, hitting, punching, and this time, Anthony intervened, dragging Simon off him.

She looked toward Luke. "Happy?"

"I had no idea."

"Yeah, and that proves you have no fucking control," she yelled at him.

Out of the corner of her eye, she saw Ryan. He flicked open a knife and went for Simon. She couldn't allow anything bad to happen to her man.

She acted on instinct, stepping in the way, and as she did, the knife slid right into her stomach.

Everything went slow.

Ryan let go of the knife as he was tackled to the ground and Tabitha stepped back. The noise seemed to be silent. The knife stuck out of her stomach.

She grabbed the handle and pulled it out. Blood covered her hands. Her blood. It wasn't supposed to be this way. Simon caught her before she went down.

****

Dried blood covered his hands.

Devil was there beside him.

Lash, Tiny, Nash, Stink, and Whizz sat, waiting for news. Daisy's face had broken out in the bruises. She looked a mess.

Simon couldn't believe what had happened.

Tabby had passed out in the car. Blood soaking through her clothes, dripping onto the seat.

She'd been in so much pain.

Sandy, Stink's old lady who was a doctor, had arrived and gone to work on Tabby.

Tiny stood and Eva let out a gasp. Miles hadn't spoken since they arrived at the hospital.

"What the fuck? She was supposed to be in her room." Tiny moved toward him. Devil stood.

"Be careful."

"Be careful? My daughter is in surgery. You think I don't know what this all means? Sandy's in there and she hasn't come back out. I know it means my little girl could be dying on the table."

"Tiny, please, no one needs this," Eva said, moving to his side.

"It's my fault," Daisy said. Tears streamed down her face. "She didn't want me to do something I'd regret."

"Shut the fuck up," Tiny said.

Daisy tensed up and this time, Anthony got up. "You don't get to talk to her that way."

"Son, sit down."

"Of all the stupid fucking things you kids could do—"

"No!" Anthony's yell was clear and carried across the entire hospital.

"Who the fuck do you think you're speaking to?"

"Someone who doesn't know all the facts."

"The facts I know is that my daughter got stabbed tonight."

"She stopped Daisy from killing the girl who beat her up. Tabitha stopped Simon from getting stabbed. One of the Dogs had a knife. She saw it, so did I. I was further away. I should be the one in the operating room."

Angel sobbed. "What your daughter did was protect the man she loves. That's all."

"I suggest you sit down."

"Actually, Tiny, I suggest you do. We don't know enough, and I'm not willing to start a war right now in our hospital."

"If she dies, I will kill your son," Tiny said, looking Devil in the eye.

"You think you'll get a chance?" Simon asked, standing up. He was broken inside. He didn't know if his wife was dead or not.

"What did you say?"

"If she dies, Ryan dies. He killed her. I'll make sure he never sees another day, and then, I will follow her because there's no point in living without her."

Sandy cleared her throat, drawing their attention. "Am I interrupting, or do you want to keep measuring your dicks between young and old?" she asked.

"Is Tabby…" He couldn't bring himself to say it.

"She is fine. Stable. There were a few complications because of her other injuries but she's going to make a full recovery. I don't even see her being in the hospital all that long. I would advise she not step in front of a knife again. It's not good for her."

Simon stepped back, collapsing into his chair. He didn't care who saw as he wept tears of happiness.

Chapter Nineteen

Tabitha sat up in bed as Darcy took a seat.

"I've been a horrible friend," she said.

"Oh, please, you've been an awesome friend."

"I don't even know what's going on in your life anymore."

Tabitha smiled and touched the ring around her neck, and then she glanced at her friend. She and Darcy had always been close, not as close as she was to Daisy. The other woman was older than her, but they were able to share secrets.

She lifted the ring out of her nightgown. She hated being in the hospital, but her parents had somehow been able to wrangle her to stay until she was fully recovered. No doubt talking to Sandy and a nice big donation to the hospital to get what they wanted. They always had been able to get away with that.

"I'm married," she said.

"Holy shit. No one else knows?"

"Daisy, Anthony, Miles, my sister."

Darcy looked at the ring. "To Simon?"

"Yep." She chuckled. "Who else could you possibly think?"

"I don't know."

"Anyway. We're married." Simon had been able to visit her sparingly and her dad was always around.

"I don't know if I want to be anywhere near that revelation."

They both smiled. "I don't mind. After the summer, I'm heading to Piston County to be with him. It is going to be a permanent feature."

"You've made your decision?" she asked.

"Yeah, I have. I decided to pick love."

"That's good." Darcy sat on the edge of the bed.

She enjoyed her friend's company, but Tiny was there to take over and Darcy hugged her tight, leaving her alone and promising to visit again real soon.

Her dad entered the room and took a seat. This time, he didn't have a book and she stared right at him, waiting.

He ran a hand down his face. "We could have lost you."

"You didn't lose me."

"What were you thinking?" he asked.

"I wasn't thinking anything other than not to get stabbed." She offered him a smile.

"That's not funny."

"I'm not trying to be funny. You want an explanation for why I tried to protect the love of my life."

"We can't lose you."

"Dad, you're not going to lose me."

"Do you think I don't know what has been going on?" he asked. "I see the way you look at Simon. I always hoped that this infatuation you had with him would fade."

"Dad, please."

"I … when you're in Piston County, I can't protect you and right now, I don't think he can."

"Do you believe that? I know Simon, and he's already dying inside that I got stabbed. Believe me, he can take care of me and protect me. I love him. Don't ruin that. Don't destroy what we have."

"I always promised I'd keep you safe."

"I'm sure Grandpa Ned felt the same way about Mom."

Tiny chuckled. "Damn, one moment you're this

sweet little girl. The next, you're getting into fights and taking a knife. Getting beat up. Where did the time go? Did I miss it all?"

She shook her head. "You didn't miss a moment. You were always there."

Tiny moved to the bed and sat close to her.

She put her head on his shoulder, closing her eyes. "I love you, Dad."

"Oh, honey, I love you too. I can't stand the thought of anything bad happening to you. It kills me."

"Nothing bad will happen. I'm fine. I'm safe."

She took comfort in her father's arms. She would always be his little girl.

"There's someone who'd like to see you. Lash agreed to the meeting as it's only him."

She frowned as Tiny got up off the bed and went to the door. Luke stood with a bouquet of flowers.

"I don't think it's a good idea for him to be here," she said.

"I come as a peace offering," Luke said.

She looked toward her dad, shocked he would agree to this. "Dad, this isn't right."

"He's spoken to Lash, honey. His dad has, and well, as you can see, we're not kicking his ass. His dad is down in the main reception. I'll be right outside the door."

She opened her mouth to tell him to stop, but it was too late.

"I don't like that you're here."

"I didn't know."

"What?"

"That they were going to attack you."

"Well, your conscience is clear. I don't give a shit what you do or don't know."

"Tabitha, please."

"What happened to Ryan?"

"He's being dealt with by his dad. I haven't gone to see him. I didn't want anything bad to happen to you."

"Luke, this doesn't change anything. I belong to Simon."

"I know that. I get it. I saw the way he was with you the other night. It looked like he'd been the one stabbed." Luke nodded. "It doesn't mean I can't apologize and bring you flowers."

"It should mean that. Nothing is ever going to happen."

"I know, and you've never given me a reason to believe it would. Can't you just accept my apologies, and know that I come in friendship?"

"You're a Dog."

"I'm also just a guy. I get that we're two different clubs, but for now, can't you just accept I'm here in peace?"

She pressed her lips together. "Fine, but if Simon wants to kick your ass, he can."

Luke chuckled. "In case you forgot, we're both equally matched."

"I did see that and no, I hadn't forgotten."

"Just out of curiosity, if Simon was never on the scene, would you be able to look at me … give me a chance?"

She shook her head. "No, because Simon has always been on the scene. We've been together since we were kids, Luke. I can't even imagine anyone else. I'm also not going to give you false hope. I'm not sticking around Fort Wills. I'm leaving after the summer. I'm going to be with him."

Luke nodded. "How are you feeling?"

"Better. I'm no longer feeling like I've been stabbed."

He chuckled. "I better go." He got to his feet.

"Thank you," she said. "For the flowers."

"Anytime, Tabitha. I know we're different but I hope you believe I never wanted to hurt you."

He left.

****

Getting out of the hospital was a welcome relief. The stitches had already come out, and other than some soreness from the beatdown she got, Tabitha was more or less recovered.

Simon wasn't allowed to sneak into her bedroom anymore. Tiny constantly visited, checking to see if he'd arrived.

It was only late at night that he did, sneaking into her room. They spent every single night together.

School finished, and they all graduated.

The bruises had faded and any pain from being stabbed was completely gone. Of course, it also meant she was now on the countdown.

Simon had taken off with the promise he wanted to have everything ready for when they returned. A small apartment, work, and she had also enrolled at the Piston County local college. Lexie had promised her a job working alongside the old ladies at the clothing store, which was only growing as the years went on.

Her life was starting to roll out in front of her and rather than be nervous, she looked toward it with relish. She was more than ready to be a part of Simon's world. He needed to start taking his prospecting seriously, and she certainly didn't expect Devil to keep paying him to come back here. He had to make a final decision and she was ready for it.

She fingered the wedding band as Daisy flicked through the college books that had come through for her that morning.

"You're lost in your own little world."

"I'm just thinking."

"Is it all about Simon again?"

"When is it not about Simon?" she said, laughing.

They both lay down, looking up at the sky.

"Can you believe we've survived high school? All of us?"

"Rachel and Markus have more time, then you have my little brother. That high school is in for a long time of Skulls kids." Tabitha took Daisy's hand.

"Promise me that no matter what happens between The Skulls and Chaos Bleeds, you and I will always be friends?" Daisy asked.

"I thought we've gone through this." Tabitha turned toward her friend. "We'll always be the best of friends. Forever."

"And we'll be our kids' godparents."

"Daisy, of course. Nothing much is going to change."

"Apart from the fact we won't be hanging out together or having fun."

"Don't. You're going to make me cry." Tabitha chuckled. "We can talk every single day. Not a day will go by where we won't talk."

"You promise?"

"Yes."

"Pinky swear?"

"Pinky swear." She wrapped her pinky finger around Daisy's, promising to be her friend forever.

Daisy's cell phone went off and she groaned. "It's my mom. She says there's an emergency."

"It's okay. I'm going to stay here for a little while."

"You can't stay here on your own, Tabs," Daisy said.

"I know. Don't worry. I'm only going to enjoy the sunshine a little bit more. I'm not ready to go back yet." She took a deep breath.

"I'll stick around."

"Don't be stupid," Tabitha said. "It is fine. I'm okay. We're okay."

"I didn't mean to leave you so long." Sadness washed over Daisy.

She hugged her friend close. Daisy hadn't forgiven herself for the ambush from Daniella and her posse. "You need to stop worrying so much. We're both here and sure a couple of people at school were terrified of you. I say good. I don't like it when people think they can walk all over you. It's not fair, and you shouldn't allow anyone to treat you that way. I'm safe and I'm walking around. I'm fine."

"You always have a way with words."

"Damn straight I do," Tabitha said.

Daisy's cell phone rang again. "I've got to go."

"Then go. Don't worry. I'm going to relax. Just breathe it all in. I'm perfectly safe."

Daisy hugged her again. "Love you."

"Love you too."

She watched Daisy leave. When she was alone, she stretched out in the grass, closing her eyes. She took several deep breaths, feeling a calm rush over her.

Tonight, Simon was due back and they were going to tell her parents they were married. He also intended to have Devil and Lexie in on the call. It was time for them to let the entire world know they belonged together. Besides, she didn't like how her father kept pushing him away. It wasn't fair.

She didn't blame Simon for anything that had happened. There was no way she would have been able to live with herself if he'd been hurt. She'd reacted to protect him.

A shadow fell over and she opened her eyes, blinking.

It was Ryan.

"Do you think it's funny?" he asked.

She made to sit up but he was suddenly there, holding her down. Panic flooded her body. She'd heard he'd been forced to hand in his leather cut until he proved himself a Monster Dog, or something along those lines. She hadn't been near Luke. She didn't believe in trying to reach out to people, especially those who had a crush, and she wasn't going to use that to her advantage.

Ryan shoved her hard.

"Let me go."

He wrapped his fingers around her throat, cutting off her air supply.

"Do you have any idea what the fuck you did? What you do? I've had to watch him fawn over you. You walked into the room and no one was more important than you. You're all he can think about and I'm fucking sick of it. You're not perfect. You're a slut, a no-good whore, and I'm sick of it. In fact. I'm going to show him exactly how easy it is to use you."

****

Anthony heard the sobbing coming from the bathroom. The clubhouse was mostly abandoned. Even his mom was out, running some errands. The sound caught at him, twisting his gut. At first, he thought it was Daisy.

He stopped, realizing it was Tabitha's room, and he stepped inside.

Something chilled him to the core. For a long time now, he'd been trusting his instincts, and he knew something was very, very wrong.

The bathroom door was right there.

Danger like this, he'd never run away from. Most of the time, he'd been intrigued by the fear people often displayed. For a long time, he'd known he wasn't like a lot of his friends or parents. His dad didn't understand him, not really. The only person in all of his eighteen years who'd been interesting for him to pay attention to was Daisy. Even as kids, the sound of her voice, it was sweet music to his ears. Watching her, being near her, smelling her, it made him realize what people thrived on. How they fought for love.

What he felt for Daisy, it was deeper than love. It was stronger than any kind of obsession, but he also knew he had to be careful.

Once he stepped through that door, he had this eerie sense that his life was about to change.

He could step back.

Ignore it.

Carry on with his life.

He'd never been a coward.

Putting his hand to the door that wasn't even completely closed, he pushed. The shower curtain hadn't been pulled back.

Tabitha was in clear view, still in some of her clothes. Her face completely covered. A pair of panties with blood caught his eye, and he knew, without a shadow of a doubt, he just knew. Tabitha had been raped, and shit was about to hit the fan.

He texted Simon, his father, and of course Daisy.

Moving into the bathroom, he stared at her, not knowing what to do. In his mind, he had flashes of her. She was his best friend.

Climbing into the bath, even as she screamed, he wrapped his arms around her. "I've got you," he said. Daisy would want him to hold her.

At first, she tried to get away.

"It's me, Tabitha. It's me. I've got you."

Seconds passed and finally, she held on to him, sobbing against him.

His heart broke for her. He couldn't stand for her to be in pain. It was the first time anyone but Daisy had affected him. He knew why. Tabitha was club. She'd been hurt for a second time, but this time went beyond a beatdown. She'd been violated in the worst possible way.

Lash arrived first with Angel. Next Daisy.

Sandy was called. Tabitha wouldn't let him go.

Holding her close, they managed to get her out of the tub and toward the hospital.

It looked like a war with the Monster Dogs was unavoidable.

****

Devil had to drive him.

Simon had read the text message again and again, his stomach twisting.

How could this be possible?

"It will be okay, son," Devil said.

"No, it's not okay." He put the phone away. "Please drive faster."

"I am."

He'd gone to get their apartment ready and to hand in her paperwork to the Piston County college. Everything had been coming together and now … what did he do? His wife, she was hurting.

Running a hand down his face, he tried to not think, but all he could see was Tabitha screaming for help. Begging him to come to her.

He'd failed her.

"Dad," he said. "I don't know what to do."

"You'll be there for her. That's all you can do."

"I…" He couldn't think of a single thing to say.

Pain sliced through him.

Be there for her.

I should have been there for her.

The time passed and when they arrived at the hospital, all of The Skulls crew were there. They were waiting.

Daisy was curled up against Anthony, who looked at him.

There was pain in all of their faces. They were all feeling it.

One of their own had been hurt once again.

She'd been beaten, stabbed, and now ... he couldn't say it.

"Where is she?" he asked.

"She's with Sandy. They're talking to the cops," Eva said.

"I need to go to her." He moved toward the doors but Tiny grabbed his shoulder.

"You can't go back there."

He pulled away. "I can."

"She needs her space, Simon. Not her boyfriend."

"I'm not her boyfriend. She's my wife!" He pulled the locket from around his neck and held up the ring. "She has been my wife since her eighteenth birthday. Ask Anthony, Daisy, even Miles. They were all there. I married her. She's my wife and she needs me. I've got to go to her."

He pulled out of Tiny's arms and walked through the doors. He didn't know where the fuck he was going, or where she would be. Knowing The Skulls, it would be in a private room.

Sandy was walking toward him. A police officer not too far behind.

"Simon?" she asked.

"Where is she?"

"I don't think—" Sandy was about to say.

He shook his head. "I don't need you to think. I need you to tell me where my wife is."

"You mean Tabitha has had a—"

Simon glared at him. He wasn't interested in hearing what this man had to say. "If you dare come between Tabby and me, I'll rip your fucking throat out and shit down your neck. Do you understand?"

The officer looked ready to arrest him.

"It's fine," Sandy said. "I'll take him." She took a step back and Simon followed, not caring who he upset. His woman needed him.

Tabby needed him.

They stopped at a room. The curtains were drawn and it all appeared private.

"She's in there. She's not in a good place right now," Sandy said.

He opened the door, closing it behind him.

Turning toward the bed, he saw her. She was fully dressed, her arms wrapped around her legs, and she looked up. There was a new bruise on her face and marks around her neck. He noticed she cringed.

"Simon," she said. She pressed her face against her knees.

"Don't," he said. "Don't be sad."

"I'm so sorry."

He went to her. "I've got you, baby. I've got you and I'm not going to let you go. I'm here." He wrapped his arms around her. She tensed up but slowly sank against him. "I've got you."

She sobbed.

His heart broke and he didn't let her go. His woman had been hurt.

"I ... it's all my fault."

He cupped her face and shook his head. "No. This is not your fault. None of this is on you. It's on whoever did this."

Her face crumbled. "It was Ryan."

"The Dog?"

"Yes. I was out in the field and I was only enjoying the sunshine. I felt at peace. We were going to tell my parents and yours, and now. Oh, God, do you even want to be married to me anymore?" She pulled away and covered her face.

Tears filled his eyes, and he didn't wipe them away. "I want you, Tabby. Always. Nothing is ever going to change that."

It was Ryan.

That piece of shit.

He slid off the bed.

Tabby looked up at him. "Simon?"

He cupped her face, staring into her eyes. "I love you more than anything."

"What are you going to do?" she asked.

Simon pressed a kiss to her lips. "What I have to."

"Simon!"

She'd flinched away from his kisses and he didn't doubt what he needed to do. He turned on his heel and left the room. He took the back entrance, leaving the hospital undetected. There was only one person who would know where Ryan was, and he was going to make sure he found him.

Chapter Twenty

Tabitha climbed out of the car as Devil came to a stop. Simon had escaped them all. Now she was with Devil, trying to find him before he did anything stupid.

She felt sick to her stomach.

Each time there was a silent lull, memories flooded her mind, and she had to keep moving. She couldn't stop. Once she stopped, that was it, she was at their mercy. She didn't have time to sit and think.

At that very moment, it was like she was two different people. What Ryan had done had happened to someone else, who in the corner of her mind was breaking apart. Tabitha's hands shook as she looked toward the Quad.

Luke and Simon were there.

Anthony and Daisy had arrived but she caught sight of Ryan as well.

"Tabitha," Devil said. "This isn't going to end well."

"I won't let Simon do something stupid." She got out of the car. Ever since The Skulls and Chaos Bleeds had aligned themselves with the Billionaire Bikers MC, and their agreement with law enforcement, they had been the good boys, not doing anything against the law, at least as far as she could tell.

"What the fuck is this?" Ryan asked. "You're working with the enemy?"

"He told me what you did. How could you do that?" Luke said.

"Oh, please, like it hasn't been playing on your mind the entire time you've known her. Even before then." Ryan scoffed. "Does she even know when we were like nine years old, we drove through fucking Fort Wills, and there she was, coming out of some goddamn store, and you were salivating, practically drooling? You've been that way ever since. Don't think we don't all see it, because we fucking do. You're all over her. It's all you do."

Devil put a hand on her arm, stopping her from moving.

She needed to get to Simon.

"That doesn't give you the right to do what you did," Luke said, yelling.

"Why? Are you jealous?" Ryan asked. "That I got a taste of her first? Don't worry, she's nothing to write home about."

Simon drew a gun. She didn't know how he'd gotten it, but it was suddenly pointed at Ryan. This had escalated way too fast and now she didn't know what to do to make it all stop.

"Simon!" She screamed his name, drawing the attention of everyone at the Quad.

The only person she cared about was Simon. The love of her life. The man she wanted to be with for the rest of her life, and if he pulled that trigger, she couldn't just leave.

"I promised you I'd take care of you," he said.

"And you will. Please, come with me. Let's go. You and me? We've got our whole summer ahead of us, remember? We made plans. It wasn't this. Please, don't let it be this. I'm begging you. Don't walk away. Please."

Simon turned back to Ryan.

She called his name again.

"I can't. I'm sorry."

In the distance, she heard a bike, but that didn't matter to her, not as the loud bang of a gunshot that went off. The smirk on Ryan's face disappeared. Simon had hit him once, then twice. The moment he got to his face, he kept on shooting.

Tabitha's hands came up to her face.

He'd chosen revenge over her. He'd given in to hate. This wasn't what The Skulls and Chaos Bleeds crew signed up for. Simon had gone against them. The bike she'd heard came riding through the Quad.

She recognized Dean instantly.

"Dude, get on, now."

Simon climbed on the bike and they rode out. Dean came to a stop as he passed her and Simon reached out, cupping her face.

"There's no way I could have let that bastard live. I love you, Tabby, and I will be back for you." He kissed her hard and before she could beg him to stay, he was gone.

Glancing up at the stadium, she saw Luke, then she looked back to the retreating lights of the bike.

The love of her life was gone.

He'd left.

Putting a hand to her chest, she couldn't contain the sobs. This was all her fault. If she'd left with Daisy, she wouldn't have been alone. She collapsed to her knees, and arms wrapped around her as she lost control.

This wasn't fair.

She and Simon, it was always supposed to be the two of them.

Now, there was nothing.

She was all alone.

Her heart shattered.

To Be Concluded...

www.samcrescent.com

Note from the Author

I think I can hear the almighty groans right now. What the hell is she doing? Why is she doing this? Why did this have to happen? The truth is, I don't entirely know why. I've always allowed my characters to tell me their story. If I try to force it, it only ends in disaster. This is Simon and Tabitha's story. From the start of me writing these two children all those years ago, I knew their story would be a labor of love. They're my babies, and getting their story right is so important to me. I hope you enjoyed this first part. For me, I always needed to delve into them as kids to show their love and loyalty, not just to each other, but to their clubs.

BESTSELLING BBW ROMANCE
SPICY ROMANCE FOR REAL WOMEN